DARK HEARTED

Other Books in The COIL Series

Dark Edge, Prequel
Dark Liaison, Book One
Dark Rule, Book Three
Dark Vessel, Book Four
Dark Zeal, Book Five

Books in The COIL Legacy Series

Distant Boundary, Prequel
Distant Contact, Book One
Distant Front, Book Two
Distant Harm, Book Three

Other Books by D.I. Telbat

Arabian Variable
Called To Gobi
COIL Extractions: Short Story Collection
COIL Recruits: Short Story Collection
God's Colonel
Soldier of Hope
The Leeward Set, Book One - Fury in the Storm
The Leeward Set, Book Two - Tears in the Wind
The Legend of Okeanos
The Steadfast Series: America's Last Days

Coming Soon

Last Dawn Trilogy

DARK HEARTED

A CHRISTIAN SUSPENSE NOVEL

Book Two in The COIL Series

D.I. Telbat

In Season Publications
USA

Printed in the United States of America

Dark Hearted/D.I. Telbat. – 1st ed; updated 9/2018
The COIL Series, Book 2
Christian Fiction, Christian Suspense

ISBN 978-0-9862372-2-5

Book Layout ©2013 BookDesignTemplates.com
Castle Drawing by Aaron Halvorson
Cover Design by Streetlight Graphics

To my brother who . . .
Faces the past by building on it . . .
Faces the present by serving through it . . .
Faces the future by yearning for it.

Acknowledgments

My thanks to my Lord and Savior Jesus Christ,
Whose Life in me I cannot help but share;
To my readers, more numerous than I imagined,
who have grown close to this adventure with me;
To Dee, my endearing and enduring
editor/assistant/manager;
To Evert and Lester, who read and gave feedback
from scribbled copies of this manuscript;
To Sean, whose paintbrush
gave my words shape and color;
To Aaron for capturing a likeness of my castle;
To Jamie and Allison,
who read and edited with care and faithfulness;
And, to the men and women who have suffered,
and will suffer, for the Name of Christ—
may they be remembered.

Xacsin Castle

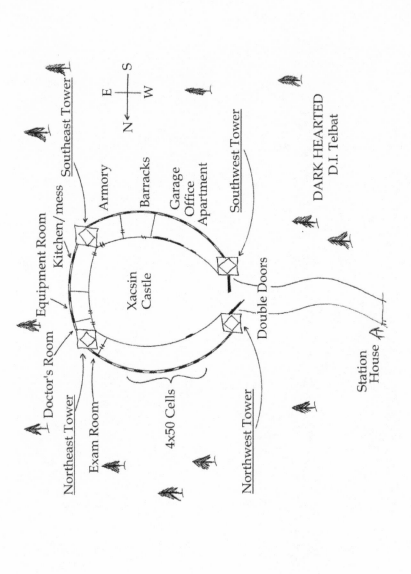

Southeast Tower

Armory

Barracks

Garage
Office
Apartment

Southwest Tower

DARK HEARTED
D.I. Telbat

Equipment Room

Kitchen/mess

N
E — S
W

Xacsin
Castle

Doctor's Room

Northeast Tower

Exam Room

4x50 Cells

Double Doors

Northwest Tower

Station
House

Quin LuDao's head throbbed as he gained consciousness at the sound of birds twittering. Looking at the thick forest surrounding him, he saw the birds weren't just in his imagination. One flew away as Quin sat upright.

He remembered being on a stealth jet. Having recently joined a Christian Special Forces team, his first mission involved the rescue of condemned prisoners in central China. A high altitude, low open—or HALO—parachute jump from a stealth jet was always risky, especially over enemy territory.

Unclipping his harness, he took account of his gear— one NL-3 tranquilizer rifle strapped to his chest, one canteen, and one satellite phone. With a grimace, thirty-year-old Quin tossed the sat-phone aside. His memory wasn't the only thing that had taken a knock during the HALO. The sat-phone was cracked and the antenna was broken, but Quin's small pack was still intact.

The other men on the jet had told Quin to pack for the worst. Quin now wished he wouldn't have acted so sure of himself. He'd told them a small pack was enough. After all, he was Chinese, and they were going to the land of his birth.

Rising to his feet, Quin leaned against a nearby tree as his head spun. The mission plans were beginning to seep back into his memory, but whatever had gone wrong during the jump still evaded him.

Checking the sun, he quickly deduced east from west. The city of Chengdu was to be south of the jump site, if he had parachuted into the right sector. But the fact that it was now morning was a problem; the team's jump was to have taken place during the darkness of night. And how had he landed on the ground without his parachute getting caught in the treetops?

The first order of business was to find the rest of his team.

Quin wasn't one to panic, not with his extensive paramilitary training. As the son of a Khingan peasant, Quin had joined the military at a young age—for the Communist Party's supposed benefits. After several years of brutal service, a covert Christian organization introduced him to a smuggled Bible. Weeks later, Quin became a convert, then fled with his family into the arms of COIL—the Commission of International Laborers—who helped them resettle in New York City.

After walking west, the forest opened before Quin. He crouched behind bushes as he spied a tiny bamboo village of three huts. Four armed masked men guarded one of the huts. *Masked men?* Quin couldn't remember any unit of Chinese military that wore masks on standard guard duty, but he'd obviously stumbled upon the target village for the mission. So, where was the rest of his team?

Nathan Isaacson, the team leader, was a tall, broad-shouldered man with an overgrown mustache and angled eyebrows. Then there Bruno, who was larger than Nathan, and definitely a comedian. Bruno had already played a couple pranks on Quin as a sort of team initiation.

A mouthy Mexican-American named Scooter spoke rapid English—too rapid for Quin to catch sometimes, since he was still learning the language. And Quin was still warming up to Milk, a slender, quiet man, who was the last of the team members. They were all Christians, which bound Quin to them eternally, and he hadn't hesitated to join the team when a position was offered.

Four guards and no team to back him up. Was it possible his team had been captured? Quin shook his head. Here he was alone on his first mission! If he had any sense, he would back away from these armed men.

Quin figured if he left now, he could reach the extraction site by noon and find a safe route out of China. Or he could choose to miss that transport and save the prisoners. There was only one right choice for Quin. Even though he barely knew the team, he was dedicated to them. Such was his grasp of Christian brotherhood—a love he'd certainly never experienced as an officer in the Communist Party. He couldn't run away or ignore the need before him, even to save his own life.

Whether his team had been arrested or not, he'd arrived at the arranged point of operation—to free the prisoners before they were executed. The four masked guards were guarding someone, and common sense told Quin that someone needed rescuing. He had a job to do.

Bowing his head, Quin prayed God would protect him. He couldn't leave the captives or his team behind. And though he was terribly outnumbered, Quin's Bible boasted of a God whose work was not restrained by numbers.

With his first order of business taken care of, Quin leveled his NL-3 tranquilizer rifle and bounded like a frog over the bushes. He advanced stoically toward the central hut, spitting pellets at the nearest guard. Though Chinese SKS muzzles with deadly rounds were aimed directly at Quin, they somehow weren't tearing him to shreds. It was as if an angel of God stood with an invisible shield stopping every bullet. But he was dismayed that his tranquilizer pellets seemed to have no effect on the masked men.

Even more disconcerting, Quin's NL-3 gun was nearly out of pellets. At a firing rate of six hundred cycles per minute, his five hundred-pellet magazine was depleting quickly, especially as he fired on fully automatic.

The guards clicked on empty, their long, forty-round magazines exhausted, the same instant Quin's pellets ran out. Quin stared at the guards, and they, behind their masks, seemed to stare back at him. How was the toxin not affecting them? He'd hit each of them many times.

Feeling his belt for a second magazine of pellets, Quin saw the nearest guard raise a hand to signal his comrades. As if the situation wasn't strange enough, did the enemy now want to talk?

"That's enough, Quin," the nearest guard said in muffled English.

English spoken in the heart of China? And by someone who knew his name?

All four guards took off their masks. Speechless, Quin looked upon Nathan, Scooter, Bruno, and Milk—his own teammates!

"We had to test you," Scooter said as the men approached a trembling Quin. "We had to know if you'd follow through with the mission, even when disoriented and alone."

"Congrats, Quin." Bruno clapped the young Chinaman on the back. "Welcome to COIL. Hey, you looked like a toad leaping out of the bushes like that! Might be some kind of handle there for you."

"Welcome to the team, Quin," Milk said.

"But, the guns . . . We are in China!"

"We were firing blanks. Our masks protected us from your pellets." Nathan tossed Quin his mask. "As for China—we're in Idaho. And we tranquilized you for a few hours to complete the façade."

"Don't feel singled out, Toad." Bruno laughed. "We've all been tested."

While the men shared stories of their own initiation exercises, the seriousness of the exercise sank into Quin's mind.

He'd been confirmed and inducted into COIL. Thereafter, the missions would be life and death operations. Quin "Toad" LuDao felt ready. Now he was one of them—a Christian Special Forces operative.

CHAPTER ONE

Corban James Dowler used binoculars to study Heathrow Airport nearly a mile away. He stood that morning on the roof of a five-story building, England's damp air penetrated his blue blazer, causing him to shiver. For the third time in as many minutes, he glanced over his shoulder. Though still alone on the roof, he sensed a presence of danger. His team hadn't captured the demonic rogue, Abaddon, during their last mission. He hoped that was the only cause of his discomfort.

Answering his satellite phone, he kept the binoculars to his brow.

"Corban here."

"It's Chloe again, Corban. You know, I just realized where you're staying and something is bothering me. Why did you say you found the key to the apartment exactly where I said it would be? When did I tell you that?"

Chloe Azmaveth, the forty-five-year-old ex-Mossad agent, ran the COIL office in Manhattan when Corban was in the field. They were all recovering from the operation in Malaysia where Chloe had also been needed. She was now back in New York, filling her position as primary attorney and public relations liaison for COIL.

"I received your memo yesterday, Chloe, with Rand

Jordan's info. You've forgotten already? Maybe you shouldn't have gone down to Asia with us. It may have been too much for you since you hadn't done field work for so long."

"No, it isn't that. Even if things didn't go as planned, at least we caught Branden and Helena, and got our boys back. But about Rand Jordan—I was busy relocating your family yesterday, Corban. Maybe someone else sent you Jordan's info to stay at the apartment there?"

"It had your text signature. I remember Jordan from the Brazilian incident two years ago. He's helped us before."

"Yes, I know the name, too. Wait. I'm pulling something up on the screen. Oh, no! Corban, Rand Jordan was found dead on the bank of the Thames eight hours ago!"

Tossing his binoculars aside, Corban slid his phone into his jacket pocket as he ran. At fifty-seven and a little soft around the middle, he still moved with surprising speed across the roof. He threw open the access door and lunged down the stairs. On the first landing, he paused. Managing his breathing, he listened for activity below. Even wounded, his men wouldn't go silently. They had recently been stolen back from someone code-named Abaddon, and already they were being targeted again!

Stepping quietly down the remaining stairs, Corban considered calling the police, but that might only endanger the peace officers. One more flight to go. He had no weapons with him, not even his thick-rimmed glasses with the tranquilizer dart, which he wore with some of his covert disguises. And he was alone. His three injured operatives in the supposed safe house had no one but him.

Reaching the third floor, Corban left the stairwell and gazed down the long corridor. There was another stairway at the other end. He could hear a television blaring and a child crying, but everything else seemed to be still. Corban jogged down the hall and stopped in front of the door to their room.

His ears burned with anger. Rand Jordan. Now that he reflected, the setup had been too easy for the enemy—a weary flight from Malaysia; the jet engine malfunction; a text message about a safe location to lay low in England. He must've been so exhausted, he hadn't thought clearly. Of course, it had been a trap! But they weren't caught yet.

Unlocking the door, Corban stepped inside. Nathan "Eagle Eyes" Isaacson, with his sickly face, thick mustache, and bandaged gunshot wounds, lay on the sofa, unconscious. Quin "Toad" LuDao, the team's Chinese operative, looked up from the dining table, a spoon in his mouth and one arm in a sling. Jesse "Milk" Patters was at the kitchen counter, the stitches on his cheek making his complexion look whiter than usual.

"We've got to move." Corban closed the door. "This place was a setup. Leave everything. Help me with Nathan."

Nathan groaned as Toad and Milk, in their own battered conditions, gathered the head of the sheet under Nathan. Corban threw an IV drip bag onto Nathan's stomach and grabbed the other end of the sheet. They lifted the hammock with great effort; Nathan was over six feet tall and heavy.

The three hobbled to the door.

"His side has opened up, Boss," Toad said. "He's bleeding through the sheet."

"He was a Marine." Corban wrestled the door open. "He's been shot before; he'll make it. Besides, the Lord's on his side."

Moving into the hallway, Corban suddenly planted his feet, stopping their procession.

"They're coming!" He shuffled toward the other stairway. "We go up!"

The three hustled with their burden to the right. As they disappeared into the stairwell, Milk looked back.

"They saw us! Four men. Armed!"

On the fourth floor, Corban shoved Nathan toward the hallway. "I'll lead them up. Find an open apartment door and hide!"

Corban dropped Nathan's feet as Toad and Milk dragged him down the hall, blood trailing. Below, Corban heard boots on the stairs. He slammed the roof door loudly to draw the enemy's attention, then dashed to the edge of the roof as the access door behind him opened. Had he bought Toad and Milk enough time?

"Don't move!" The hammer of a gun clicked.

Looking over the edge at the street, Corban saw a reefer truck parked directly below him. If only he could—

"Turn around!"

The man had an accent. Not British, as Corban had expected. Maybe East European. He hit Chloe's speed-dial number with his thumb and turned slowly, both hands in the air. Four bald men clothed in black spread out and aimed handguns at him. One had a long butcher knife in his belt.

"Where are your friends?" The one with the knife moved toward Corban.

"Friends?" Corban heard his phone connect with Chloe. She would hear everything now. "I have no friends. Why are four white men with Eastern European accents and shaved heads aiming guns at me?"

"Corban! I hear you!" Chloe said on his phone. "Just play along. Try to stall them. I'm calling the police!"

The gunmen heard Chloe's voice as well. They glanced at one another. The leader nodded, and Corban knew he had no more time.

With a short prayer, he bent his knees and threw himself backwards off the roof. He saw sky, then landed hard on his back. His head and knuckles slammed onto the roof of the reefer truck. The four gunmen appeared at the edge above and fired down at him. Rounds peppered the roof as the driver pulled the truck away. Gasping for air, Corban reached for his sat-phone underneath him, but found it shattered. Sounds and light faded as he slipped into unconsciousness.

Xacsin McLeery stared at a blank video conferencing screen. He sat in a rock room with water dripping methodically nearby. After meditating for more than an hour, he felt a dark, powerful presence drawing closer. Shivering with exhilaration, he saw a face appear on the screen next to his own bald, pale reflection.

Yes, it was Abaddon! Xacsin closed his green eyes, savoring his time.

"You have done well, my son," an unearthly voice rasped from the speaker. "I am proud of you."

"I am your servant."

"You must increase your efforts to hinder my enemies."

"Yes, my master. Give me guidance."

"They wish to destroy me before my time and they wish to destroy you as well."

"Protect me, O Abaddon."

"I will guide you, my chosen one, against the chosen of my Foe."

"Beautiful master, I will act as you will."

"You have dealt a great blow to the agents of mercy."

"Yes, I have succeeded in this for you."

"Mercy is weakness."

"I understand."

"Now you must follow through, my beloved, whatever the cost. Use whom you will. I permit it."

"I am your servant."

"Double your forces at the castle, the fortress I have prepared."

"Yes, master."

"Rest assured that I am inside the organization of our most hated enemies."

"Yes, great one. COIL will never suspect you."

"I am close to their leader, Corban Dowler, and he suspects nothing."

"I am your servant."

"Even partial success toward our objective is total victory. Do you know why?"

"Because we have drawn the enemy from their cherished plans."

"Keep your wife at your side. She will inspire you with vengeance for what my enemies have done to her sister."

"Vengeance. Yes."

"It is a simple, weak mind that loves. But the beautiful mind conquers and reigns."

"Yes, I am a ruler."

"Let my gratitude for you drive you forward."

"I will, O great one."

"Dwell on my fury for those who call themselves saints."

"I hate them as well, my lord."

"When danger closes, I will guide you away in safety."

"I believe."

"I am your protector."

"I trust in you, O Abaddon."

CHAPTER TWO

Six months later . . .

Boris quickened his pace through the cobblestone streets of a small Swiss village. Darting suddenly into the shadow of a doorway, he studied the alley behind him. He squeezed his burning eyes closed for a moment and thought of the long night he'd had protecting the package, watching his inn door for the slightest movement.

Looking in the other direction where he was heading, all seemed to be quiet. This was why he liked meeting soon after dawn. The only people awake were bakers and those milking their goats.

He scratched his chest casually, but he was actually adjusting the package under his shirt, making sure it was secure. The package was more important than his life, Karol Ngolsk had told him. Of all the errands Boris had run for the Romanian archivist and interceptor of electronic information, she'd told him that only twice before. And both times, people had died for the contents in the package.

Fifty-five-year-old Boris didn't understand how data could be more important than his life, but he knew better than to argue with Karol. She paid him well. And she'd been paying him even better since she'd become a Christian. Boris decided that she gave Christianity a good name, because money was all that mattered to him. Well, money and loyalty, and neither one was valued above the other since they could both buy him different satisfactions.

Checking his watch, Boris saw he was a few minutes early, but leaving the inn had been a wise move. They were probably in his room at that moment, tearing open the decoy briefcase and scratching their heads at the information the Romanian gypsy had given him to leave. He'd read through the informational bait because it always made him chuckle to see what newly acquired secret the thieves would "steal" and take back to their lair to sell.

This time, it had been an assortment of large molecule diagrams of a renowned chocolate manufacturer's secret recipe. The recipe was real, and it was a secret, so anyone caught trying to duplicate the patented recipe would be severely prosecuted. It was a trap, of course, to expose the black market buyers and corporate thieves.

The fact that Karol had gone to so much trouble to prepare a believable decoy, had made Boris think twice about peeking into the real package. Though she'd allowed him to peek before, he didn't dare this time. Here, money and loyalty had to be weighed on an honest scale. If he were caught and tortured after handing off the package, he knew he would talk. He knew this because deep down, he was a weak man. Thus, he wouldn't peek. It wasn't worth it. The two had never been involved romantically, but he loved Karol too much. Never would he betray her; it was out of the question.

Boris stepped out of the doorway and moved cautiously through a courtyard surrounded by tall townhouses two centuries old. The smell of pastries made his stomach growl, but there'd be time for food soon.

Leaving the courtyard, he walked through another cobbled alley, stepping aside for a horse-drawn cart to pass. At the end of the alley, he emerged into the town square. Here, the village was awake.

The pastries were delicious while still warm, Boris remembered. He'd made a package transfer in the same square a year ago, and another time four years before that. Long ago, he'd been able to blend in with the young, fit skiers visiting the village between ski runs up the Alps passes, but he was no longer young and he certainly wasn't fit anymore. Now, his cover was as a middle-aged investor. His suits were simple and barely in style, but they were convenient and affordable for the majority of his travels through Europe.

"Uncle Boris!" A young man stood from one of the patio tables. "So good to see you!"

"Alfred!"

Neither man had seen the other before, but they embraced. The man known as Alfred was under thirty and wore an Austrian flag button on his coat front. It was placed lower than anyone else would ever wear a button—which was their signal. The two sat down together at the table.

Gesturing at the pastries he'd bought, Alfred shoved one toward Boris.

"These are the best! A taste explosion, Uncle! My mouth was watering, so I ate one. I ate two. I ate three! But my mouth is still watering! They're delicious!"

Alfred was speaking loud French, which Boris barely

knew, but it didn't matter. He'd already pulled the package from under his jacket and passed it to Alfred. Now, it was Boris' turn to distract any onlookers. Leaning forward, he took a giant bite of something filled with cream, then he moaned with pleasure.

"Oh, it is excellent! We must meet like this more often! Really, we must. I have tasted pastries from all over the world, and these are the best—or am I just hungry? It doesn't matter. I'm buying the baker!"

Both men laughed. Alfred had the package hidden. After eating and an appropriate amount of small talk about the weather and mountains, they stood together and shook hands heartily.

"We'll do this again soon."

"It's been a joy."

"Absolutely."

Their smiles remained on their faces as they parted. Boris left in one direction. Alfred shouldered a pair of skis, slung his ski boots over his other shoulder, and headed toward a ski lift in another direction.

Unlike Boris, Alfred blended with the tourist crowd, complete with goggles, gloves, and ski hat. On the west side of the village, he swapped his boots for his ski boots, hung his snow boots by the laces over his shoulder, and stepped into skis. A gondola ride took others farther into the Alps where fresh powder had fallen overnight, but Alfred had a schedule to keep.

He skied down the eastern slope—a route he'd been skiing all week, waiting for this day, watching faces, learning who were regulars in the area and who weren't. At the bottom of the mountain was another village. Alfred changed back into his snow boots and left his skis and ski boots in a stand near a skiers' lounge. After waiting for a bus to empty its dozens of skiers, he climbed aboard and sat in the back. The bus route went from village to village, picking up the Alps' most important commodity: tourists.

Four others boarded the bus after Alfred—a young woman and her boyfriend, a man wearing a headset, and a man still in ski boots, who sat across from Alfred. Nobody traveled in ski boots, Alfred mused, but he acted as if he hadn't noticed.

And he also pretended not to notice when the headset man made eye contact with the ski boots man—a communicating look. They'd boarded separately, but they seemed to be together.

Alfred was sure the two were after his package. Even though they couldn't know what was in the package, they somehow knew he had something worth stealing. It was the way they acted. He'd moved material for Karol Ngolsk before, so he knew she worked with only the most sensitive information in the world.

As he slyly studied the two, Alfred surmised why they hesitated in attacking him. At least one of the two would be armed, he was sure, and they probably wouldn't hesitate to kill him, but they didn't know if Alfred had a weapon or not. There were also three other unknowns on the bus: the bus driver, the boyfriend, and his girlfriend. The two thieves couldn't be sure if one or more of the three were a backup for Alfred.

They probably wouldn't suspect the driver, which was why Alfred had decided to use the driver as his backup. If the thieves had done their recon as Alfred had done his field prep, they would've seen their bus driver wasn't the regular one. The current driver was actually a pilot Alfred used on certain missions, and his pilot friend certainly had no problem filling the shoes of a cautious bus driver as he drove on the snow-packed roads.

"Those two are together," the driver warned Alfred in Finnish. "You recognize them?"

Earlier they'd decided to take a chance that no one else on the bus would know Finnish. The two interceptors looked bewildered at one another, and Alfred knew his plan was working.

"The one on my right was staying at my hotel." Alfred slowly applied Chap Stick to his lips. The thieves watched his every move. "I've not seen the other. They could be German. I doubt they'll attack now that they see I'm not alone."

The exchange between Alfred and the driver was complete, and the two thieves seemed alarmed enough to settle into their seats. Outnumbering Alfred, they may have had a chance, but not now.

At the next stop, all of the passengers disembarked except for Alfred. His Finnish driver companion drove them to an airfield covered in snow. The real driver of the bus was waiting there. Alfred paid and thanked the man as his pilot ran diagnostics on a 35 Bonanza Beechcraft plane. The distinctive V-tail was designed to reduce weight and drag, as well as buffeting from the wing and canopy wakes. It was an old plane, a model discontinued in the last century, but its design was perfect for flying through the Alps' passes with their frequent up and down drafts.

They flew south and west to Lake Como at the southern base of the Italian Alps. The upper-class resort community was frequented by Hollywood's favorites, as well as the rich and famous from other countries.

After spending the night in accommodations on the waterfront, Alfred boarded a plane for Germany. His Finnish friend boarded the plane late and sat two rows behind him to cover his partner. At no time did they look at one another. If there were more enemies about—and there always seemed to be—his partner would notice first and step in. But the flight was without incident, and Alfred was able to relax.

In Berlin, Alfred took a taxi to the borough of Wedding, an industrial center north of the city center, where he picked up a car. Though he'd made no calls and communicated with no one other than his pilot for two days, he was on time for a meeting with forty-eight-year-old Rupert Mach, a man he'd not met before, nor did he know what he did for COIL. Each man pulled into a restaurant parking lot at the same time. Rupert had tar-black hair, combed and greased straight back, with eyes that always seemed to be squinting.

As if rehearsed, Alfred and Rupert stepped out of their identical gray coupes and shook hands. Though Alfred was formal, Rupert remained light-hearted and steered a decoy conversation toward a bogus house he was building, making grand hand gestures in case anyone was watching the lot.

Finally, they shook hands again, and unless an enemy

were paying close attention, he wouldn't have noticed the two men parting, each in the other's vehicle. The two had switched cars, the package now under Rupert's seat. Alfred and Rupert both had backup drivers watching nearby. They, too, left separately.

Rupert drove into the city center, wound his way through another borough, and then returned to Wedding. He parked behind COIL's office building, which was in the basement of a newspaper company. It was easy for Rupert to stay up on news and trends simply by going upstairs through the fire escape and chatting with the rag's editor, a man in whose conversation Rupert particularly delighted.

But before Rupert sat at his own director's desk, the package was handed off to his backup man, Johnny Wycke, an American who worked as a field prep agent for COIL's more aggressive operations in the most dangerous countries. Since Rupert had been in and out of the intelligence business for twenty years, he didn't bother to ask Johnny what was in the package. Besides, Rupert and Corban Dowler were good friends from the past Cold War years, and Johnny was Corban's operative, so no answers were needed.

Johnny barely caught a flight to Paris. From there he hopped a jet for New York City. Though all traces of any dangerous tails seemed to be long gone, he was still cautious in his travels. Besides, he figured his six-four, two-hundred-fifty-pounds would deter most attacks. He decided it was safe enough to relax a little, but he rested with one eye open. Any real shut-eye would have to wait until he completed the final stage of his mission.

CHAPTER THREE

In the shadows of a German cafe, a man with a shaved head stood in combat boots. He watched two men in black as they sat on the patio outside. The winter chill didn't seem to bother the two. Their round black hats sat snuggly over curly sideburns. Sundown had passed on this Sabbath day and both Orthodox Jews seemed lost in thought after their evening synagogue meeting.

The bald man watched the two religious men for ten minutes, then made a call on his cell phone. When he hung up, he drew a sidearm and held it close to his thigh.

A dark suburban drove up the quiet street, right on schedule. The few pedestrians on the sidewalk didn't pay any mind to the vehicle with tinted windows. The suburban stopped in front of the cafe, and three men, also with shaved heads, exited the vehicle and approached the two Jewish men. The religious men saw the aggressors, but they didn't panic. Instead, they stood boldly to face their attackers.

With little resistance, the two men in black hats were forced into the suburban. The vehicle sped away from the cafe. The man with the gun remained behind to ensure there were no witnesses. Then he walked away, a smile breaking across his grim face.

Corban Dowler's intercom buzzed, but he didn't answer it right away. Using his fingers, he tallied how many Christian missionaries COIL—the Coalition of International Laborers—had extracted from dangerous Portuguese-speaking regions. He hoped they might be able to transplant some of them into Brazil. Brazil had one hundred eighty-three million people with two hundred sixty-five people groups. It was estimated that over one hundred eighty of those groups had yet to be reached with the gospel of Jesus Christ. The most important job for those missionaries was to teach the Brazilians to reach their own people. Much of this was accomplished through the network that hard-working missionaries had previously founded. But they needed more hands, more laborers. COIL had much work to do behind the scenes.

The box buzzed again. Corban pressed the button.

"Yes, Kaylene?"

"Chloe and three guests to see you, sir."

His calendar showed he had no appointments scheduled, but if Chloe was accompanying a party, it was probably a legal matter. Or trouble.

"Send them in. Thank you."

Chloe opened the door and gave him "the look." The look was a signal to let him know to brace himself because something was afoot. A bold, Syrian-born Jewess with curly, black hair and brown eyes, Chloe had also served as a Mossad agent for twelve years. She was both professional and cautious.

Two women whom Corban had met followed Chloe into the room with a man he didn't know. The first woman was

Quin "Toad" LuDao's fiancée, Fon. She was a brave Chinese woman who worked for COIL in an unofficial capacity as an interpreter. Toad had rescued her from China and established her in the city thereafter.

The other woman was Eve Patters, Jesse "Milk" Patters' wife. Corban shook Eve's hand first. He knew the hair on her head was not her own, but a wig. She'd been diagnosed with cancer and the chemotherapy was hitting her hard. But still, with COIL's sponsorship, she ran one of the largest prayer chains in the country via the Internet, all from her home in Ohio.

"And this is Eve's brother-in-law, Joseph Patters," Chloe said. "Milk's, er, I mean Jesse's older brother."

Corban shook the meaty man's hand. He was as white as Milk, but taller.

A look of worry mixed with frustration showed on all three visitors' faces. When they were seated, Corban sat down and folded his hands on his desk. Chloe remained standing to his left. Though he knew why they were there, Corban didn't know how to begin or what to say. Three times he opened his mouth, but nothing came out. He preferred to be in disguise in a Muslim extremist compound than face the stern looks on their faces.

"Mr. Dowler, maybe you'll allow me to begin," Eve offered.

"Please." Corban sat back.

"It's been six months, Mr. Dowler, since the incident in England. Every week, Chloe sends us the same letter, saying that you're still looking, but there's no news yet. And we appreciate even that much. It's certainly more than the government offers the women of lost service members. We've come to hear it straight from you, Mr. Dowler. Where are our men?"

Under the pressure, Corban struggled to keep his face expressionless. He didn't have time to coddle the wives of his missing operatives; that was Chloe's job. But these women had been more than patient and he had to give them something.

"Maybe you could tell us what you know so far, Mr. Dowler," Fon said. "We realize you have security concerns, but we can keep things to ourselves. We just need to know."

"So far . . ." Unfolding his hands, he rubbed the whiskers he'd missed on his chin that morning. He'd been feeling the stress, too—along with sleepless nights. And he'd even run two different operations alone in Europe to track down an old enemy to see if that foe was responsible for the kidnapping of his men in England. All he'd found so far were dead ends, but he couldn't share that lack of hope. "What I do know is that a trap was set for us in England as we returned from the Malaysian rescue operation."

"*A trap?*" Eve gasped. "But two of our men are missing! I thought you were with them!"

"Corban . . ." Chloe gave him another look, this one of stern concern. Even though COIL wasn't a government agency, they usually kept intel to themselves to protect those in the field.

"You want it straight and tough? It won't be easy." Corban stared at his three guests in turn. "I've been protecting you from the worst of it, trying to give you some hope."

"Mr. Dowler, I'm only a poor farmer," said Joseph. "When I have a hard year with the crops and I'm listening to the weatherman, I want him to be honest and open with me, even if it means the year's crops are going to get even worse. That's what we need from you right now, even if it hurts. Even if it's the worst."

"Okay, you're right. They were on a rescue mission in Malaysia and it went bad. Everyone on the team was injured. We were on our way home afterward, but a trap was set in England for us."

"We understand that much now." Joseph set his jaw. "Miss Azmaveth has implied they may not even be in Great Britain anymore, where they were last seen."

"The intel we've gathered does support that, yes." Corban said a brief prayer in his heart. "An elaborate scheme was contrived to ambush our team. A communication was sent, making us believe it was from Chloe's cell phone. Then while our plane was being supposedly repaired, we stayed in a safe house we now believe was part of our adversaries' plan to capture us. To some degree, we believe those responsible for our Malaysian injuries were also responsible for the trap set in England.

"When Chloe and I discovered the trap, I tried to draw the enemy away from Jesse and Quin. But I fell off a building as they shot at me, and I was knocked unconscious. After coming to, I returned to the building, but our boys were gone. The police were there, but whoever attacked us were too slippery; they'd covered their tracks and disappeared."

"And someone sabotaged your plane to keep you in England," Fon said, nodding with understanding.

"You say you couldn't find our boys." Joseph shook his head. "What does that mean? Do you think they're alive? Dead? You have a better sense of this enemy than we do. What are their intentions?"

Sighing, Corban looked out the window. That window was bullet and sound proof for a reason. COIL was always under attack by those who didn't want the Word of God shared in distant lands. He couldn't begin to explain the hundreds of foes and dozens of countries that had COIL in their sights. Though appearing to be a simple organization occupying two suites on the fourth floor of a Broadway apartment building in Manhattan, COIL had a network that spanned the globe, a network based on his old CIA network.

"You should know that the leader of our primary field ops team was also kidnapped." Corban knew Chloe was already unhappy he'd disclosed intel that need not be shared, so he avoided looking at her. "He was wounded and bleeding from the Malaysian op. Quin and Jesse were with him. The last I saw—"

"Wait. There are *three* missing?" Eve stammered and reached for Fon's hand. "The team leader? You're talking about Nathan? Nathan Isaacson? Does his family know? Why haven't they been in contact with Fon and me? Why have you kept this from us? This is what we're talking about!"

Corban stared blankly at Eve as she and the others waited for him to respond.

Most American Christians had no idea what measures

Christians around the world had to go through just to read their Bibles, if they even had one, and the risks they took to get one. The previous year, an enemy he was still trying to find, code-named Abaddon, had hired an Italian assassin named Luigi Putelli to kill Corban. Luigi had chased Corban throughout Europe and Asia before Corban finally trapped the assassin. Thinking he was about to die, Luigi offered his life to Corban if he would only let him live. Corban had allowed Luigi to live, and Luigi had proved valuable to Corban, even assisting in the rescue of Corban's wife and daughter. But Luigi Putelli seemed to have gone rogue again, and was off the radar.

Suddenly, Corban wondered if he could find Luigi, the old assassin who chewed more gum than any human should, in an effort to give up cigarettes. If Corban could locate Luigi, then Luigi might be able to track down the missing COIL agents through the ex-assassin's European contacts. If only he had a lead as to where to find Luigi!

"Nathan doesn't have any family," Corban said. "As you said, many things are too sensitive to disclose. But you should know that Quin and Jesse were helping Nathan, carrying him, when they were taken. They were doing what they were supposed to be doing: caring for one another."

"Nathan has no immediate family," Chloe said, "but we're his family. The team is all Nathan has."

"And to answer your hard question, we don't know who is alive and who isn't. Nathan's injuries from Malaysia were the worst—a wound in his side and leg. Quin was shot in the shoulder. Jesse had some superficial shrapnel in his back, which made him the most mobile of the three. But there is one other issue." Corban took a deep breath. After countless missions and many lost soldiers, this part was never easy. "We are certain that one of the three is dead. And we don't know the status of the other two."

"Wha—?"

Their mouths gaped.

"Well, which one died, Mr. Dowler?" Eve asked. "Please, I have to know . . ."

"We don't know which one. I couldn't stay long in the building to investigate. If I could've gotten a sample of blood, then maybe. There was a lot of blood. Too much was lost for the person to have survived. The police who arrived on the scene were more interested in catching who'd caused the injuries than identifying who'd been taken. And I couldn't tell them our agents' real names, which would've placed all of you in danger."

"Maybe it was one of the bad guys' blood?" Fon asked.

"Not likely." Chloe shook her head. "You know our men don't carry lethal weapons. And traveling like they were, they didn't even have any of the NL weapons with them. We don't kill the enemy. They're always left alive."

Eve began to weep with one hand over her mouth. Fon squeezed her other hand.

"So, who were they?" Joseph asked. "We know COIL makes enemies when they extract believers from these dangerous countries. Maybe it's something to do with Malaysia, you said. You can't narrow it down?"

"We have some leads. Good leads. Yes, I'm narrowing it down, using every resource I can muster to find them and bring them home."

"Jesse said you used to work for the government," Eve said. "Can your old friends help us?"

"There are field operatives risking their lives to find those boys, even as we speak. It seems so simple, but prayer is our most powerful tool. Even in the worst circumstances, God has His angels. Jesse, who we nicknamed Milk, says that about the team. None of us are going to give up on—"

Corban's intercom buzzed.

"Sir, you said to let you know when Johnny Wycke arrived."

"Oh, right, Kaylene. Thank you. See if he'll wait."

"He says it's good news about Operation Rahab, sir."

"Okay, Kaylene. Send him in."

"Should we come back later, Mr. Dowler?" Fon said, her eyes red.

"No, you can stay. This concerns the boys. You know about everything now, anyway. It's important you don't speak about the status of any of this, even at church. The devil knows how to use us against ourselves, unfortunately."

The door opened without a knock. Johnny Wycke's bulky frame stepped around the three seated people without glancing at them. Even though Johnny had prepped for Jesse and Quin's Flash and Bang Team, Fon and Eve didn't know him. Johnny bent down and whispered in Corban's ear. Corban nodded. Then, Johnny reached under his shirt and produced the package. It was a manila envelope, thick with bubble wrap, torn and stained.

"Thank you," Corban said with a nod.

Johnny turned and, with his gaze on the floor, he walked

out of the office, closing the door behind him.

"Operation Rahab?" Joseph leaned forward. "That's something to do with Jesse?"

Corban didn't answer, which was an answer in itself. Turning the package over, he silently thanked God that it had arrived. Couriers had risked their lives to see it safely delivered.

He inserted a letter opener into one corner of the envelope and drew it across the top fold. After peeking inside, he dumped the contents onto the desk. Three photographs slipped out. There was nothing more. Each photo appeared to be exactly the same—a high-resolution image of Bucharest, the capital city of Romania, with its Danube River tributary in the background.

The view of Romania confirmed to Corban that the data encoded in the images was from Karol Ngolsk. When she was younger, the information specialist had been in contact with the one code-named Abaddon, but now as a Christian, Karol worked with Corban to fight the spiritual darkness.

"What is it, Mr. Dowler?" Fon asked. Everyone, including Chloe, craned their necks to see his desk better. "What's in the pictures?"

"Nothing is as it seems." Corban studied the photographs for a few more seconds, then shoved them back into the envelope. "It's nothing that can be understood at this time, but I'll have more news for you in a day or two. Chloe will be able to tell you then."

"But those pictures are . . . good news, right?" Eve asked with hope.

"Absolutely. The fact that I received them at all means

that someone, at least one of the three boys, is still alive."

"But . . . you don't know who?"

"No. Not yet."

CHAPTER FOUR

Taath Merari shivered against the damp, rock wall. His scrawny fingers clung to his thin shoulders where a blanket ridden with lice was pulled tightly against his bare skin. Up the middle of his back, his spine protruded hauntingly, his ribs and other bones punctuating his malnourished state. Other than the blanket, the twenty-year-old man was naked, unless the sores that blistered his body could be counted as covering.

Hearing footsteps coming up the corridor, he scurried like a rat against the wall in the opposite direction. He'd never been in this part of the dungeon, but he'd heard screams coming from this level—screams like from the other levels. Since there were no windows in the walls, he guessed he was still on an underground level. If only he could find stairs...

A hand reached out and clawed at Taath's blanket. Taath hissed and leapt clear of the cell door, ripping his blanket away from the stranger.

"Find the keys!" the unseen man said in German. "Move, you fool! Find the keys! Get us out of here!"

Once, on Oranienburger Strasse, Taath had been a student. That was a lifetime ago, though. Now, he didn't know where he was. He opened his mouth to speak back to the man, but no words came. They'd taken his speech by cutting out his tongue. But they hadn't needed to do that since the cancer with which they'd infected him had long since eroded his throat.

He shrank away from the man in the dark cell. The man cursed Taath in whispers, then he was quiet. Taath followed a single line of light bulbs that illuminated the corridor, strung by thin wire where cobwebs and mold seemed to ooze from the rock. Stairs. There had to be stairs somewhere!

Then, he found them. Testing the first step, he stopped and sniffed the air, barely believing this wasn't a trap. Did they know he was loose yet? He sniffed the air again for some signal, but it was no use. His senses were too damaged to smell if that slight breeze was fresh air or re-circulated air. Fresh air or not, he had to move on. It was simply a matter of time before they locked down the dungeon to hunt him. Taath glanced at his hand where he'd cut it horribly when the scalpel had broken. The tool had been his lock pick. The door had opened, and he'd stepped toward freedom—or so he hoped.

As quickly as possible, he ascended the stairs, but the simple act of breathing was difficult for him. The doctor had removed part of at least one lung for one of his experiments. Afterward, Taath hadn't healed from that surgery, and the raised, pink scar along his spine was still tender.

In a stumbling pace, he arrived at the next landing to discover yet another level, same as the last, with cells lining the left side of the corridor and a stone wall to the right.

There weren't as many screams emanating from these cells, which Taath figured might mean it was probably nighttime somewhere outside the walls. The screams were worse during the day, especially in the morning. That was the only way to tell the time. Their keepers kept the captives disoriented by an irregular feeding schedule.

Taath shuffled past the cells. They'd removed one of his Achilles' tendons, but he could still move quickly when he was feeling well. He hadn't felt well for a few months, though. If it was only physical illness, he thought he could live with it, but if he was permanently damaged psychologically from their cranial experiments, he didn't want to live. That was his most recent decision. At other times, when the misery had been so unbearable, he hadn't wanted to live at all. But right now, he was driven more by instinct than common sense. Animal instinct—that base impulse to be free.

"Friend!" a voice whispered.

Startled, he looked to his left. He wanted to keep moving and find the next stairs, but he knew what it was like to be inside the cells, looking out. Taath could imagine what the others saw from their steel door windows. For countless days, they'd stared at the rock wall and occasionally glimpsed men in full biohazard suits who passed by. Thus, Taath paused for a moment in his quest for freedom. In this cell, a bright-eyed tall man eyed him from the window that was only large enough for Taath to see a third of the man's face. This man was bearded and appeared to still be healthy.

"How'd you get out?" the man asked. He seemed much friendlier than the last man who'd tried to steal Taath's blanket. Since the man's German was accented, Taath guessed he was a foreigner, maybe an American.

Taath made the motion for the stranger to reach out his cell window toward the door's lock. The man understood and shoved his arm out the window, but his arms were still too fleshy. It had taken Taath months to lose all the sinew in his arms. Now, he was bare bones. Only when this man lost his weight would he be able to reach the lock. Even then, he'd need a tool, like the scalpel Taath had used.

The captive drew his arm back inside, scraping it on the edge of the window.

"I can't fit. Did you have a key?"

Taath shook his head.

"Did you use something? A piece of metal?"

He nodded.

"Do you still have it?"

Shaking his head again, he wished he'd thought to pick up the scalpel to give to this man. But it was time to continue.

"Wait! I have something for you to take!" For a moment, the man disappeared. Taath heard a clang from one of the lower levels. Someone was coming! The man was back, shoving a piece of cloth out his window. "Here. Take it! Tell others where we are. I'll pray for you." The man's voice choked. "Go! God be with you, Friend."

Taath crept up and snatched the cloth. What was it? It was barely the size of his hand. If it contained a message, Taath couldn't see it. The lighting here was dim, but they'd nearly blinded him in one eye. He tucked the cloth into his armpit.

"Go," the man said. "It's in your hands now. Hurry! Someone may come soon."

Nodding, Taath moved on, passing twenty more cells where others slept. With caution, he peeked into one to see if it was empty. A man was curled in the far corner with his own filthy blanket. These men hadn't been afflicted yet. Their bodies were still whole, still healthy. Taath had been there the longest. What they'd learned after experimenting on Taath they would use on these newer captives. But he pitied them all. They wouldn't be strong enough, as he'd been. The doctor had spoken to the guards with satisfaction about Taath. For a time, pleasing the doctor who cut him and implanted germs had been Taath's only comfort, clinging to even that small piece of attention and dignity, besides the pain and his blanket. Other captives had died or committed suicide by swallowing their blankets before they had endured half of what Taath had experienced.

There was a ramp instead of stairs at the end of this corridor. He limped upward and through a door that was ajar this night. Yes, he could feel the cold, fresh air on his sunken cheeks now. This was the right direction. At the top of the ramp, the floor leveled out to a bare hallway with one window on either side. Pulling his blanket tighter, Taath approached the left window. His trembling increased from the chill. The window, with no glass in its rock frame, faced a courtyard of a castle keep.

Above, the sky sparkled with millions of diamonds. Taath saw a lit window above a garage across the keep and wondered what warmth flickered within. Two garage doors bordered the rock-layered ground. But then a shadow moved in front of the window—the silhouette of a big man. Shrinking away from the open window, Taath crossed the hallway to the other window and gazed at a tall forest that stood thirty meters from the castle wall. About ten centimeters of snow covered the ground there. The pine and birch trees creaked in the night breeze. It was the only sound until a scream from one of the other levels made Taath jump.

Morning must be near, he figured. The screaming would be worse and he didn't want to hear another minute of it.

Taath turned from the window as a vehicle zipped past below him. It was a man on a four-wheeler with a rifle on his back. Maybe they were already looking for him.

As soon as the guard was out of sight, Taath climbed onto the windowsill. After dropping his blanket to the ground below, he lowered his body out the window until he hung by his fingertips.

His feet stretched for the frozen ground below, then he let go. The ground was farther than he thought. When he landed, he fell in the snow and rolled over to right himself. Brushing ice crystals from his shoulders, Taath picked up his blanket. He'd dropped the piece of cloth from his armpit as well, but he picked it up. Still, he wondered what strange message was written on the cloth. Maybe the man had been crazy, Taath pondered. There was nothing in their cells with which to write. But Taath tucked the cloth under his arm, anyway. In some small way, it gave him added purpose. The cloth represented the other lives for which he was escaping—not only his own.

Barefoot, Taath ran across the snow into the forest.

Under a birch tree, he paused on bare ground to look back at the castle. Shivering, he muffled a cough into his fist. He wasn't well at all, but he wouldn't ask the good doctor for help. Taath wouldn't miss this place. If he died in the forest, he hoped his body was never found so no one could see what horrid things they'd done to him, and the open sores he still had from a number of injected chemical tests.

To the right of the castle, he could see an access road leading away from the complex. To the left, the castle wall continued into darkness. The four levels that made up the dungeon were below the ground in that direction. Beyond the wall, he noticed a number of towers, but their windows were dark at this hour. If it wasn't for the four-wheeler he'd seen, he could've imagined being sent back to another century.

Taath coughed again. Running deeper into the trees, he put his back to his past of terror. Where there was no snow, his feet crunched on pine needles and twigs that snapped, but he didn't consider the noises he made. He wished only to avoid the freezing patches of snow where the careless footstep might leave a trail for pursuers. His bare feet were calloused from months on the dungeon floor. But the rest of the skin on his body was sensitive to the winter's brutal elements, especially since his bones had no fat or muscle to insulate his walking corpse. With determination, he told himself if he kept moving, he'd be okay. If he could only keep his body heat up, even from the single potato he'd been given the day before.

Not far into the forest, he turned left in an attempt to parallel the access road to the castle, but Taath was not a woodsman. In the foreign surroundings, he was soon lost. Or maybe the road had curved away from him. He stubbornly pressed himself to continue, hoping he wasn't walking in circles.

Much later, possibly two hours, his lips were numb and his body was in danger of complete exhaustion. He was past hypothermia; parts of him felt warm. Taath didn't notice as the sky began to brighten toward sunrise. At a crawling pace, he pushed onward.

When he cracked his brow on a gully rock after tumbling down a gradual slope, it somehow registered in his mind he was near death. Crawling out of the gully, but unable to gather the strength to stand again, he rolled under a bank of earth. Roots as thin as hair tickled his cheek as he rested on his side. Strangely, the dirt around him wasn't frozen.

Taath reached up to the earthen ceiling and clawed loose clumps of dirt to cover his body. Lifting a leg, he weakly kicked more soil free to bury his legs. In minutes, Taath's body was covered by rich soil. Only a circle for his face was exposed to the winter morning air.

He didn't remember falling asleep, but he woke with a start. The sun was up, but not visible behind the clouds that dropped fluffy whiteness.

That was odd, Taath mused. It was snowing in his dungeon cell.

As he lay there watching it snow, his escape gradually came back to him, but he couldn't remember all of it. The animal within him had pushed him. Delirium had overwhelmed him and he couldn't remember finding his earthen shelter that felt so warm.

After shaking his right hand free of dirt, Taath grabbed at the fresh snow and stuffed some into his mouth. *Fresh snow.* It tasted so good. Maybe he could live the rest of his life right here in this paradise.

Falling back to sleep, he woke again possibly minutes later to the sound of voices. It couldn't be voices, he told himself. Had he not escaped the mean voices, the cold steel, and the numbing medication? But there were voices coming from the forest, and the sound of dogs, as well. Hunting hounds were tracking him. For an instant, Taath considered emerging from his den and running down the gully through the snow, but how far would he get? They had dogs. He didn't even have shoes. And he was so warm where he was.

Taath didn't move. Closing his eyes, he tried to focus on a happier time, before he'd been kidnapped from the campus, before the months of shivering in the empty cell, before his body had become foreign to him. His mother— she was icing a cake. Was it his cake? No. It was his sister's birthday. He stabbed a finger into the icing when his mother wasn't looking. But his father had seen him sample the creamy sweetness. His father winked, said nothing, and continued reading his paper.

A tear rolled from Taath's eye and was soaked up by the thirsty soil packed next to his ear. Crying wasn't safe, he knew, not when he needed to retain his body moisture. He'd learned that months ago when he realized he was given only two cups of water a day. Preserve the moisture. No crying. But he had snow now, he remembered, so he cried.

He turned his head and watched four men stride into the gully. Two hounds on long leashes led one of the men.

Stopping at the bottom of the gully, the hounds sniffed in Taath's direction not ten meters away.

"There's no way he came this far," one man said. They had rifles and sidearms. "Your dogs are worthless in this snow. We're probably on the scent of some deer! We'll double back."

"My dogs can track through a quarter of a meter," the canine owner said in defense. "It makes sense he came this way. The town's only two kilometers away."

"The longer we stand here talking, the deeper this snow gets! We're going back. Those dogs were a waste. We should've never waited for you to get here! Dr. Stashinsky said as much."

The men tromped back up the gully, pulling the dogs along. Taath didn't cheer or even smile at his good fortune. He was thinking too clearly to believe his hardships were over. If he were two kilometers from some town, which way was it? Unless he found something for his feet, he'd never be able to travel barefoot over so much snow. But then he remembered the snow would be in patches under the trees. As much as he hated to leave his shelter, he knew he should travel while it was snowing so the few tracks he had to leave would be covered. And the day would be warmer than the night.

It was time to move, but two kilometers in which direction? That wasn't too far; he'd find the town. Taath ate more snow. He'd leave soon. Just a few more minutes in the warmth.

CHAPTER FIVE

Corban and his wife, Janice, strolled hand in hand down the Atlantic City boardwalk on the coast of New Jersey. The surf splashed gently onto the beach. Twenty kite fliers twisted and pulled on their airborne creations far above.

It was a relaxing, carefree scene to everyone except Corban and Janice. There was the saltwater taffy vendor who kept badgering the boardwalk's visitors—everyone except the Dowlers. The vendor drifted along with them or behind them. And there was the civil servant with the tool belt, tapping on the planks, yet he had a habit of glancing over his shoulder and moving away every time Corban came too close.

The question wasn't whether Corban was being watched or not; the question was, for whom were they working? A number of government agencies had kept tabs on the ex-spy since he'd left the Agency. He knew if he could spot these two, there were probably others in relay, as well.

Ever since the ambush in England, Corban had been carrying an NL-1 tranquilizer everywhere he went, even in the US. And though the non-lethal pistol only fired pellets and was nothing against live rounds, it still gave him a sense of security. COIL and its workers were under siege.

He wouldn't admit it to Janice, but Corban preferred COIL's enemies to focus on him rather than on other Christians in the field. Missionaries were easy targets. They stepped out in faith and risked their lives daily for Christ in whatever environment they were led. These servants truly carried their crosses daily. Trained to fight covert foes, Corban felt it was his responsibility to draw attention from the field workers.

More than the attention, however, were the blatant attacks upon COIL in the last two years. Since COIL made every effort to protect the field servants of Christ, someone had been targeting COIL specifically. Corban was certain the central enemy instigating and funding these attacks against his agency was the entity or person code-named Abaddon. His team also suspected Abaddon to be the demon mentioned in the Book of Revelation, and perhaps Abaddon's attacks on COIL were in preparation for the coming of the Antichrist.

The unknowns about the attacker made Corban uneasy. He was used to having superior intel, and he hoped solid information that day would give him grounds to act.

Janice pulled Corban to a stop and laughed while pointing at the sky.

"Look at that one! A shark with four fish streaming behind the tail!"

Corban chuckled at the kite and pointed at something silly about the last fish's facial expression. But neither Janice nor Corban were truly interested in the decorative kites.

This wasn't the first time Corban had brought his wife as

cover on an operation. Once, she'd been sent as a nurse overseas with the International Red Cross to deliver documents to him. Other times, she traveled to distant countries to check on missionaries, or to pick up and smuggle back important packages. Janice loved fieldwork, though Corban tried to keep her out of the most dangerous operations. She was too inexperienced to handle tails or a hunter-tracer team, so Corban took special precautions to send her on only the most casual missions. Besides, Janice preferred to remain at home with their adopted blind daughter, Jenna.

If it were up to Corban, he would've had Luigi Putelli as his backup on the boardwalk that day. Every time Corban saw a gum wrapper in an ashtray or on the ground, he wondered if Luigi had been there.

As the couple watched the shark swoop and dive after the fishes, the taffy vendor and boardwalk maintenance man paused as well. One was behind them and one was in front. Corban was becoming annoyed at their performance; they were such amateurs. He guessed they were junior feds of some sort—information gatherers. Though Corban and Janice had switched cars twice before arriving in Atlantic City, it would've been easy enough to figure out where they were headed.

"Should we get Jenna a souvenir?" Janice tugged him toward the gimmick and gadget store behind them.

"Yeah, you pick something out." He kissed her hand. "I'll use the bathroom in the back."

They entered the boardwalk store and browsed a rack of postcards together for a minute. The lighting was choked by the press of crowded shelves and racks of Atlantic City gizmos: water guns, stuffed animals, stationary, beach buckets and shovels, magic tricks, and clown noses.

The cashier appeared to be a freckly-faced teenager, but Corban knew he was a trained agent. Corban caught the young man's eye, and there was a brief look of acknowledgement. His eyes glanced behind Janice at the plank worker who lingered outside the door. The taffy vendor was there, too, but neither tail was wearing the right costume to assume the ploy of a curious shopper or tourist.

Giving Janice a kiss, Corban whispered for her to stay close to the cashier, and he made his way quietly to the back wall covered with stuffed animals. He paused before the wide wall. They always put the clown in a different place, that ugly one no one would think of purchasing. Where was it? After finding it on a low shelf to his right, he checked over his shoulder, then squeezed the clown's left shoe three times. There was a whirring sound, then a click and a section of the shelves of merchandise popped loose. Corban reached down, gripped the bottom shelf, and heaved upward. The secret door was counter-balanced and swung up easily. The stuffed critters were barely unsettled. Ducking inside, he used a steel handle to pull the door closed until it clicked again.

"How'm I supposed to get any work done when you bring feds to my doorstep?" a voice asked behind Corban.

Corban faced a man at a desk. The desk was so tightly placed between the inner and outer walls, the man must've climbed over it to access his cluttered office and chair. Beyond the first desk was another. They each had a computer on them, and both were running diagnostics or downloads. Above his head, two mainframes hung on cables. A high-resolution scanner and a filing cabinet completed the underground office.

"Good to see you, Miles." Smiling, Corban shook the man's hand over the first desk. "You staying in the Word?"

"Can't live by computer chips alone." Miles settled into his chair again. "How long's it been, Corban?"

Miles Grady was a young CIA contractor who ran his own research office. Since he was also a Christian, Corban had fellowshipped with him when Corban had been in the Agency. As a contractor, Miles chose his own assignments, a luxury he preferred so his faith wasn't compromised by ungodly strategies.

Sitting on the edge of the desk, Corban pointed at the next desktop screen which was split into four surveillance frames. Each frame showed a different angle of the gimmick shop and door.

"Friends of yours or mine?" Corban asked of the two tails outside on the boardwalk.

Zooming in on the boardwalk maintenance man, Miles took a snapshot of his face. The monitor flashed a personnel file onto the screen. He did the same with the taffy vendor.

"National Security boys," Miles said. "Friends of neither, but I've seen them before. We pretend we don't know the other exists. The NSA is always wondering what the CIA is sending me by way of national secrets."

Corban studied their profiles and memorized their vital agency statistics.

"Some feds followed me into the city, but these two look

like they could be Atlantic City-based."

"Whoever followed you into Atlantic City probably contacted these two locals to tail you since they know the area. I doubt they even know who you are. Not really. Probably know your face only. Maybe an alias or two. They're small fries, monitoring me and my visitors, mainly. What brings you to my shack, anyway?"

Pulling the manila package from under his shirt, Corban handed it to Miles. Miles donned a pair of rubber gloves before he dumped the three photographs onto the desk. This wasn't the first time Corban had brought him something to decipher. Since Corban had met Karol Ngolsk six months ago in Romania, she'd sent him a number of cryptograms to assist in his investigation of the disappearance of COIL's three operatives.

Picking up a magnifying glass, Miles studied the three photos for a few seconds.

"I give up," Miles said. "What's the key this time?"

"The sum of A-B-C. A transparent overlay should give you a fourth image."

"Okay, we'll go high resolution. Hmmm . . ."

Miles got to work, scanning each image in turn at over fourteen hundred dpi. He turned the primary graphics screen so Corban could watch him work.

"Now, I transparentize them . . ." Miles said.

"Is that even a word?"

Shrugging, Miles began the overlay, each frame upon the other, then ran a compare and contrast algorithm on all three frames to expose their unique differences. A small box highlighted a portion of each frame and Miles zoomed in ten times in the frames before slight squiggle marks became visible. Then, he overlaid each contrast square on a clean spreadsheet. All three images contained a fraction of a microscopic message or code. Separate, they were mere squiggles. Merged, however, they became a six-letter word. On the screen was the word, "*Xacsin*."

"That's everything?" Corban asked.

Neither of them would say the word aloud. Whatever it meant was so important that Karol had slyly concealed its delivery. Men had risked their lives across Europe for that single word.

"That's it." Miles highlighted all of his work, the frames and the word, yet unsaved, and held his finger over the delete button. "You got it?"

"Got it. Thanks."

Miles worked quickly to erase everything from his hard drive, then checked for any backup caches to be certain. Next, he cut the three photographs up with a pair of scissors, added a couple bogus photos, and burned them all in a tiny furnace the size of a shoebox.

"Later, I'll dump the ashes in the toilet." The technician glanced at the store's front screen view. "You'd better scoot on out of here before those two out front get too curious. Say, how's your daughter doing?"

"She's good." Corban moved to the false wall. "Take care, Miles."

"Can you shake those guys or do you need my guy out front to give you a hand?"

"I could do it with my eyes closed. Well, your back door will help."

Back in the store, Janice had bought a dozen postcards and a stuffed character called Taffy Andy for Jenna. With a knowing nod from the cashier, Corban and Janice exited through the back door and wasted no time escaping along the back avenue to their parked car.

CHAPTER SIX

"Good morning, Mrs. Azmaveth." June Ellerman, the young investigative reporter, greeted Chloe. "Thank you for coming."

"Thank you for having me, June." Dressed in a modest pantsuit, Chloe seated herself before June and three cameras. "Please, call me Chloe."

An old hand at public relations, Chloe brushed her curly hair aside so the cameras could catch her pretty face. June Ellerman, a fit thirty-year-old, had been badgering Chloe for an interview for months. Corban had finally given his permission, giving her no restrictions as to what could be said outside her own discretion.

"Very well, Chloe. We've been doing an assortment of exposés on covert organizations. I believe the public should be aware of those clandestine persons who prowl through the night and seem to have no rules to follow, no laws. Some even have an international license to kill. No matter how much our world governments deny it, we know these teams exist. The public should have full disclosure. Don't you agree?"

Chloe smiled back at the reporter. June's dark hair was up in a tight bun and she wore a stylish outfit. The young reporter had knowing eyes, as if she knew all the answers before she asked the questions. Good ol' reporters, Chloe thought to herself. They didn't really care about the public. Media outlets had their own agendas. She wondered what June's agenda was.

"You can't imagine a time or situation where secrecy is needed?" Chloe asked.

"Certainly, with military operations, but when it comes to citizens' privacy, we need to keep the governments in check, right?"

"I don't disagree."

"But you work for a very different type of organization. You call it COIL. C-O-I-L. Can you tell our viewers about COIL?"

"COIL is an acronym that stands for the Commission of International Laborers, based on the Bible verse in Luke 10:2—'*The harvest is plentiful, but the laborers are few.*' Those were the words of Jesus referring to the plenty that are in need of salvation in Him, but so few laborers actually enter the field. One of COIL's greatest endeavors is to monitor volatile situations for Christian missionaries and workers who take up that charge and become laborers. We provide these people with early warning systems so they can safely and successfully exit a foreign country before they're harmed. In some cases, we ensure their safety so they can stay in the country without harm."

"And because this series of interviews regards covert operations, what is it about COIL that is considered covert?"

"Not much, I suppose." Chloe shrugged. "Our greatest concern is the safety of our international missionaries, so most of the work is done on the phone by case workers who monitor adverse countries. Nothing covert about that."

"Give our viewers at home an example of an adverse country."

"Okay. The Kingdom of Saudi Arabia is one."

"You have missionaries there?"

"We monitor missionaries and other Christian workers there, yes."

"Are they in danger often? Be honest."

"No, not often." Chloe paused for effect and noted the triumphant look on June's face. "Not often, but *always*. It's an Islamic state, considered a radical one, at that. The country hosts their religion's most holy sites—Mecca and Medina. Thirteen hundred years ago, there were many Christians in Saudi Arabia, but most have been expelled or executed since, dozens in this decade alone. Arabia's government hires public relations firms in the US to cover up their atrocities against Christian converts and other so-called political criminals. As one popular monitor stated, any person who does mission work or converts a Muslim to Christianity faces jail, expulsion, or execution. It's common knowledge that Bibles are not allowed in Saudi Arabia, under penalty of stoning in some areas. So, are Christ's ambassadors in danger for sharing His love and peace? Absolutely. Daily. But the opposition clings so severely to the cruel bondage of Islamic extremism that we're forced to use some clandestine avenues to support believers there."

"Outside of Muslim countries, does COIL deal with anyone else?"

"Every country in the world has problems with true

Christianity being preached openly, even this country."

"Excuse me, Chloe, but this is a free country."

"Where a teenager is expelled from high school for praying over her food in the cafeteria? Really, June, you know better."

June forced a smile through her reddening face.

"What does COIL do for Christians in these difficult circumstances?"

"The Bible says that anyone who truly lives for Christ shall suffer persecution. It doesn't take a theologian to understand that persecution will exist with or without COIL. There are many forms of persecution, though. We stick to the physical—sticks and stones—concept, but words cannot hurt a Christian."

"I don't understand. COIL steps in under the threat of sticks and stones?"

"Or fire-bombing, or machete, or bullet. Yes. We try to keep the missionaries alive."

"And you'll do anything to keep them alive?"

"Anything? Of course not. Some missionaries, even in the face of grave danger, don't want to leave their posts. Others who choose to leave, we assist them through peaceful means only."

"But you have covert teams operating to extract these missionaries by any means necessary."

"You're not listening, June. *Peaceful means only*. I read all the field reports. We've never caused a death while extracting a missionary family or individual—unless you want to count our own people getting killed while trying to help others."

"Are you saying these covert teams are not armed?"

"Only with—"

"Careful, Chloe. I've read many reports and research about COIL."

Chloe bit her tongue. She took a deep breath before answering calmly.

"Our teams—and all of our operatives—are armed with non-lethal devices only. Stun guns and such."

"Not real bullets? They use nothing lethal whatsoever in their operations?"

"No. Never."

"These reports, the field reports that you receive, are they available to the public?"

"Do you mean are they available to you? I really doubt the public is as concerned about the safety of foreign thugs as you are, June."

"I simply want to hold COIL accountable, as well as other covert organizations."

"Of course you do. Do you know the song, '*Amazing Grace*,' June?"

"Sure. Everyone is familiar with at least the first verse, I think."

"If you went to Saudi Arabia right now, as a woman, not only would you be forbidden to drive, you'd have to wear a veil or go to jail if you weren't publicly beaten first. And if you went to the supermarket and started to quietly sing '*Amazing Grace*' to yourself and a male Muslim heard you, you could be stripped to the waist and publicly whipped on the back. Forty lashes or blows with a cane might teach you the lesson. If, by some act of God, you were able to contact

COIL as you were being dragged into the town square for your shameful beating and scarring for life, COIL might be able to whisk you out of the country, if one of our agents or contacts could get to you in time."

"So, these field operatives would rescue me without violence?"

"There might be a couple smoke grenades involved, but it beats the alternative of bloodshed, right?"

"I can't believe your people rescue these believers from the jaws of death, with the enemy armed to the teeth—without violence."

"The Word of God, the Bible, tells us to love our enemies. All of them. Now, we wouldn't be showing them much love if we were killing them, would we? That's true Christianity."

"But it seems you are prejudiced, if not violent," June stated. "You've said over and over how you rescue Christians. What about other religious missionaries? Jehovah's Witnesses and Mormons are in danger, too. You refuse to help them?"

"That's a good question, June." Chloe reached over and patted the younger woman's hand. "When we were writing our mission directives, this was a major concern because we wanted to help everyone, though we have barely enough resources to help only the true Christians. We prayed about this extensively. This was almost three years ago. The situation, however, worked itself out."

"How is that?"

"Well, you see, there's only One God. Those who don't stand on His saving grace during the most extreme persecutions can't continue their apostate work. It's difficult to die in a foreign land for a god that doesn't exist. The Book of Galatians, chapter six, verse twelve, touches on this fact. False teachers are more concerned about personal safety than correct doctrine. It's that simple. Other religions and cult missionaries simply pulled out of the most dangerous places when this recent rash of world persecution began. There were once millions of missionaries in the name of Mormonism, for instance. It's not so, anymore. They have abandoned their posts because they don't have anything real on which to base their faith. It's not the One True God of the Bible in which they believe.

"Keep in mind also, June, that persecutors are driven by darkness, and the true darkness wants only to kill the true Light. More often than not, Christians are the only ones who are targeted in these foreign lands. The devil wouldn't get anywhere if he were targeting his own false teachers. He'd be destroying himself."

"You're quite the fanatic, Chloe. Listening to you, I'd say you're an extremist. No one would condemn your operatives for taking out a few torturers, you know."

"June, we don't do what we do for public opinion. We serve God in Jesus Christ's Name by the power of the Holy Spirit and His guidance. And though we don't serve man, we do desire that all men, women, and children recognize the joy that comes in serving Christ."

"Let's talk more about your covert operations and less about your religion," June said. "Countries certainly wouldn't allow you to move across their borders freely. Don't international laws mean anything to you?"

"COIL tries to exhaust all diplomatic measures before anything covert is ever exercised. Of course, laws are important. The Bible says in Romans that we are to live peaceably with all men as much as possible, and to obey the government—and we do—as much as we can."

"But you still sneak across countless borders every time a follower of your Jesus cries for help. You have no accountability."

"If we were really violating international laws, June, we'd be shut down. Several intelligence agencies around the world watch us very closely. We make no compromises. It's commonly understood that countries that violate human rights must be handled differently. When we parachute into Duba, Saudi Arabia, to save Christian women from forced circumcision, borders don't exist. There's no border that condemns such mutilation, so there's no border that can keep assistance out."

"You seem to really hate Muslims, Chloe."

"What a horrible thing to say, June! Even though the Koran instructs true Muslims to persecute and wipe out any non-Muslim, a true Christian would never wish ill or do harm to anyone of the Islamic faith. Muslims spend billions to eradicate everything but Islam, therefore, their presence is quite an obstacle. In many ways, they are in the forefront. But Islam is regional. In Central and South America, our greatest obstacles are guerrillas who kidnap missionaries to ransom them. In Mongolia, we face Lamaism, or Tibetan Buddhism. In North Korea and China and Cuba, we deal with communism and atheism."

"We can talk all day about how holy COIL is, Chloe, but

let me ask you this: would you allow me to accompany a covert operation to witness your organization first-hand—in action?"

"Are you serious?" Chloe gasped. "I mean, you'd want to go that far?"

"I was in the Army Reserves for four years. I could handle it. But, of course, you won't allow me to accompany an op because you have things to hide—maybe even untruths you've told our viewers today, skeletons in the closet, and such."

"No, no. Um. Wow. On the contrary, uh, June. We'd be delighted to take you along on something real. I must warn you, though—they rescue the persecuted in the face of death, nothing less. And we often lose operatives."

"You're saying you'd actually allow me to go with one of your teams? No one has ever allowed me to accompany them before."

"Since you have military experience . . ." Chloe shrugged. "We have nothing to hide. I can't promise you'll make it out alive, but if you're willing . . ."

"And your teams are well-trained, right?"

"They're the best of the best from all over the world—Navy SEALs, paramilitary from China, Belgian commandos, you name it."

"But they're all Christians."

"Now they are. Many have, well, pretty hard-core pasts, but God can change anyone's heart."

"And where will I go? Who will I go with? Let's give the viewers a little teaser."

"It's tough to say right now, but we'll stick you with one

of our rescue teams in a real situation."

"With your . . . Christian commandos?"

"Yes, with our Christian commandos."

CHAPTER SEVEN

The morning after the interview with June Ellerman, Chloe eased into Corban's office. She cleared her throat only when she realized Corban hadn't noticed her entry.

"Oh. Chloe. Come on in."

"Don't tell me you were here all night again." As she sat down in front of his desk, she noticed three plastic bowls and spoons on the shelf behind him. "Janice's catering service?"

Corban set his computer mouse aside and focused on his public relations manager.

"Yeah, we made a family event of it. She brought Jenna since she had another snow day yesterday. Half the city's shut down. Nothing else for them to do. How's Zvi making out?"

"He's stuck in Pittsburgh. I don't even know why he went up there. It seems I see this office more than I see my own husband. How about our three boys overseas? Any clues?"

"Ever heard of Xacsin Castle?"

"*Xacsin.* I've heard that name, but it's been years." Chloe cringed. "Please don't tell me that sadistic guy's involved!"

"Afraid so. Interesting story about this Mr. Xacsin." Corban placed a photograph in front of Chloe. "Looks like he's another one of Abaddon's men. It's been confirmed through my European contact—the attack in Malaysia, my family being abducted, now our three boys in England. Xacsin's been up against us for over a year and we're only now learning of his involvement. He's been keeping his head down. How familiar are you with his origins?"

"I know he started in Ireland. He was the IRA's basic terrorist trying to crumble England for a while. And I know he had enough influence that when he went rogue on a couple bombings, the IRA didn't rein him in; he was too powerful. They exiled him instead of killing him. Word was he went to Germany and found a new calling, some sort of white supremacist group. The Mossad was watching him for a few years, probably still are, because he sponsored hate crimes against Jews all over Europe, but nothing anyone could prove. I didn't know he had a castle. You did say Xacsin Castle?"

"Yep. It seems he's broadened his scope to include Christians now. Jews and anyone who's pro-Zion or pro-Israel could be a target. I'd sure like to sit down with him and ask why he took my wife and daughter last year if his beef is with me."

"You know why, Corban. He can't attack you head-on, so he finds and goes after your weaknesses." Chloe bowed her head, knowing Corban was aware of all this. After the attack six months earlier, he'd been fortunate to get his family back at all. The Lord was gracious. Now, finding another contact of Abaddon's who was involved in that attack was opening old wounds, not to mention the fresh wounds of the three missing operatives. "Well, COIL has never held back our support for Israel's right to exist. They're God's Chosen People. And *forever* in the Bible means *forever*. That's probably why he's targeted our people and the operation in Malaysia. It's a whole lot more complex than we thought. And we're not just being targeted because of our work to support missionaries in dangerous lands. We're being targeted for our support for Jews, as well."

"Zack McLeery," Corban spat aloud as if it were a curse word. "That's the name he uses, but I guess he goes by Xacsin McLeery, too. He likes to include that 'sin' suffix, evidently."

"Creative."

"Why didn't the Mossad take him out a long time ago?"

"I don't know. It was never on my plate. This Zack, or Xacsin, probably has a dozen loyal followers. If anyone removed him, he'd just be replaced by someone with the same ideals, all sponsored by whoever this Abaddon is. So, are our boys in this castle of his?"

"It's the best lead we have so far, Chloe, and I'm confident enough in the source that I've set things in motion already. He and his compound have a website; they're claiming to be the original Germans by way of their Wend heritage. The Wends were a first century Slavic people."

"His alias is Irish, but he's claiming German descent?"

"Hate-filled ideals can be blinding. And they have no shame about their hatred. He seems to have a mess of skinheads from America and Europe working for him, probably more than what you'd guessed."

"Where's the castle?"

"Midway between Berlin and the Baltic Sea."

"That's a cold region. Deep forests, most of it. Some farming land. I was through there years ago."

"Don't even think about it, Chloe."

"What?" She frowned. "Am I still on probation for the Malaysia nightmare?"

"There's never been any probation. If I thought you were at fault over Operation Helena, Chloe, I would've fired you. You're feeling responsible for our boys' injuries, I know, but don't. I really need you here to run things and coordinate."

"And you're going to Berlin?"

"I'm calling it Operation Rahab. After six months of searching, I believe we're ready to move. The more I learn about Xacsin, the more he scares me. I need you to dig up everything you can on this castle."

"You're certain he's working with or for Abaddon?"

"Somehow, yes. Our Romanian contact used to communicate with Abaddon when she was young, so she was able to confirm this much. She sent me Xacsin's name specifically. There've been others who delved into satanic means to accomplish their agendas. They worked with Abaddon, so this could be the same enemy. We can only pray that our boys aren't too—"

"You don't need to say anything more, Corban."

"Right. Well, from what we've learned in the past, the one we know as Abaddon gives his followers directives. I'm meeting with CIA Deputy Director Buchanen to find out what he knows about Xacsin. Then Operation Rahab will commence."

Chloe studied his face. It was so expressionless, and yet so full of spy secrets, but she'd learned how to read him.

"What aren't you telling me? What's concerning you beyond the obvious?"

Stalling and avoiding her eyes, he went to the window and stood looking out, his hands in his pockets.

"It's not good, Chloe."

She closed her eyes and mouthed a silent prayer.

"What is it?"

"A . . . naked man stumbled into a North German town yesterday. He died before anyone could communicate with him. Not that he could communicate, anyway. Someone had cut out his tongue."

"How'd he die? Exposure? They're having a tough winter there."

"Partly from exposure, but mostly, he died from about two dozen experiments performed on his body. Everything from minor lobotomies to nerve transplants. Rupert Mach, Berlin's COIL director, was able to get into the investigation from the start. He says they identified the man as Taath Merari, a Jewish student from Berlin. He's been missing for eighteen months."

"Xacsin did this, I know it. It's his signature. He's been suspected of mutilations and torture before. This was only yesterday, though? How'd we hear about it so fast and connect it to Xacsin? Rupert knows what we know?"

Corban faced Chloe.

"No, I haven't told Rupert anything. The poor Taath boy

had a piece of fabric with my name on it."

"Your name?"

"Right. Written . . . in blood. Rupert rushed a test on a hunch. It was Nathan's blood."

"Okay." Chloe's bottom lip trembled. "This means Nathan didn't die in London. He's one of the two still alive. I mean, he wrote his own blood on the piece of fabric, right?"

"Perhaps. But we know someone died in London. So it's down to Toad or Milk now."

Chloe nodded sadly, but was still relieved that it seemed Nathan hadn't died. All of the men were special to COIL, but Chloe knew Nathan had always been closer to Corban than the others were. Nathan wasn't just the commander of the best extraction team COIL had, he was also an emboldened Christian leader.

"Yes, you said either Toad or Milk lost too much blood to survive in London. We can only imagine what Taath's escape from the castle has done to the compound's security. Corban, we need to act now! Please tell me you've sent someone in already . . ."

"Of course," Corban said. "I did the minute I heard the name Xacsin from our contact."

"Why won't you let me go, Corban? I want this as bad as you."

"Involve yourself all you want, just do it from here."

"No wonder you've been pulling night shifts." Chloe sighed. "Did you watch the interview last night?"

"Oh. No. Sorry. Janice gave me the highlights, though."

"Do you want to yell at me? I should've known that

reporter would ambush me like that."

"I think you handled that June woman fine, the way I hear it, Chloe—until the end."

"The inclusion of her in an op. I panicked, Corban! I was ready for everything she threw at me until that. The opportunity to prove ourselves was all I could think of, but I regretted it the next minute. I'm sorry."

"This isn't a dictatorship, Chloe. I don't have to agree with everything. Maybe it'll work out."

"So you don't want me to step into the waiting room and tell her it's all off?"

"What? She's here?"

"Yeah. June says she doesn't want us to set up anything special just for her. She wants in on a genuine op."

"Boy, she has no idea what she's asking. What are her intentions?"

"She's a conspiracy theorist and she wants dirt. I've checked her other reports. Her goal is to prove COIL as an illegitimate covert organization."

"Because I don't have the time to put kid gloves on for her, she'll get what she wants and more than she bargained for," Corban said.

"Just try to keep her alive. I'll make sure she signs a waiver."

"Do that. And tell her to be here tomorrow morning with an overnight bag only."

"A one-night op?"

"I've never heard of a one-night op. I'm saying that's all she's bringing. If she wants to play reality TV, she'll take no more than the rest of us."

"So, you're already off to Germany? Operation Rahab?"

"Yeah, and I'm not coming home until I have some bodies—our boys, dead or alive."

Juan "Scooter" Blanco had requested to be a part of the operation that would free Toad, Milk, and his friend Nathan from whomever had taken them in London. But now, the short muscled operative for COIL wasn't so sure he had what it took. Feeling like the bionic man, Scooter raised his arm over his head and winced as he painfully rotated his new joint. The doctors had rebuilt his shoulder after he'd taken a round in the armpit while escaping the Fhatl Lasam Prison in Malaysia during the last op. Since he was still on the mend, he wondered why Corban had pulled him from his physical therapy.

Scooter studied a slip of paper as his boat was piloted down the Dnieper River in Kiev, a city of two million in north-central Ukraine. The paper had an address on it. He wasn't too thrilled about the treasure hunt Corban had sent him on, but Scooter hoped Nathan was at the end of the trail. Milk and Toad were like brothers to Scooter, and he cared for them greatly, but he'd known Nathan longer than anyone else in his life, even longer than he'd known his own wife. The two men had been the most decorated Marine sniper team before they'd left the military as Christians. Scooter had even grown a thick mustache to memorialize his missing friend, but it was nothing like Nathan's wild handlebar.

The boat bumped against the side of the river's cement containment wall. The driver rattled off a couple sentences in Ukrainian and pointed south. Scooter paid him a handful of *hryvnias* and climbed out of the boat. Stretching his shoulder again, he wondered if he should've brought his sling. No, he decided. He hated the sling. It made him feel weak.

After several operations in the Marines across the Middle East, Scooter spoke Arabic pretty well. That language didn't help him now, though; he didn't speak a lick of the languages of the half-dozen countries he'd visited over the past week. Even when he'd been an active field agent with the Flash and Bang Team, he hadn't traveled this much. And all the cloak and dagger stuff seemed so mundane and tiring, even useless.

First, he'd gone to Serbia a week ago. Then he'd delivered a package to the COIL office in Berlin. Norway had been next, and then a package to the Czech Republic. But why had he been in Greece yesterday? Oh, yeah—to get the address for here.

Maybe Corban was touring him around Europe to test him to see if he was up to the challenges ahead. Could he be counted on after a near fatal injury and six months of down time? Scooter ran his fingers over his fresh crew cut. Yeah, he was back. He was just a little tired and edgy, but he was back.

Gazing to the south at an industrial-class neighborhood, Scooter hoped this was the last stop. He walked nearly a mile before he came to the block with the address on his paper.

From across the street, Scooter studied the house he was about to approach. Traps could be anywhere, too many for one man to see. Corban had told him to trust nothing, for nothing was as it seemed in the spy world. He'd shaken a dozen tails in the past week alone, so he knew Corban wasn't being paranoid. COIL had real enemies. Scooter didn't have a clue who those enemies were most of the time, and he rarely spoke the languages to ask them. As a short Mexican, he stood out more often than not, but he tried to pass as a Spaniard or Italian when he could get away with it.

The house before him was a brownstone, sharing walls with two other narrow, tall residences. The region had a troubled past, but unlike the neighborhoods across the river, these houses appeared to be relatively untouched by the last century's wars and communist rule.

Three stories high, the house appeared to be normal at first glance, but he knew better, so he sought out the subtle details about which Corban had warned him. There was a camera on the light pole to his right, the lens pointed at the front door. A man swept the cracked sidewalk to his left, but he wore combat boots. *Combat boots?* It was a dead giveaway. Seeing as it was early afternoon, the man should've been at work. But he was home sweeping his sidewalk wearing combat boots. Farther down the street, a woman one-handedly hung clothes on a short clothesline while holding a toddler on her hip.

Scooter crossed the street, a careful eye on the man sweeping the sidewalk. He knew he would be safe inside with whoever lived in the house. Well, *safer*. Dangers were part of the job. The sweeping man didn't look his way, but Scooter tucked his hand into his jacket all the same. Feeling the hard plastic of the NL-2 machine pistol, he flipped the selector switch to fully automatic. He was ready.

Suddenly, bullets like killer bees whipped over his head. He didn't stop to face his attacker. Like a rabbit, he ran and dove behind three garbage containers, the only cover available. The bullets pinged into the containers. Some of the rounds passed through the first two bins. Fortunately, they were filled with garbage. The rounds from the opposing gun were silenced, therefore subsonic, which meant a small caliber, but still deadly.

With two hundred and fifty pellet-rounds in the NL-2, Scooter showed no hesitation. Holding the trigger down, he sprayed the sidewalk with pellets before he stood and spied his attacker. Surprisingly, the man with the broom and combat boots was scrambling for cover, with only the broom in his hands. Scooter redirected his fire at the woman who'd abandoned the baby doll on her hip, as well as the clothesline, and now held a Russian automatic pistol. Shooting from a crouch, he peppered her with pellets until she slumped unconscious, without injury, onto the side of the street.

Even with silenced weapons, they'd made quite a bit of racket. Scooter eyed the neighborhood windows for a second attacker. He saw several closed curtains—neighbors probably wanting nothing to do with the wild gunman in the street who held a strange-looking weapon. They were sure to think the woman thirty yards away was dead, as well as her doll baby. Backing away, Scooter sidestepped up the brownstone's stairs and tucked his NL-2 back under his jacket.

Knocking on the door, he waited anxiously, his eyes

studying the street. Hearing no sirens, he realized these were working class people, all too familiar with the old days of KGB raids and midnight arrests. They didn't trust the authorities any more than they trusted him, and that worked to Scooter's advantage. A bug tickled his ear. Rubbing his lobe, his fingers came away wet with blood. Only then did he feel the sting of a bullet's graze.

The door swung open suddenly. Scooter jumped around to face another possible attack. An elderly woman snapped Ukrainian at him and gestured for him to enter. He stepped inside. Old enough to be his grandmother, she closed the door and dropped a heavy bar across the frame.

"Good you are careful!" She grunted her approval as she examined him. "Come!"

She led him through another door, which she also locked behind them, then into a small, darkened living room that smelled of sweet pipe tobacco. When she turned on a lamp, Scooter saw a man as old as she was, dozing in a soft chair, his head back with his smoldering pipe still between his lips. The woman pointed to a chair next to a giant cello case. As Scooter sat down, she took the old man's pipe and tapped it over an ashtray.

The tapping brought the man from his slumber. Scooter guessed the two were in their late seventies. The man yawned, his eyes on Scooter, then he leaned forward.

"You no look American."

"I'm Mexican-American, born in California."

"I know California." The man looked afar off. "Gold in California."

"Yep, it's a golden state. You ever been there?"

"Nah. Much sex and roll and rock."

"I suppose it's gone downhill over the years."

"Trouble for you to come here?"

"Some." Scooter opened his coat. "But, I was ready."

"Ah, NL-2. One of my favorites."

Scooter raised his eyebrows in surprise.

"You know the series?"

"Six-hundred-rounds-a-minute rate. Range: fifty meters—or about fifty-five yards in American. Two-hundred-fifty-round capacity. Who you think make them, da? They do not hang from the trees."

"So, you're the one. I always wondered."

"I rather make deadly guns, but . . ." The old man shrugged. "Your people pay well, so I make these toys for you. I am Lars Klistova. My wife, Monique, my pear, as you say in America, da?"

"Your peach, I suppose you mean."

"Peach, pear, apple." He waved his hand. "Moni, show him the cello. It is why he comes."

The old woman dragged the cello from between the chairs. Scooter began to help her, but she slapped his hand away. She opened the cello case and strummed the beautiful instrument's strings.

"This is a most difficult order," Monique said. "We ruined two other cellos to find right housing. It is good?"

Scooter narrowed his eyes. *The right housing?* What was he looking at? What did Corban want with a cello? The instrument was as tall as Scooter!

"Yes, it's perfect," he said, but he had to know more. "Show me."

Monique reached around the side of the cello and clicked a switch. The top of the cello opened to expose two disassembled long rifles, their barrels parallel and crammed amongst a dozen ammunition boxes and magazines. Since he'd been a Marine sniper years ago, Scooter knew a long distance weapon when he saw one. Unable to stay in his chair, he knelt on the floor and ran his fingers over both rifles, their scopes, their lightweight carbon and aluminum fabrication. He touched one of the ammunition rounds. They were standard brass casings, twice as large as a .223 cartridge, but the noses of these cartridges were transparent plastic. Inside each nose were five, tightly grouped darts.

"It is NL-X1, first generation," Lars said proudly. "First non-lethal sniper rifle I ever design. Four-by-twenty scope. See?"

"I see."

"Twelve-round magazine. Bolt action. Special casing. 1,000-meter range, no more. Each round carries five biodegradable darts with spread of five feet at maximum range. One hour of sleep, each dart. Water-soluble toxic silicon—only these are solid in original form."

"Amazing. We've needed something like this. The NL-3 is good for shorter ranges, but with this . . . How fast do the tranquilizers travel?"

"Eighteen hundred feet a second. Our son tested. Very accurate."

"The darts have a five-foot spread at one thousand meters, you said. What does that mean exactly?"

"As the darts fly, they spread. You can take down two or three targets at once under the right circumstances."

"Outstanding."

"Yes, it is. I only wish I see it in action." Lars clucked his tongue.

Carefully, Monique closed the cello's housing, then the case. The instrument was ready for transport through customs—to wherever Corban wanted Scooter to go next.

CHAPTER EIGHT

It had been ten days since Alfred had posed as the Swiss downhill skier and delivered the package for his unknown employer. Now he was executing yet another assignment as a freelance agent for the same employer. Whoever the man was, he'd first asked if Alfred was a Christian, and only after Alfred responded to that encrypted email was his assignment confirmed. This time, Alfred was simply asked if he was free for another mission. Alfred accepted, hoping the second mission would be as enjoyable as skiing. However, when he received his orders, he saw it would require considerably more dedication and preparation.

As a thirty-year-old Christian, and an operative for ten years, Alfred trusted God to keep him and protect him. He prayed every morning for God's will to be done in his life and that God would use him to make a difference where it mattered most. If that meant Alfred would have to give his life to save others, he was spiritually and mentally prepared—and trained—for that possibility.

Now in north-central Germany, Alfred turned off the highway and drove east on a snow-packed road. His four-wheel-drive Jeep was made for this terrain. He checked his mirrors. There were no headlights, but those at the castle were sure to know he would be arriving tonight.

Steering with one hand, he pulled up the sweater sleeve on his left arm. The fresh tattoo of a snake's head emerged just past his wrist. The snake's body coiled up his forearm, around his elbow, over his shoulder, and somewhere on his back was the other end of the snake—where a second head hissed. Green, orange, and black ink. Even if he could have the tattoo laser-removed after the assignment, he'd be scarred for life.

The tattoo had taken eight hours to apply by an artist, or "slinger," in Berlin. He would never have used a local slinger, but this was one through the very agency who had given Alfred the assignment. Alfred wasn't sure which agency it was, but the assignment order itself gave an indication to their character:

"Infiltrate Xacsin Castle. Alias: Snake, a well-known arsonist from the Netherlands. Locate Christians and Jews to extract from captivity. Support team incoming. Secure sat-phone number below."

Memorizing the phone number, Alfred then studied an included photograph of the front and back of a tattooed man with his shirt off. He had realized he'd have to duplicate the man's tattoo—the man known as Snake. Stealing someone's identity and going undercover was risky, but the real Snake in the photograph was lying on a steel table. Since the actual Snake was dead, at least he didn't have to worry about running into his duplicate.

He ran his hand over his shaved head—the final part of the costume. That . . . and the steely-eyed glare. Though Alfred had been a Christian for fifteen years, he could still play the bad-guy. To make a difference in the war between Light and darkness—it was why he'd become an agent.

Alfred slowed his Jeep in front of a guard station where two men with automatic rifles stood watch in the winter cold. The iron gate across the road was anchored firmly on both sides, but it didn't extend into the forest on either side as a fence would. One hundred yards ahead and to the right he could see the corner of a stone castle—Xacsin Castle.

"Little late to be out here driving around," one guard barked in German. "This is private property."

"Shut up and open the gate," Alfred said. "I'm expected."

The other guard held up a clipboard.

"Name?"

"I'm Snake. That's all you need to know."

They shined a flashlight in his face, studied his features, his bald head, and glimpsed the snake's head emerging from his sleeve. One guard retreated two steps as the other lit a cigarette and watched Alfred closely.

"You want me to take that cig from you or you got another one?"

The guard grit his teeth and lit a second cigarette, then passed it to Alfred. Alfred wasn't a habitual smoker, but it had been a superficial prop more than once for the young agent. He took a long drag, knowing his every move was being scrutinized.

"I heard of you," the guard said. "Thought you were in prison. Amsterdam or somewhere."

"Well, I checked out." Alfred smirked. "But you can still smell it on me, can't you?"

Alfred chuckled as the guard nervously backed away to the other man's side.

"Let him through." The other guard waved. "It's too cold to stand here like this!"

The gate was raised and Alfred flicked his cigarette at the station house as he drove by. He laughed as the guards cursed.

Driving up to the castle, Alfred took in everything. His orders hadn't told him to gather intel exactly, but the phone number wouldn't have been included if Alfred wasn't supposed to recon for whatever extraction team was incoming. Though he had a secret scramble-phone, he wouldn't make any calls until he had something worth reporting.

The castle appeared to be dark. As he approached the massive, wooden doors, he saw the silhouettes of armed men against the night sky. They stood on the ramparts above him with their winter coats and rifles. He counted three near the front and a fourth sentry farther down the wall.

The double doors swung outward electronically. The doors, as thick as his fist, appeared to be wooden at first, but upon seeing them open in his headlights, Alfred noticed the wood covered a steel core. He drove through the opening into a stone-laid courtyard—the castle keep. Spotting a garage to his right, he parked in front of the doors next to two four-wheelers. Collecting his duffel bag, he stepped out of the Jeep. Since he'd skied and been otherwise active his whole life, his six-foot frame was athletic and muscled, but not overly stocky. When he wasn't on assignment, he was always training in one capacity or another.

Two men, both with shaved heads, approached him from across the keep.

"You Snake?" one asked in English.

"That's right. Got a place I can collapse for the night? I'm exhausted."

"I'll take that," the other said, and made a move to carry Alfred's duffel bag.

Alfred's hand shot forward and stabbed the man's larynx. The second man reached under his coat for a weapon. Kicking with his steel-toed boots, Alfred connected on the man's right knee. The man doubled over, but only to meet Alfred's up-coming knee. The man's head snapped back, his nose smashed and pouring crimson. The other man was still on his feet, clutching his bruised throat and gasped for breath.

Ready for their retaliation, Alfred stood with his feet slightly spread for action, still holding his duffel. A man whistled on the wall behind him.

"Hey, Snake! One of those fools fetches coffee for us, so don't mess them up too badly."

"They'll get more from me if they don't learn some manners." Keeping his eyes on the two, Alfred didn't look over his shoulder. "Where's Xacsin?"

"Where everyone is at this hour—sleeping. Barracks are through the door next to the garage. Find an empty cot; it's all yours."

The two men in front of Alfred recovered and backed away to give Snake distance. Alfred walked to the barracks door and entered a long, narrow hall filled with single bunks—twenty in all—but only half were filled with snoring men. If Alfred hadn't already made an example of someone, he would've woken one of these men and picked a fight. But he'd already made his statement. First impressions were important. Nobody would mess with him now. He was in. He was Snake.

After finding a bunk on the end, he lay on his back for a time before he fell asleep, and prayed that he wouldn't be forced to do anything too horrible in his undercover assignment. After slapping a couple guys around, he hoped that would be enough. Now, the most he wanted to do was put on a scowl and find the captives in the castle who needed his help. From what he'd learned of the fortress, it had once been a prison—housing two hundred Prussian inmates on four levels. But the castle had surely been renovated since those harsh days.

On the sidewalk outside, Investigative Reporter June Ellerman was focused on the Manhattan COIL office building entrance. Her dark hair with hints of red highlights was pulled up into a tight bun and she carried a tote bag. She had no reason to acknowledge the average-looking, middle-aged man passing her as he exited the building.

"Come on, June," the man said without stopping. "I'm your escort."

Surprised, June paused, then followed the man who'd spoken to her. He carried a silver briefcase and had a backpack over one shoulder. She tried to see his face but he was already climbing into the driver's side of the Pontiac parked close by. June set her bag in the back seat beside the man's pack, then climbed into the front passenger seat. Glancing at the expressionless man beside her as he drove, she remained silent until she realized they were going to the airport.

"Please don't tell me we're leaving the country."

"Yes."

"I thought I was going on an exercise around here. I wasn't told to bring my passport."

"You don't need it." He pointed at the dash. "Glove box."

She opened the glove box to find a rubber band around a small bundle of identifications. Thumbing through them, she saw they were all for her, with alias names.

"These are flawless," she said.

"That's because they're real. Have them memorized before we get to Paris."

"If they're real, then COIL must have some serious contacts. Who are you exactly?"

"My name is Corban, but I'll be Christopher Cagon on this trip."

"Corban . . . Corban Dowler. You founded COIL."

"Did I?"

"Wow, I get escorted by the legend himself! I'll be on my best behavior."

At JFK Airport, they boarded a commercial jet and sat several rows apart. Corban seemed to have staged it that way. June wasn't even able to get an interview on the flight over the Atlantic. He was letting her watch, she figured. She'd learn more watching than listening to him ramble, anyway!

In the Paris airport, she followed him by a few paces through the terminals and eventually through a personnel exit, which led them directly onto the tarmac. He walked to a massive blue hanger wherein sat a number of private jets. No one except a handful of plane mechanics was around. Corban led June to a bench against one wall to wait. The bench was near a bathroom and a coffee machine. They took advantage of both, and only then, out of earshot of the mechanics, June finally opened her mouth.

"So, am I gonna get the silent treatment for the whole operation or can we talk now?"

"You don't have any recorders on, do you?"

"No, I'm running cold turkey on this, if you must know."

"It wasn't my idea for you to tag along, Miss Ellerman."

"Yeah, I know. It was mine. And you can call me June. As for tagging along, this isn't my first exercise. I've done this sort of thing before."

"I know what you think you've done before. I know what you did in Bogota, and I know you survived in the Andes while injured. Those exercises, as you call them, were in the company of heavily armed units and patrols. You were a reporter, you were wounded, and resistance fighters rescued you as they fled guerrilla fighters. You're lucky they didn't leave you for dead, but I guess we know why, don't we? Your producers paid them off to get you home. The people we're up against, June, won't take money, any amount, to cease their cause. They're committed to the death."

"So, you know about me. And you know I can handle

this . . . whatever this is. Actually, I'm glad we're in Europe. I can't stand the jungle."

"You're not one of us; you're an outsider. Some of the fellas are going to be a little irritated you're coming along, me included, until we get used to you. I expect you to follow orders and help out where you can. If you can't step up, we drop you."

"I can take orders." A moment passed. "We're joining a team?"

"A team is joining us—if they haven't all been killed trying to get here."

"C'mon. We're in that much danger just sitting here?"

"A lot of people want us gone. They want us dead because we've saved the lives of Christians they wanted dead. Yes, we're in that much danger. Things have been done recently that we're about to expose. Our foes will do everything they can to keep their evil hidden in the darkness."

At that instant, a short, muscled Mexican with a crew cut and ungroomed mustache walked around the tail of a jet and approached them. Beside him, he rolled a cello case almost as tall as he was. His face was solemn and tired-looking, and his ear was bandaged. He parked his cello against the wall and relaxed on the bench opposite June.

"Are you a musician?" June asked.

The Latino, about her age, gave June the once-over.

"It's okay, Scooter," Corban said. "She's with us."

"Well then, no, I'm not a musician. I'm actually tired of carrying this thing around."

"What's in the case, then?"

"A cello." Scooter pulled the case in front of him and opened the cover. He strummed the strings of the beautiful instrument. "See? It's quite a beast, huh?"

June looked closer.

"Naturally, I'd say there's something inside the cello."

A smile crept across Scooter's face.

"She's a smart one, huh?" he said to Corban, then addressed June. "Excuse me, ma'am, for ignoring you. Boss, who exactly is this? I thought you said this was an inside job, that I'd know everyone—just me and the boys."

"My name is June, and I'm a civilian observer tagging along. I don't think I gave your boss much of a choice in it, either."

"Oh, I get it." Scooter's eyes narrowed. "You mean you're here to audit us, maybe as a reporter." He scoffed. "Believe me, I know the look. I saw plenty of your type in Iraq and Afghanistan. Think this is going to be some sort of party? You know how many men we've lost in the last two years? Sure, we've saved a lot of people, hundreds, but standing next to us with a camera isn't worth it, lady. What's going on, Boss?"

"I haven't shared anything with anyone yet. We'll brief once we're on location. Until then, June, meet Scooter."

The two chatted casually, June prying so delicately, but Scooter avoiding so expertly. Then another man arrived who looked like a pilot, or mechanic, his knuckles still greasy from what was probably jet engine lubricant. June caught his eye. He was tall, blond, in his early thirties, and had a gentle air about him. Behind him came a giant of a man they called Bear.

Corban briefly introduced the blond as one of their pilots, Fred "Memphis" Nelson. And the other man, Bear, was another pilot, Johnny Wycke.

The two pilots were livelier than the others were, and brightened the mood. With eyes sparkling at the potential news sources, June realized right away she was in the presence of seasoned military types who didn't often have someone with whom to share their stories. And they seemed to have the approval of Corban to talk if they felt like it.

June kept a careful eye on Corban. He seemed on edge and sat by himself on the end of the bench, sipping his coffee and watching the mechanics across the hangar. Oddly, he spoke little to the others. Quiet and distant, he was the boss, and the men were respectful of him. She knew respect didn't come easily from military types. Corban had proven himself, though she couldn't imagine how. It seemed there was more to him than his ordinary appearance let on.

A black man as large as Johnny Wycke came in next. This was Bruno, she was told. He had a quietness about him, sad eyes, and his big hands hung at his sides. Bruno gave a quick pat on the back of each man as if it was a family reunion. When he came to Corban, he shook the older man's hand, then jerked him upright for a mighty bear hug amongst laughter from all. Corban took the comedy in stride and polished the big man's bald head with his forearm during the embrace.

Memphis and Johnny crossed the hangar to run diagnostics on the jet they were about to board. June remained at Corban's side as he greeted the final two members of their team. Rupert Mach was introduced as the head of COIL's Berlin office. She was informed that nothing happened in Europe that he and his agents didn't track. He had a Gestapo air about him, since that was his training before joining COIL. His squinty eyes seemed to analyze June as she tried to get more out of him, but she failed.

The man who arrived with Rupert was Brauch Schlenko, who Rupert introduced as one of his operatives. Brauch only glanced at June, but didn't speak to her. He was a wiry man in his late-thirties, and wore glasses over what June thought of as icy eyes.

With introductions behind them, everyone began to board the jet. June stayed back with Corban until they were alone.

"That Memphis guy. What's his deal? He's one of the only guys not wearing a wedding band."

"What're you doing, spouse hunting?" Corban scowled.

"Fine. I'll talk to him myself. What about this Brauch Schlenko? Not the kind of guy I'd trust with my life, by the creepy look of him. Just how does he fit into things? What's his specialty?"

"He's a man with a past. Like all of us. Be glad he's a Christian and on our side now. You ready for your first life and death situation?"

June blinked at him in confusion. Corban wasn't moving from his bench.

"What do you mean?" She tried to read his body language since she couldn't read his face. He didn't seem the type to joke around. "What's wrong?"

"Our lives depend on your ability to follow orders in the next few minutes." He looked into her eyes. "Are you ready?"

"Yes." She swallowed, her heart beating faster.

"Walk calmly to the jet and find Scooter. He's the first one you met."

"Right. The non-musician with the cello."

"Tell him, whisper to him in secret, that the mechanics sabotaged the plane, and he has to take them out."

"I . . . thought you guys didn't kill," June said nervously, her eyes wide.

"Already questioning? Watch and learn, June. We have our own mechanics, yet those boys were wrenching under our fuselage. Can you find Scooter?"

"But I'm only an observer."

"If the mechanics are waiting for us to gather on the plane before they ambush us, then they'd have us all in one place, especially if I have to approach the plane to tell Scooter myself. I didn't put it all together until a minute ago. Go, June. You're not only an observer anymore. They'll kill you as sure as they'll kill us if you don't do what I say now."

She nodded. The weariness from the flight had vanished. Her eyes darted about, and she couldn't stop her hands from trembling.

"Calmly, Miss Ellerman. Casually."

Corban studied the mechanics near the tail section of the COIL jet beyond June. There were four men, but he could see only the legs of two of them at the moment. He could also see an open toolbox on the ground at their feet. In the hour that Corban had been on the bench, the mechanics had stayed close to that particular toolbox, but they'd never retrieved anything from it. Occasionally, one or two of the men would tinker with one of the jets, but the others remained near that box, chatting as if they were taking a break.

June reached the COIL jet. She appeared calm, Corban observed, though maybe a little rigid. Nothing detectable by anyone else, he figured. Climbing the steps, she disappeared inside. Corban could see Johnny and Memphis through the cockpit glass. Suddenly, Scooter appeared in the cabin's door where only Corban could see him from across the hangar. He stared at Corban until Corban nodded three times. Three clicks on their radios always meant, "Yes." Scooter understood and vanished again.

Slowly, Corban stood and stretched nonchalantly. Since he wasn't armed, he couldn't join the fight. Their gear had been placed inside the jet. But it meant he would need to find cover for when the shooting started. The wheel of another jet was twenty paces to his right. It would provide enough cover, as well as offer a front-row seat. If he was needed, he could dash forward. He began to wander toward his cover, trying to time it with Scooter's attack. Corban visualized Scooter flinging open the NL-3 and NL-2 cases and tossing the weapons into the men's hands. What would his old friend and ex-assassin, Luigi Putelli, do in this situation? The old Italian would be a good asset here, Corban mused, if only he knew how to find the man.

Leading the assault, Scooter emerged from the jet first,

descending the stairs with an NL-2 hidden against his ribs. Bruno was three steps behind him. They were the only ones left of the original Flash and Bang Team since the other three had been taken in London, but they weren't beginners. Johnny, and then Brauch, came next to back them up. Four against four. As soon as Brauch's foot touched the hangar floor, Scooter spun toward the mechanics, who still didn't suspect anything. Scooter laid down cover fire with his machine pistol, working to his right toward Corban. The other three swung NL-3 rifles horizontally, and were able to make precise shots with their longer, more accurate barrels.

The mechanics initially dove for cover, then crawled from behind machine parts for the toolbox on the floor. They dispersed their own machine guns to one another amongst the shower of toxic tranquilizer pellets. One mechanic fell, then another. The other two who hid behind machinery could be heard cocking their weapons.

But Scooter and Brauch made fast their charge on the enemy's flank. Both had surely seen more action than all four of the mechanics put together. Brauch and Scooter flanked the final two mechanics as Johnny and Bruno covered them. Standing up, the two mechanics let loose a volley of live rounds over the machinery. Johnny and Bruno hit the deck since they had little cover, but Scooter and Brauch were close enough to fire down on their assailants, only paces away; they couldn't miss. The toxic pellets burst on impact. Inhaling the vapor, the mechanics pivoted on their knees, then collapsed, their guns clattering onto the floor.

No one moved for a few seconds. The thunder from the

live rounds still rang in their ears. Corban jogged up to the COIL jet as Rupert and Memphis emerged. June, though pale and trembling, was on their heels.

"Memphis, figure out what they did to the engine," Corban said. "Bruno, tie 'em up and separate 'em from one another. Rupert, find out who they are as soon as they come to."

"You got it." Rupert marched away from the plane, a smile on his face. Corban often sent new COIL agents to Rupert for interrogations. After a few hours of threats with Rupert, Corban knew each of his agents' breaking points. But they didn't have hours today. That meant Rupert would have to work quickly as soon as they woke up.

Bounding up the jet's steps, Corban moved to the back of the cabin. He selected an NL-2 from a padded, silver case and stuck it into his waistband. Never again would he be caught unarmed, not on this mission. Exiting the jet, he found the mechanics bound, ankle and wrist. They wouldn't wake up for another fifteen minutes. That was plenty of time to prepare for departure—assuming the jet's engine wasn't damaged from sabotage. Most of the mechanics' deadly rounds seemed to have passed out of the hangar's massive door and ricocheted off the tarmac outside. Johnny joined Memphis to examine the engine, fuselage, wings, and landing gear.

Bruno and Scooter dragged each mechanic to a different area of the hangar. As evening closed on France, there were no other airport personnel present in that section of the airport, but the team remained alert, prepared for anyone to happen upon them.

Brauch gagged the last of the mechanics and stepped back as Corban was joined by Rupert. The Berlin chief handed Corban four identification cards, each with the man's picture.

"German IDs," Rupert said. "Doesn't mean they're all German, though. Probably German-based. It's obvious enough they underestimated us. They wouldn't have had identifications on them, otherwise."

Corban knelt next to the nearest mechanic who wore a gray, stained beret. He seemed different from the other three—more fit with a hardened look. The beret fell from his head to reveal he was shaved. The other three had hair and were probably locals, Corban guessed. This bald one appeared more professional, probably sent from Xacsin to make sure the job in Paris went down without a hitch. Replacing the beret, Corban stood.

"Who are they?" June asked.

"Hey, Boss!" Memphis jogged up to Corban, smiled at June, and then focused. "We found an altitude detonator. Johnny says it's trinitro-something."

"Is that it?"

"Isn't that enough?"

"Memphis, search the whole plane. There might be something else." Nodding, Memphis jogged away. Corban turned to Brauch. "Handle that TNT, but salvage it. We might need it later for prosecution."

Brauch strode away without responding.

"TNT?" June gasped. "We were on that plane! What's Brauch going to do with that explosive, exactly? And what're we going to do with these guys?"

"Rupert?" Corban faced his German counterpart and switched to speaking German. "This guy's a pro. You won't get anything out of him. Talk to the other three. Find out who they are. Since we're letting them live, they'll be going straight back to their employer, so I don't want them to see anyone else's face close up."

"I can make a call, have them arrested."

"Not a bad idea, but not yet. Whatever we decide, if they're really Xacsin's men, he'll either bail them out or have them killed if he thinks they'll talk."

"You're sure they're from the castle?"

"The shaved head, the German IDs, the sabotage . . . Obviously, Xacsin or someone close to him suspects we know what he's up to. The sooner we can get to Berlin and disappear, the better."

"Maybe we have a leak?"

"That's not impossible, but I've kept everything close to my chest. You and Chloe are the only two I've shared any of this with. Rather than a leak on our side, I'd say Xacsin is getting help from Abaddon. And we must remember, we're not working entirely with flesh and blood here. Like all of our missions, we fight against principalities, and darkness, and powers of the air. The devil knows we're coming, and if Xacsin is as close to that darkness as I think he is, he's got an advocate bigger than us. But not bigger than Jesus Christ. We need to keep our hearts pure as we move forward. First, work on these three."

"I'll do what I can."

It was ten more minutes before the explosives were removed from the fuel tank on the starboard side and the jet was deemed safe to board. All except Rupert sat down in the jet's swivel seats. June sat next to Corban and looked out a port window as Corban and Brauch admired the brick of TNT and the altitude component. Memphis and Johnny Wycke readied the jet for departure. Bruno and Scooter did inventory of the gear and reloaded the NL weapons.

"This is digital," Brauch explained to Corban in German. He pointed at an LED screen the size of a watch face. Wires strung from it to a small battery, then a blasting cap—all planted in the explosive compound. "It's set for five thousand feet. An altimeter is planted behind the face panel. The needle sinks, the pulse goes boom. I've built similar ones before. Nothing too fancy, but your men missed it on their first check. The components are Russian. The TNT, of course, is Czech. Even though it's not special ops, the maker was no dummy."

"Thanks. Stow it. And be careful. I sense danger close."

Brauch moved away to deal with the bomb. June pointed out the window.

"What's he doing out there? What won't you let me see?"

"Rupert was once a Gestapo trainee. He's scaring one of the mechanics right now, I suspect." Corban chuckled. "But he won't hurt anyone. It's been proven that the prospect of injury is worse than any physical torture during effective interrogation. And it's not that you can't watch. We'll be in Germany for quite some time. I don't want them to see any of our faces—no more than they've already seen—to identify us down the road. Don't worry. You're not missing anything—just a grown man crying for his life, which we're not even endangering in the least, anyway."

"If he talks, won't his buddies kill him? You didn't think of that, did you?"

"That's why we separated them, June," Corban said with patience. "None of them will know who said what, if anything, and we won't expose the rat. It's basic interrogation."

She turned her face back to the window.

"Here he comes. Can you guys please talk in English so I can—"

"No."

Corban moved to the cockpit door and informed Johnny they were ready to leave. Rupert spoke in hushed German to Corban.

"They're from the castle, all right. Xacsin sent them. Apparently, there's some medical experiment or project going on, headed by some Estonian doctor. The guy who talked didn't know his name. Sounds like a biochemist, though. Older, like in his sixties maybe."

"So, our suspicions are true. The one you found naked in the town to the northwest of the castle was from the castle, and that's where Nathan is."

"Yeah, I agree." Rupert shook his head. "They're very racist men, I should add. There's much hatred in their hearts."

"I expect no less, Rupert. How's your French?"

"No better than yours."

"Go ahead and make that call. Convince the French police to hold them indefinitely, pending an investigation into a terrorist plot. Send them the TNT by courier."

"There's a guy I know in the French secret service," Rupert said. "I'll take care of it, but like you said, they may still be released in a day or two. We may see them in a week at the castle."

"Do what you can. I don't want Xacsin to know too quickly that this attempt failed."

As soon as the jet was airborne and eastbound, Rupert called the French authorities. Corban sat amongst his men and studied a German law book, which only Rupert and Brauch could identify since no one else knew German.

"Excuse me, Boss," Scooter interrupted. "I can appreciate the confidentiality aspect, but I've been running all over Europe for over a week. Mind telling us what's going on?"

"I thought I was the only one in the dark," June said.

But Corban didn't look up from his book.

"Let's wait until we can all hear it together, Scooter."

Bruno handed everyone a snack-pack of cheese and crackers, and Brauch reviewed a few basic German greetings and phrases with the team. The flight was a short hop over the border. They'd barely reached cruising altitude when Johnny announced their descent.

Berlin was asleep when they touched down.

CHAPTER NINE

Nathan "Eagle Eyes" Isaacson lay curled in a ball on the floor of his cell. The captured COIL operative was naked except for the sackcloth blanket covering him from thigh to shoulder. The cloth didn't seem to thwart the chill, but he dared not move, anyway. The rock beneath him shared his body heat, keeping him somewhat warm. He paced every few hours across his cell to keep up his strength and to work out his cramps, but he didn't want to leave the rock for more than a few minutes. It took too long to heat up, otherwise.

Though his eyes were closed, Nathan wasn't asleep. His lips were moving. Only God could keep a man from going insane in here, he whispered to himself. The screams toward the morning hours confirmed his thoughts about men who tried to survive by their own wits. Nathan hadn't screamed yet, but he hadn't been tortured yet, either. He knew his turn was coming, though. That's what he'd learned from his neighbors—mostly Germans—in the cells next to his. They dared to speak only when the men in biohazard suits weren't in the corridor. If the captives were caught communicating with one another, their meal for that day was forfeited.

The man in the cell to Nathan's right had gone for a

blood test three nights prior. Nathan knew he was next.

In the six months since his abduction in England and captivity, Nathan had lost thirty pounds. It was the first time he'd weighed less than two hundred pounds since junior high. The sickly feeling of malnutrition scared him. But he could do nothing about it, other than eat the two cups of rice, or oatmeal, or noodles, or whatever they were fed once a day. He'd even eaten a few bugs that had ventured under his steel door. Nathan had rescued and spoken to enough prisoners around the world to know how to make the most of the days and months, but it was still only God on whom he depended to preserve him.

More than the weight loss, though, was the presence of something deeper and more sinister within his body. At first, Nathan had ignored it, even denied it, but the more he saw the men in white, biohazard suits, the more he knew he'd been exposed or contaminated to a serious bug. He'd felt it in his lungs first—shortness of breath and sharp pains every few days if he happened to sneeze. Then the headaches had started. Since they hadn't begun experimenting on him directly, Nathan concluded he'd been contaminated by something airborne. The food or water could've been poisoned, too. Whatever it was, it was all part of their testing.

Nathan's once-pronounced handlebar mustache had lost its form as a beard had overgrown his face. His eyebrows, from which he'd gotten his handle *Eagle Eyes*, were shedding and thinning, as was the hair on his head. Amongst the lice, his hair was turning gray, though he wasn't yet thirty. Using a piece of straw, he picked at his teeth, but gingivitis had overtaken his gums and his teeth felt furry.

A heavy foot kicked Nathan's cell door. He jumped awake, not realizing he'd drifted off. Sitting up, he looked at the small window in the steel. A masked face stared at him. Nathan stared back. Unless they were dropping off the meal slop, these suited men had never come to his door. Though only a shadow of his former self, he was still Eagle Eyes, and he met this man's gaze without flinching.

"Come here!" the man ordered in German, his voice muffled through the filtered mask. "Put your back to the door. You won't need your little blanket."

The food tray slot opened midway down the door. Obeying, Nathan backed up to the cold steel. His hands were cuffed tightly behind him. He eyed his bed, which was nothing more than the rock space in the corner. Sorrowfully, he prayed it stayed warm and hoped he wouldn't be gone long. He'd left his blanket, minus one corner, to cover the rock. That missing corner of the thin blanket had gone to the mute man who'd escaped a week ago—or was it two weeks now? Nathan had lost track of time. Time didn't pass the same in the cells.

If the man had gotten out of the dungeon, it was still a far stretch that the cloth had made it into the right hands. Maybe his captors had caught the escapee and found the cloth corner, Nathan considered. They could easily match it to his blanket, or match the cloth's message to his blood type. Nathan tried not to hope too much, but hope was all he had in this sea of despair. Hope and prayer.

Behind him, the steel door swung open on creaky

hinges. A gloved hand gripped his arm securely. Though he was naked, Nathan wasn't ashamed. Nor was he trembling from the cold. After all, he'd been cold for six months. Searching for the positive, he appreciated that he was finally out of his cell. That was something new! Ever since leaving England, he'd wondered if others from COIL were in the dungeon. In the first week, he'd discovered he knew no one on his level. But the other captives said there were more levels, though no one knew how many. Finally, he was getting a look around for himself. He praised God for this small blessing.

Nathan limped as his guard escorted him deeper into the dungeon. His leg had been lightly bandaged for the first month he'd been there, but the bullet that had clipped the bone in the Malaysia operation had forced the limb to heal wrong. Calcium had grown over the damaged bone, interfering with ligaments, muscles, and tendons. The other bullet wound in his side had healed into a puckered scar— matching a half-dozen others on his body. But this one still held the bullet somewhere deep inside.

His masked escort led him down a flight of rock stairs, along another cell-lined corridor, then they descended to yet another level. The deeper they went, the worse the odor became. And Nathan started to hear whimpering, too. Here were the those who'd been receiving the worst treatment— having been there much longer than Nathan had been. Now, it was his turn.

He suddenly halted, surprising his escort. Though he'd lost weight, Nathan still outweighed the man holding onto his arm.

"God knows your pain, brothers!" Nathan yelled in German, his voice echoing off moist rock.

Someone cried out in response from a cell, but it was indiscernible.

"Try that again," Nathan's escort said, "and I promise, you'll lose your tongue."

Smiling, Nathan felt a little taller as he was tugged forward. But behind his smile, Nathan's eyes were wet. The place was too horrible for him to comprehend.

They stopped at a door that buzzed and clicked open electronically, then after moving through, it sealed with a hiss behind them. The next room was completely white, and by the look of the medical equipment, it doubled as a crude operating room. The room was heated, though, and Nathan relaxed in the warmth, knowing there was nothing else he could do, anyway.

There were two other men in biohazard suits in the room. Nathan looked through one mask at an elderly man with sunken cheeks and thick glasses. Behind the glasses were deep-set, dark eyes, sunk into a narrow skull, which gave him an inhuman appearance. The man wore a smile, and he licked his lips as if admiring his newest victim.

"Quite a specimen, yes?" the dark-eyed one said. "Let's get him up on the table."

The second man stood behind the doctor, but Nathan didn't get a look at him through his mask, as the doctor and the escort helped him onto the table. Though Nathan realized the older man was the doctor responsible for all the suffering, Nathan could do nothing more than whisper a prayer for preservation.

Taking off his handcuffs, they forced him to lie on the table. He was strapped down until he couldn't move, and partially covered with a clean white sheet. Then the doctor approached and stepped onto a stool to examine him.

"You're a healthy one." The doctor referred to a clipboard. "Almost one hundred ninety days, and you still have a little muscle on your bones?" He pinched the inside of Nathan's leg where the bullet had left its mark. "Oh, yes. I do remember you now. You didn't come easily, so I don't expect you to go out easily, either. Working out, are you? Exercising? What are you doing? Pacing? Pushups? Yes, I know. There's so little for you to do in your rooms."

"You remember when I came in?"

"Sure." The doctor pulled a tray of syringes up to the table. "Though you were barely conscious, you still gave us a difficult time. Tell me: how is your health otherwise?"

"I'll tell you that if you tell me how many men arrived with me."

"No, no. I'll give you no such news." The doctor squirted one needle into the air and tapped the syringe. "Tell me how you've been feeling."

"Well, I could use more to eat, but I feel pretty good besides that," Nathan lied. He had no desire to help this man's experiments.

"Nothing raspy in the lungs? Headaches? How about stomach flu? I can give you medicine, so be honest."

The doctor ran through a checklist, each of which had traumatized Nathan in one way or another over the months in his cold cell, but he denied each one. He didn't believe for a second he would receive necessary treatment. Maybe some of the others had believed that and told him their symptoms, but their health still hadn't changed. Nathan wouldn't be so fooled. The doctor took careful notes on his chart, then set it aside and took up the first syringe again. He gave Nathan an injection, but it didn't seem to change Nathan's sensation. Then the doctor took up a syringe with an interchangeable vial.

"I just gave you a blood thinner so I can draw blood. Lots and lots of blood. Hold still."

Filling one vial, the doctor then attached another, and yet another. What he was doing with all the blood, Nathan could only imagine. Next, the doctor picked up a syringe of clear, green liquid. It seemed to glow. Nathan couldn't help but fidget.

"What's that?"

With one hand on Nathan's biceps, the doctor hesitated.

"Do you believe it would be easier if you knew?"

"I only want to know what to expect."

The doctor's empty eyes narrowed insightfully.

"You're not like the others, but you will all meet the same fate." He clamped down hard on Nathan's arm and plunged the needle into a ropey vein. "Your destiny is to share what I give you. That is all."

Grinning, the doctor watched as the liquid was forced into Nathan's bloodstream. Nathan's body convulsed involuntarily as the foreign matter invaded his system. The vein in his arm bulged under the pressure of the liquid. It was cold and seemed to claim his circulatory system with a chilling presence. His heart stopped, a valve sloshed through a pulse, then started beating again. The pain from the heart attack caused Nathan to pass out for a few seconds. When he was able to focus his eyes again, the doctor was still grinning, his face two inches from Nathan's face.

"How do you feel?"

Nathan couldn't respond. As the poison swam through his brain, his mind clouded. Something was wrong, but he couldn't struggle. Everything burned like ice. His face felt flushed. He wanted to vomit; something was choking him. Fear swept through him like waves of nausea. Others had suffered horribly for their faith. Whether they lived or died, they lived or died for Christ, leaning on Him through their anguish. He had to do the same!

"Please . . ." he whimpered involuntarily.

"Yes? Please, you say. You want more, and I have more. After today, you'll stop praying to an imaginary God in your cell. You will pray to me for mercy, for my attention, for more . . ."

With eyes rolling back, Nathan mercifully lost consciousness. When he came to, he found himself alone in the room. His whole body was soaked with sweat, the sheet over him sticking to his body. Even though the room was warm, he couldn't stop shivering. He wondered if the rock in his cell was still warm. All he wanted to do was sleep. A tear rolled from one eye. There was an ache in the pit of his stomach, something deeper and more severe than hunger, as if he'd swallowed a frozen baseball whole.

For the first time in his life, Nathan wondered if allowing himself to die was the answer to end his suffering. But a voice inside his tormented skull told him this was temporary, to hang on, that this too, would pass.

"Lord God, help me," Nathan whispered, and drifted off to sleep again.

Sometime later, he woke as a door opened and three in white biohazard suits entered.

"And this is where we treat the disease with, well, disease," a tall man said, as if guiding a tour. Nathan recognized him from his green eyes to be the man who'd stood behind the doctor earlier. "This man on the table now is of particular interest to us. He's a Zionist, a lover of Jews, and therefore chief of the disease."

Through the mask, Nathan could see the tall man had a shaved head, but his eyebrows were red. He had a hard face and perfect teeth, like someone Nathan had seen in a photo once back in the States, a wanted man perhaps. The tall man stepped away and another bald man looked Nathan over, peering down into his face.

"Even with your suit, Snake, I wouldn't get too close," the tall man warned, but Snake didn't retreat.

"What's his name, Xacsin? If he's so special, shouldn't I know his name?"

"We don't go by names for them, anymore," Xacsin said. "These don't deserve names. Numbers only. See? This one has a fresh number." He pointed at Nathan's arm, and Nathan felt the sting of a tattoo for the first time. "But numbers or not, this one's a prize, don't you think, Hannah?"

The third suited stranger stepped closer. Hannah had short blond hair and blue eyes. She sneered down at him.

"Yes, it's Nathan. I didn't recognize him at first from my

sister's photos. But he's the one she shot in Malaysia, all right. Can he even hear us? He seems drugged."

"He's only had his first treatment today," Xacsin said. "His senses are a bit blurred right now, I suspect."

The one called Snake lingered over Nathan, studying his face. Snake's eyes seemed to twitch and narrow, to communicate. Nathan did his best to focus, but his eyes kept wandering.

"How long until you release the infected ones to the public?"

"Dr. Stashinsky believes he'll be ready after ten more subjects. I work him night and day as it is, but he loves this science. It's not really work to him. More like a hobby in which he takes meticulous notes. A sick man, he is, but one of the best."

"Will Nathan be one of the ones released?" Hannah asked.

"I suspect not," Xacsin said. "He's still in the trial stage, though I'd love nothing more than to send more of these Jew-lovers back to America, especially back to those cursed COIL people. But I doubt he'll live that long. I think of them as petri dishes since all they do is culture organisms. You should really read Dr. Stashinsky's journals, Snake. He makes Dr. Mengele look like an angel of light."

"Yes, I'd be interested in those notes," Snake said. "Only wish I'd gotten here sooner. Finally, we're striking at the heart of the disease."

"Come, I'll show you the levels. There are four." Xacsin's tall frame moved to the door on Nathan's right. "Be glad you can't smell the air here, Snake. These animals smell worse than hogs on a farm."

A moment later, Nathan was alone again. The air slowly dried the moisture on his body and the internal discomfort gradually subsided, but the mental disorientation continued. He tried not to think about the disease pumping through his body, catching on his organs and burrowing into his tissues. *A petri dish?*

Squeezing his eyes shut, tears rolled down his sideburns and into his ears. His mouth was dry and thirst plagued him, but there was no one there to help him. Again, he prayed for God's hand of mercy, then drifted into a fitful sleep.

Blowing a bubble with his gum, Luigi Putelli stood next to a townhouse and peered around the corner at another residence. The moon reflected off of his bald head, and his gaunt face showed signs of recovery from his last sacrifice for Corban Dowler. Luigi had taken a number of bullets in the chest trying to protect Corban's wife and daughter, but the family had been taken anyway.

Holding a small scope to one eye, Luigi trained it on the house across the street. Corban had rescued his own family from the grips of an enemy that Luigi hadn't been able to identify. That was six months ago. Luigi didn't need to know anything about Corban's enemies. All of them were the same. They all wanted to hurt Corban—the protector and guardian of the weak. And since Corban was so cautious and sly, his enemies targeted his family instead.

It was an easy error to make, Luigi reflected. He'd been hired months prior to kill Corban and to bring COIL to its knees. But Corban had simply turned the tables on Luigi, an expert assassin, and given Luigi a second chance at life. Corban said he'd given him his life back because Jesus had given Corban a new life. Luigi didn't understand that fully, but he was learning. And ever since that fateful day in a Lebanese desert, standing above a grave he'd dug for himself, Luigi had vowed loyalty to Corban.

The shame of his past seemed to stalk Luigi. He'd murdered by poisoning, shooting, or knifing individuals, for mass amounts of cash. But for some reason, he felt most ashamed for failing to protect Corban's family. That's why he was back at their side, though unsuspected, once he'd found where Corban had relocated his wife and daughter. Luigi wouldn't allow them to be harmed again. There were always enemies around someone like Corban. A darkness seemed to follow him, seeking to destroy the goodness that flowed from his courageous soul.

Shoving two more pieces of gum into his mouth, Luigi dropped the wrappers on the ground. Two days ago, he'd rented a van and parked it down the street. That was his headquarters for watching the Dowler house. But the night was warm and the neighbors were sleeping, so he was stretching his legs. Besides, it didn't hurt to get another view of the house. He simply had to stay alert. An enemy could come at any moment. Luigi couldn't be moved from the vow he'd made to the man who'd given him back his life. And yet, he still didn't communicate with Corban.

CHAPTER TEN

Corban crossed his arms as everyone filed into the office area set up in a warehouse in West Berlin. Behind them were a number of vehicles, as well as several crates of gear for Operation Rahab. All had been prepared by Rupert Mach and the Berlin office, or other COIL operatives. Some of the gear was Russian, some American, some Israeli, but most of it was German-made. There were no chairs in the warehouse, only a metal table with a giant map of Germany, so the field agents stood around their makeshift battle grid.

Opening the silver briefcase he'd carried since New York, Corban pulled out a stack of stapled papers divided into eight sections. He passed out each section, the eighth for himself. June Ellerman seemed surprised that he'd prepared one for her.

"This is Operation Rahab," Corban said. "We're in the heart of enemy territory. Don't trust anyone outside this room." Pausing, he took time to look each member in the face to stress the importance of his order. "Turn to page two. This is the person we know as Xacsin McLeery. As others this past year who've attacked COIL directly, this Xacsin character is serving the one we know as Abaddon. The photo of Xacsin is a little grainy, but you can still see what he looks like. His hair was red, but he keeps it shaved now. He has green eyes, he's over six feet tall, and weighs over two hundred pounds. This fellow has taken the position as leader of a group of men who believe they represent the Wends. He indoctrinates his followers with a mixture of white supremacist ideals. Xacsin recruits Caucasians from all over the world, but seems to prefer criminals. Turn to page three.

"Here we have Xacsin Castle. A few hundred years old at least; it required renovations in the recent decade. You're looking at a week-old satellite visual. Old documents support the fact that there are numerous levels underground. Among other things, the castle was once a prison that held around two hundred Prussian inmates, mostly political prisoners awaiting execution. Xacsin owns it now. It's his center of operations. I believe he set up the Malaysian ambush from here, and the England kidnapping—maybe even my family's abduction last year.

"Page four gives us more detailed info on the castle rooms, towers, height of the ramparts, and certain other dimensions as they were years ago after a realtor's survey. Be familiar with this info, but don't take it to the bank because of the possible renovations.

"Look at page five. This man is not sleeping; he's dead. His name was Taath Merari. He was missing for several months, but almost two weeks ago, he was found in a village a few miles west of Xacsin Castle. We understand he escaped the fortress, which has once again become some sort of a prison. Taath was found with a piece of cloth. A name was written on that cloth—my name. And the writing on the cloth was in blood. Nathan's blood."

"Nathan's?" Scooter gasped. "What? He's in the castle? What about Milk? And Toad?"

"Who is Nathan again?" June asked. "And Milk and Toad?"

"I'll brief you more later, June. Just listen for now, all of you." He directed his gaze at Scooter. "Yes, we believe Nathan's in the castle, but he's not well. Blood tests proved positive for a number of airborne agencies—tuberculosis and other things I can't pronounce. Taath, the one on this slide, was barely twenty-years-old. His insides looked like a grenade blew up in his abdominal cavity, and his heart and lungs were no better. Xacsin plagued him with everything in the book. To list the diseases would only make us sick. He was a walking germ.

"So, why was Xacsin slowly killing young Taath? He wasn't. He wanted him to live—though not forever. Only long enough to infect others. That's what we can assume— that Xacsin is implanting contagions in the people he hates: Jews and Christians.

"It all goes back to Abaddon and the darkness he's served for years, which I've detailed on the final page. Xacsin is perfecting his human virus bombs before he releases them to the public. In the last three years, over three hundred Jews and Christians around Berlin have been abducted. If we were finding bodies, that would be one thing. But we're not finding bodies. Taath was the first. It seems reasonable to assume that Xacsin has test subjects numbering in the dozens if not hundreds. He's holding them until release time, whenever that is."

"Why don't we get the authorities involved if it's such a large operation?" Rupert asked. "I think I know why, but tell us anyway."

"A few reasons. First, there's not any legal evidence yet that Xacsin is responsible for Taath's condition and death. We're a private, foreign organization that has contacts in this country, but no real leverage with the law enforcement. Second, even if we did have evidence, Xacsin has a small but powerful following somewhere near the top that must be protecting him to some degree. Though we're not here to topple a corrupt government, I'll be making an effort to isolate Xacsin from his supporters by showing he compromises his own ideals.

"Furthermore, Xacsin hasn't been caught and charged as a deadly killer already because he serves a supernatural darkness in this world. I remind you all again that this is not only a physical adversary, but also a spiritual one."

"Uh, I don't understand his cause, exactly," June said.

"His cause is to eradicate Jews and those who stand with them." Corban continued. "That's not all, though. Satan has always tried to stop the spread of Christ's message of salvation, so his mission is really two-fold: kill or discredit those who God loves—the Jews—and those who carry God's message—the Christians. It's hatred at the base level. But unlike the one who came before Xacsin—Hitler, in this region, anyway—Xacsin isn't interested in world domination. He wants lives, and he wants the Christians and Jews to be blamed for the disease and illnesses that take those lives. By doing this, Xacsin gains support, as does Abaddon, whoever he is. What we suspect he's doing is so disturbing that the general public wouldn't believe it, so we're keeping it quiet. However, if he truly has a couple hundred in captivity, and many, if not all of them, are as infected as Taath, we'll have to call in a disease control center to handle it appropriately."

"But what about Toad and Milk?" Bruno asked.

"We know Nathan was alive when he wrote his blood on the cloth. And we know one of the three was killed in England. Whether that was Toad or Milk, we have yet to find out."

"Who do you mean when you say 'we'?" June asked.

"I'm referring loosely to a number of intelligence reports from various sources."

Scooter elbowed Bruno.

"The boss already has someone on the inside!"

Corban frowned at Scooter, and the operative quickly closed his mouth. June looked from Scooter to Corban.

"Wait, can we read these intel reports? How are you getting your information?"

"No, those reports can't be shared. Not now, probably not ever. Some of the reports were prepared by deep cover operatives, yes. Most of the intel has been destroyed. If you, June, were to be taken captive, you would surely be tortured to give up your sources. The fewer who know those sources, the better. I don't even know them all, and I prefer it that way. Having said that, we know very little about Xacsin Castle, our target. Other thermal imaging views from space show as many as twenty soldiers on guard around the castle. These aren't lazy guerrilla fighters, either. These are soldiers, all killers, all criminals, and all armed with deadly weapons. Our job for the next couple weeks is to gain intel, run recon, and so on. But don't do anything to draw attention.

"Before we attack, we need to know everything about the castle. Do they have motion sensors in the surrounding forest since they have no discernible perimeter beyond the castle walls? How long are their sentry shifts? Detail their security efforts. Plug into their frequencies if you can. Find their weak spots. If they have prisoners, they must be feeding them. Find out their food sources, and we can estimate their captive count. That's what the next to the last page details. There's a lot to do before we storm that castle. When you've read and understood your assignments, slide your copy back to me."

"We can't keep these?" June frowned as the team started to read.

"No, June. You can't keep them."

One at a time, they gave their briefs back to Corban. When he had them stacked in front of him, he opened his silver briefcase again, and opened a false bottom. He turned it toward the seven.

"Here are eight cocktails. We are sure to make contact with some of Xacsin's diseases. This vaccine won't guard against them all, but it'll shield against some of them. If you feel any questionable symptoms, Rupert will have a doctor on standby at COIL's Berlin headquarters. But this is our H-Q. We're not drawing the local COIL office into Xacsin's line-of-fire, besides Rupert here, though Xacsin seems to already know we're coming. Probably because he knows me. And we can expect no less attention and danger than what we've already experienced in Paris.

"Now, Rupert has our hotel designations, which will be altered at least once a week. Watch for tails. Keep your heads down. Trust no one. And keep the faith, because above all, we serve a God who works for and with His people. We've been through a lot, all of us. There's a purpose for everyone in this room, even you, June. Now we have to live up to our potential. Let's get our boys home one way or another and get back to the basics of our calling: making sure the Gospel is spread worldwide. Abaddon has done a good job of pulling us from our mission statement. We're about to remedy that."

Selecting a syringe from the briefcase, Corban pulled off the cap and stuck it into his deltoid muscle. Johnny Wycke was next. Everyone watched until each one had taken a turn. June went last, but she bravely followed suit.

Corban closed the briefcase. He eyed his team, then with a nod, he bowed his head and prayed for the safety of his team and for God's blessing upon them.

"Okay, let's get to work."

Bruno took his time installing a pinhole camera lens in the hotel room assigned to him and Scooter. The camera was mounted behind the picture of a goose, and the lens peeked through a hole he'd delicately drilled into the frame. Both men were weary. Scooter was in his queen-sized bed watching Bruno work and waiting for the light to be turned out. They'd already installed a similar camera in June's room a few doors down, as well as in Corban's, as a precaution. When they left their rooms to gather intel on the castle, if someone crept into their rooms, they'd know. Memphis, Rupert, and Brauch were sharing two rooms at a different hotel.

Scooter picked up a two-way radio from his bedside table. It was more than a radio, though; it was a satellite device that used scrambled frequencies. All eight members of Team Rahab had a radio and were to keep it on them at all times, which wouldn't be difficult since the devices were as small as cell phones.

"I think Corban installed GPS systems inside these babies," Scooter said. "You think he's spying on us too much?"

Finished with the motion-activated camera, Bruno lay on his own bed.

"Can you blame him? He feels responsible for losing three men."

"You think anyone's monitoring the signal right now?"

Yawning, Bruno clicked off the lamp.

"I think it's safe to say there are a lot of boys and girls involved in this op, no matter what Corban says. And you know Chloe wouldn't sit this out, so either she's in Germany undercover, or she's the one coordinating all of our movements from the head office. It's a machine effort."

A quiet moment passed.

"You think Nathan's still alive?" Scooter asked.

"I don't know. We'll bring him home, either way. Go to sleep."

"He may not want to live if they do to him what they did to that Taath kid."

"Nathan's no beginner," Bruno said. "This is Eagle Eyes

we're talking about. Remember when he was captured by those thugs in Sao Paulo?"

"Yeah, I remember."

"Almost ten million people, and we were supposed to find him there?" Bruno chuckled. "None of us spoke Portuguese and we were out of cash. And remember what happened?"

"He found us."

"That's right. He got away from those thugs, escaped with two other hostages, and found us at that cheap motel. Think about it. God's looking out for us, man. If it was you or me in some prison, we'd go crazy, but Nathan's an old whiz at this."

"What about Toad and Milk?"

Bruno hesitated.

"You're thinking too much, Scooter. We'll take that castle down, this Xacsin character, too, and we'll get 'em all out. Anything else is out of our control. God may have arranged this so we would take down this Xacsin character. And maybe it'll all lead to whoever this Abaddon guy is. Nathan, Toad, and Milk would sacrifice themselves to save others. You know that. And at what time has God ever abandoned His people? If the rest of the Flash and Bang Team is alive and awake right now, I bet they're praying. They know where their strength comes from."

After taking a few minutes to pray together for the captives and their mission, the two men drifted off to sleep, only to be awakened an hour later by a light knocking on the door.

Scooter was out of bed first, an NL-2 in his hand.

Moonlight from the window gave them barely enough visibility to give each other a couple hand signals. Approaching the door from the side, Scooter knelt down and aimed up at the door with one hand, then gripped the door handle with the other.

He whipped the door open as he held his breath. The hallway was dark, but he could see enough to reach up and grab the arm of the prowler. Jerking the man inside the room, Scooter twisted him around onto his belly, and covered his mouth as he struggled and tried to scream out. Scooter kept the intruder pinned down with his weight and closed the door softly with his foot.

"Lights," Scooter ordered Bruno.

Bruno kept Scooter covered as he clicked on the lamp.

"June?"

Taking his knee off June's spine, Scooter stood above her, and they lowered their weapons at the sight of the investigative reporter. They offered her nothing as she caught her breath and rolled to a sitting position. Her hair bun had come loose. She brushed her hair out of her face but didn't try to stand since she was clearly too shaken.

"Obviously, she needs to know our secret knock," Bruno said. "Or remind her we have radios for late night communication."

"Mind telling us what couldn't wait until morning?" Scooter stretched his arm and held his shoulder. He still wasn't used to the man-made socket.

"I wouldn't have even come to your door if I hadn't heard Corban sneaking out of his hotel room."

"That's Mr. Dowler to you," Scooter said.

"You're saying the boss isn't in his room?" Bruno asked. "And what business is that of yours?"

"If he's telling us to keep our heads down and stick to our assignments, why is he running around secretly? I want to know what he's up to." June crossed her arms, pouting.

"Did the boss say he was going anywhere?" Scooter asked Bruno in Arabic, the Flash and Bang Team's secondary common language. They'd all picked up the language when they served in Middle East campaigns before joining COIL and it served as the perfect code language.

"Nothing was said to me." Bruno shrugged. "But he's the man; he doesn't need our approval. I think Germany's like a second home to him. He was here a lot in the Cold War days."

"I don't like it. It's dangerous, him going off alone. The rest of us are working in pairs. Who's watching his back?"

"It's none of our business," Bruno said in English to June. "You have a lot to learn about Mr. Dowler. There's a lot more to him than some middle-aged guy who could pass for a car salesman."

Getting up from the floor, June sat on the foot of a bed.

"Well, while I'm here and since we're all up and awake, why don't you guys tell me what makes Mr. Dowler so special?"

"It's too late for this." Scooter rubbed his eyes. "We'll have plenty of time in the days ahead, believe me. Working surveillance is nothing but time."

"Come on!" June growled. "Every time I ask a question, you all avoid the answers!"

"June, I think it's time for you to go back to your room." Bruno glanced at Scooter, then at the NL-2 weapon in his hand. "Go ahead, Scooter. I don't think she's going to go voluntarily. She's in her reporter mode again."

"Why me?" Scooter gestured to Bruno's own NL-2 tranq gun. "It was your idea. You do it."

"Do what?" June threw her hands up in frustration. "This is what I'm talking about! Cryptic talk! Every time we—"

Bruno shot June on the chin, only one pellet. Jerking, she touched her chin with one hand. Fury crossed her face as she started to rise from the bed, but she'd already inhaled the pellet fumes. She slumped over on the quilt.

"You shot her." Scooter shrugged. "You carry her back to her room."

Smiling, Bruno shook his head.

"Oh, no. We're both going, and on our way back, we're stopping by the boss's room to see if he's really gone."

CHAPTER ELEVEN

On the other side of the world in New York, it was daylight. Chloe Azmaveth was in her COIL home office doing concentrated online research for Operation Rahab. In a few hours, she knew the team in Germany would be waking up and beginning their first official day of gathering intel to sabotage Xacsin's network around Berlin and Hamburg.

Every few minutes, Chloe glanced at another screen dedicated to tracking the handheld radios via satellite. The team was asleep in their assigned hotel rooms and not moving, but still, Chloe was watching over them. Too much had gone wrong in recent years to not keep an eye on their status.

"Oh, no," she mumbled when she noticed Corban's radio beacon on the screen begin to move. "What are you up to, Corban?"

She focused her attention to watching Corban drive through Berlin on the northbound autobahn toward Lubeck, the port city. Once she realized he was headed toward the thick forest around Xacsin Castle, she reached for her own satellite radio.

"Christopher Cagon, what are you doing? Over."

"Just a little recon, Az. Can't sit still."

"Don't you do it, Cagon," Chloe said. "Wait for the others to back you up. Over."

"I'm going silent, Az. Out."

"Cagon, come in! Cagon!"

Chloe dropped the radio and stomped her foot. Corban had turned off his radio, but she could still see his beacon since he hadn't disabled the power source. She contemplated calling Janice to tell her that her husband was taking dangerous and unnecessary risks without backup. But she couldn't do that. He knew what he was doing, she hoped. Besides, Janice didn't even know he was in Berlin for the next couple of weeks. Then she considered alerting the others on the team to get up to the castle to help Corban, but she knew that would only bring a reprimand. There was a reason he'd gone alone.

When Chloe saw Corban's beacon move off the highway west of Xacsin Castle, she could stand it no longer. She reached for the radio and cued Brauch Schlenko's radio specifically. If Corban wanted something done quietly without the team knowing, he'd often called on Brauch, who'd once been a spook at the highest level in the German underground. Chloe had met him once and thought he looked like a geek with his glasses and sunken cheeks.

"Brauch, come in. This is Mother Rahab. Over."

A few seconds passed. Watching Brauch's radio beacon in the Berlin hotel room, Chloe saw it move ten feet, presumably into the hall.

"Speak, Mother. I know your voice. Over."

She smiled at the German's accented English. He was all business and just what she needed right now.

"Father Rahab has gone to the castle alone. Do you copy? Over."

"Understood. What is your request? Over."

"He must've gone alone for a reason, but he has no cover. Can you go solo to keep Father quietly warm? Over."

"On my way, Mother. Out."

Chloe sighed and set her radio down. Watching the signal, it told her that Brauch returned to his room, prepared for the trip, and then left alone. She studied the other radio beacons belonging to Memphis and Rupert at the same hotel, but theirs didn't move.

Five minutes later, Brauch Schlenko was driving north on the autobahn to back up Corban. Staring at the screen, Chloe prayed she hadn't made a mistake in sending someone. Corban simply wasn't a young agent anymore who could run off alone to infiltrate enemy compounds!

Fifty miles north of Berlin, Corban crept through the forest. He carried a night vision scope and an NL-2 pistol. Slung across his back was an NL-3 rifle, but he hoped he wouldn't need to use either one. Though he was taking a huge risk approaching the castle alone, he'd come so far after so long. How was he supposed to sleep knowing his men were held captive so near? This time he had to throw caution to the wind, as well as Chloe's concerns. Sure, it was a reckless move, especially since he wasn't sure if there were tremble-sensors in the forest around the castle, but it was an impulse he couldn't deny; he had to look around.

Corban paralleled the road to the castle. He stopped short at the sound of a man's cough and swung the NL-2 toward the sound, though he didn't pull the trigger. Bending down, he peered under the boughs of several trees between him and the source of the cough. That's when he saw a lit station house and gate across the road not thirty yards away. Two men smoking cigarettes mumbled to each other, too quietly for Corban to hear. They wore parkas to ward off the twenty-degree weather and both carried assault rifles.

It was three in the morning and the castle was obviously alert. Through his night scope, Corban watched them for ten minutes before moving south and deeper into the woods. Then he circled to the east, walking slower now, pausing more often, and patiently examining the terrain around him. There could be a patrol marching through the woods at any moment, and the four-wheeler tracks in the snow suggested Xacsin took his security seriously.

The castle finally came into sight through the trees. Corban remained deep in the forest, hiding behind a thick pine for extra cover, and studied the castle through his night vision gear. Since he'd approached from the south, he could see only one side, but the four towers were prominent. The double-door gate was on the west end of the castle complex. On either side of the gate was a tower, each thirty feet tall. But the real estate paperwork had told him that much.

Two men stood in each tower, which was evidenced by their glowing cigarette butts. On the southeast corner was a forty-foot tower, also with two guards. Then, farther away, there was another forty-foot tower, but this one was roofed and had windows rather than parapets. No doubt, someone was keeping watch from within that tower as well. No, not *someone*. Xacsin seemed to keep his men in pairs. If Corban crossed one, there was sure to be another nearby.

Everywhere else on the fifteen-foot rampart between the towers, two men patrolled, each spaced about fifty feet apart. There were sure to be more sentries on the other three wall sections. At least fifteen men keeping guard even at night? Xacsin was obviously hiding something.

Corban figured the walls were probably taller than fifteen feet at one time—most likely twenty or more all the way around. But after the wear of several hundred years, the heavy rock had sunk into the ground. So, tunneling into the compound would be out of the question.

Hearing a motor, Corban hid his white face behind the tree as a four-wheeler rounded the castle wall from the west on a perimeter path that Corban hadn't seen until now. The four-wheeler slowed and revved its engine loudly. Two men rode the all-terrain vehicle. As Corban watched, they stopped in the hundred-foot clearing between the forest and castle wall. They climbed off the machine, leaving the engine to idle, and checked their rifles without a sense of urgency. Certain he hadn't been seen, Corban guessed this was a random perimeter check, a patrol exercise.

Light suddenly beamed across Corban's position from his far left. Like an amateur, he looked directly into the single headlight of another four-wheeler that had approached from the west, its engine noise disguised as the other idled nearby.

Temporarily blinded by the headlight, Corban dove to the snowy ground on his right as bullets took chunks out of the tree where his head had been. They weren't using silencers, so the thunder of gunfire alerted everyone to the danger of an intruder. And there were no homesteads around for miles, so no one would be calling the police about the shooting.

Rising to his feet, Corban dashed south, deeper into the woods. Bullets whacked tree limbs over his head. He fired at the nearest four-wheeler as he ran. Several pellets harmlessly slapped the top of the driver's helmet. Desperately, Corban dove behind a rotting log half covered by snow. Men were yelling in German and English. They were getting organized.

Stupid! He chastised himself. Though he'd been careful, he'd not been careful enough. Only now was he considering the footprints he'd left in the snow from where he'd parked his rental car. That had to be how they found him. There was no going back to the car now, but he didn't need to. It was clean, rented under a bogus name through Rupert Mach in Berlin. And he couldn't fight these men if they kept their motorcycle helmets on, protecting them from the tranquilizer pellet fumes. But they couldn't track and chase him through the forest with the helmets on, either. They'd have to take them off eventually to use their night vision, if they had any, then his pellets would be effective.

Corban jumped to his feet and ran two paces before he fell into a snow-covered hole. He expected to hear his leg snap from the natural trap, but he freed it in time to tumble against a fallen tree. Rounds zipped near his head. Ducking low, he dashed west. Though he wasn't returning to his vehicle, they would think he was since he was stupid enough to leave tracks.

He didn't stop for three hundred yards. Finally, he drew

up to catch his breath. While watching his back trail, he noticed four lights. Maybe some of them didn't have night vision after all, Corban hoped. But then he heard two men crashing through the brush from the station house, closing fast, and they didn't have flashlights.

Moving cautiously to the south, Corban doubled back to the castle, fully aware the men were following his tracks through the snow. Tucking the NL-2 away, he took the NL-3 assault rifle off his back. It was more accurate, though a little more bulky. Clipping his night scope onto the top, he swept the rifle from left to right until he spotted their flashlights. Two had already passed him. The other two were pursuing more carefully. Corban aimed at the first man. They'd left their helmets behind. *Perfect!*

Firing a burst of five pellets, he then pivoted toward the next man. Too late. With bullets spraying overhead, Corban dropped to his belly on the snow.

"Over here!" someone yelled in German.

Knowing the language from his youth, Corban put his hand to his mouth.

"He's going back to the north!" he called out in warning.

Crawling, Corban headed south while men crashed through the forest to the north. As soon as he was clear, he jumped to his feet and jogged. They'd know he was a professional by now. Only a pro would double back and ambush a superior force. Though they would surely track him down again soon, they'd not be so careless next time.

A mile later, he stopped and scoped his back trail. The forest was thick here, the snow barely hiding debris that would make it too dangerous to ride a four-wheeler through the trees very fast. For now, they were far behind, but surely reorganizing. They certainly knew better than he did that there was nothing but winter wilderness and then farmland to the east, and a couple of towns over ten miles away to the north and south. To the west was the autobahn that connected Berlin to the Baltic Sea. The enemy would be all over the highway. He considered doubling back to the castle again, maybe even sneaking inside the walls. No, he should never have come alone in the first place. Nathan was so close, as was one of his other agents, held in captivity and near death, but Corban had to be patient.

Digging into his pocket, Corban palmed his satellite radio and set the frequency for all channels.

"Bruno, Scooter, come in. Come in, Flash and Bang."

"This is Brauch. Talk to me," a familiar voice said in German.

Corban smiled. It was so like his team to be fast asleep—warm in bed where he should've been—but the local spook was wide-awake.

"How fast can you get to your car and drive to the castle? Over."

"I'm about three minutes out. Over."

"Three minutes from climbing into your car? What? Over."

"No, three minutes from the castle. You're not invisible as long as you're carrying that radio. Where do you want me? Over."

Being vague, Corban gave him directions where he could meet him, but not so close that Brauch would be in harm's way. He switched off the handheld, stuffed it into a pocket, and started jogging east. Chloe was certain to be behind Brauch's coming to the castle, and her clear thinking may have saved his neck! God was watching over them all.

After a mile, Corban turned south again. Suddenly, he came upon a *feldweg*, a dirt road that led to a square patch of cleared land where homesteads and farms were stationed by the government. Stopping, Corban listened and watched the road for a couple of minutes. His vantage point in the trees wasn't clear enough to see far down the road, but he sensed danger.

Cautiously, he walked up to the edge of the snow-packed, dirt road. There were no fresh tire tracks, at least not since the last snow, but that didn't mean the castle guards weren't nearby. Surely, they would've driven ahead to cut him off. He couldn't stay there forever, waiting for them to show themselves. After dashing across the road, he reached the trees on the opposite side and looked back at the road. They should've started firing already if they were there. Xacsin had too much at stake to allow an intruder to slip away.

Jogging southward, Corban weaved through the trees and leaped over logs. Only rarely did he deviate from his heading to skirt a frozen creek bed or small clearing. It wasn't long before he came to another *feldweg*. Though less traveled than the last, it was no less dangerous. And since this was the forest road on which he'd told Brauch to meet him, it was even more dangerous. While watching what little he could see for five minutes, he kept his ears perked for the slightest sound. Against his wishes, he was putting Brauch in harm's way. He assumed the castle guards would've tried to close the net around him by now or stop chasing him. The castle was miles behind him.

Starting forward, he was about to cross the road when he smelled tobacco. *Smoking during the hunt?* Xacsin's men were careless. Corban spotted the shape of a man standing next to a tree on his side of the road about twenty yards away. The smell of tobacco drifted on the clean, morning air.

Not moving, Corban was surprised he hadn't already been noticed and killed. And if there was one of them, there was certain to be another. Pairs. That's how Xacsin worked. But where was the second man? With Brauch certain to be coming up the road to give him a ride out of there—and the other castle guards following his tracks through the snow from behind—Corban had to move.

He slowly raised his scope to his eye. The ambusher was motionless and stared directly north. Corban could've cleared his throat and gotten the man's attention, but the man turned his head away from Corban and nodded. *Nodded!* Scoping beyond the nearest man, Corban hesitated to attack without knowing exactly where the other man was. It was also possible there was another pair nearby, perhaps across the road in the trees waiting for him to cross. But try as he might, he couldn't find the second man, and he dared not move another step for fear of detection.

A branch snapped a distance behind Corban, close enough that he could hear one man curse and another apologize for his clumsiness. They were on his trail, tracking him faster than he'd anticipated—so confident in their tactics that they were making careless noises. Two flashlights came into sight, bobbing through the trees, then disappearing behind a thicker stand of timber, swiftly approaching his tracks. Though reckless, they'd be upon him in seconds.

As now, Corban had been in tight situations before, and most of those times he'd been outnumbered and outgunned. However, he'd be a fool to be unconcerned. His experience told him that if he had live rounds, he could permanently take out these men, yet he wasn't that kind of man any longer. It wasn't his place as a man of God to kill others. He took his faith seriously, even if he had to keep it concealed at times.

There seemed no choice but to attack and expose his position. His selector was still set on five round bursts. That was perfect for the NL-3 until the enemy closed on him. Then, he'd bring the shorter NL-2 into action. It was the only plan he had.

Carefully, he aimed at the visible ambusher's neck. The men on his trail were thirty seconds away now, which left little time to take this pair out and brace for those approaching. Gently, he squeezed the trigger.

Pa-pa-pa-pa-pa. The soft clicking of the NL-3's action seemed loud in the quiet forest. His target toppled over and squeezed off a burst of his own rounds into the base of a tree as he faded into unconsciousness.

That was all it took for the forest to come alive. Corban saw the second man rise up forty paces away. Too quickly, Corban aimed his rifle as an SKS assault rifle spat fire at him. He pulled the trigger, but his pellets were wide and to the right. Sensing danger close by, he rolled in the snow and heard boots running on the road—besides those in the forest behind him.

Rising to one knee, he fired at a prowling shadow no more than five yards away on the road. The man was too close to miss, but the pellet's vapor had that dangerous second or two time delay that sent Corban scrambling into a bank of snow as a live round screamed through the skin above his temple. Sprawled on his belly, he landed on his rifle with the stock stabbing into his gut. The barrel buried itself into the frozen ground.

Another man loomed on the road, sweeping with his rifle for a target. Rolling to his back, Corban fired up at the man, but the NL-3's pellets were compacted into the snow and soil stuck in the end of the barrel. Corban rolled over again and threw the rifle at the enemy. The man ducked under the weapon and straightened up to aim at Corban, but Corban had already leveled his NL-2. He pelted the man with a dozen pellets straight in the face.

With his position now compromised, Corban heard three or four men from two directions rushing toward him. Instead of fleeing, he ran straight at the closest foe, firing before they saw him. Ducking a blow from a fist, Corban gripped the man's gun hand and forced it down over his knee. The man's machine gun clattered against a snowy boulder. With a grunt, Corban hooked his arm around the man's neck and twisted around to fire the NL-2 at two men running abreast toward him.

Searing fire ripped through Corban's coat and across his ribs on his right side. Not once did he think about using the man he held in his arm as cover. He simply kept firing at the aggressors. They fell as they charged, one running face-first into a tree and another falling headlong into a ditch.

Corban turned in a circle, dragging the man hooked in his arm with him, but the woods were quiet again. Hurling the man onto the ground, Corban posted a heavy foot on his chest and aimed at his face as the man caught his breath from the chokehold now released.

"Snake, come in," a muffled earpiece in the man's ear crackled loud enough for Corban to hear. "Snake, you there? I heard gunfire. Come in."

Keeping his foot and weapon on the man, Corban reached down and forced the man's left sleeve up his arm. *A snake tattoo.*

"Answer him," Corban whispered.

The man hesitated, then raised his right hand to his ear.

"Yeah, this is Snake."

"What's going on? It sounds like a battle out there!"

"We . . . ran into an ambush. Everyone's down, I think, but me."

"How many were there?"

"Eight, maybe ten. Mr. Xacsin, I think they're still out there."

"All right. Stay where you are. I'm coming to you with reinforcements."

Corban calmly stared down at the man, then sighed, took his foot away, and offered his hand to Snake.

"James and John," Snake tested before he accepted the hand.

"Sons of Zebedee," Corban responded in code.

Snake took the hand and Corban pulled him to his feet.

The agent was several inches taller than the veteran spy.

"You'd better get out of here." Snake pointed across the road. "There's a couple ATVs over there. Go east. Another unit's coming from the west by way of the highway. I'll call you if you're who I think you are."

A vehicle engine sounded in the night air. Brauch was right on time, especially since Corban was injured too badly to continue on his own.

"Just tell me this much, Snake—did I send you to the right place?"

"It's worse than you even imagined. Shoot me now, and wipe out the tracks in the snow here that show we stood together."

There was so much Corban wanted to ask him, but there was no time.

"We're praying for you, Snake."

Firing a burst into Snake's chest, Snake took a deep breath of vapor, then fell to one side. Catching him, Corban laid him gently on the snow. Using a tree bough, he brushed out the snow tracks before dashing toward the road, scooping up his disabled NL-3 as he ran.

Thankfully, a dark sedan crept up the narrow road—a vehicle that didn't belong in the forest. The window was down and Brauch held an NL-3 out the window. He leveled it at Corban until Corban was close enough to identify. Corban fell against the car as it came to a stop, smearing blood on the paint job.

"We have to leave the car, Brauch" Corban said, pointing to the west. "Xacsin is sending men up this road from the highway. Come on. You'll have to help me get back to Berlin, though. I'm a little . . . banged up."

Stepping out of the vehicle, Brauch shouldered a small pack. Armed with an NL-2 and NL-3, Brauch appeared to be prepared for the elements. As Corban waited against the hood of the car, Brauch opened the car's gas cap and shoved a rag into the hole. He used a lighter to light the rag on fire, then went to Corban.

"Which way do you want to go?" Brauch supported Corban.

"There's a couple four-wheelers . . . across the road there." Corban pointed, feeling weaker by the moment. "We'll take only . . . one of them, though. You'll have to use . . . my belt to tie me . . . to you. I won't be conscious for the . . . whole ride, I'm afraid."

Brauch half-dragged Corban into the trees where they found the two ATVs. Behind them, the car exploded in a burst of heat and light.

"Was that really necessary?" Corban tried to chuckle, then gripped his side.

"That'll give Xacsin something to explain if anyone asks questions. Besides, we needed a little light to do this."

It took the two of them a couple of minutes to fasten Corban securely to the back of Brauch as they straddled one of the four-wheelers. Sticking a knife in the tire of the other ATV, Brauch then drove their machine onto the road. With the car burning behind them, they sped east, deeper into the forest.

CHAPTER TWELVE

"I'd like to speak to Mr. Dowler, Chloe," Eve Patters requested sternly.

Before Chloe could get around her desk, Eve was marching toward Corban's office. Unlike last time when Joseph and Fon had accompanied her, Eve was alone, and in her loneliness, she seemed bolder, or maybe desperate. She obviously missed her husband.

From her desk, Janice Dowler watched as the wife of Jesse "Milk" Patters gripped Corban's office door handle, but it was locked. Chloe caught up to Eve.

"He's not here, Mrs. Patters. That's what I was trying to tell you. Please, let's go somewhere to talk. It's time for me to take a break, anyway. How about we go—"

"Just tell me where he is, Chloe!" Eve fought to keep a sob under control. "I'm tired of your lies and patronizing! I want to know what's going on! What's being done for Jesse?"

Janice saw Chloe's face turn red in frustration, which was rare. Chloe was quite familiar with frustrated men and stubborn operatives, but here was a hurting woman making demands. And adding to the discomfort was the fact that many case workers in the suite were watching and listening. Biting her lip, Chloe took a deep breath.

While her daughter was at the school for the blind, Janice often used the COIL office to coordinate medical supply drops overseas. But she sensed another need now, and rose from her desk.

"Perhaps I can help," Janice offered.

"It's okay, Janice," Chloe said, excusing her.

"It's not okay!" Eve shouted, her voice breaking. "I have to go back to Ohio in the morning to continue chemo, and my trip here hasn't made one bit of difference! *Six months!* That's how long I've been waiting for something! Anything!"

"Eve, let's go into the waiting room to talk. It's usually empty this time of day."

"No! Do I have to find Jesse myself? Tell me what Corban Dowler is doing for him! Tell me right here! What's being done?"

"Now, that's enough!" Janice shook her finger at the troubled wife and glanced at Chloe. "Chloe, I'll handle this, okay?"

"Janice, no offense," Chloe said, "but you don't know what's going on."

"Oh, don't I? I may not be one of your operatives, but I've lived with one since you were in diapers, so I know a thing or two." Then Janice softened her voice. "It's all right, Chloe. Go ahead."

Chloe forced a smile, tucked her head, and returned to her desk.

Taking Eve by the arm, Janice led her to a chair against the window, then Janice sat down, facing her.

"Your name is Mrs. Patters, right?"

"Yes, Eve Patters. I want to speak to Mr. Dowler, even if it's over the phone."

"My name is Janice Dowler. I'm Corban's wife. Why don't you tell me what's going on?"

"Don't you know about the men who went missing in London? They were COIL employees."

"I heard about it because Corban asked me to pray for them. You have to understand that our men and women are being killed or kidnapped all the time around the world as they help others. But tell me, one of them was your husband?"

"His name is Jesse." Eve nodded. "They call him Milk. And he wasn't only another agent, either. He was on Mr. Dowler's lead extraction team. So, I don't understand how you can help me, Janice, if you don't know what's going on."

"You said you're going through chemotherapy right now, too?"

"That's right."

"Wow, you're certainly dealing with a lot. But, young lady, being unreasonable toward Chloe isn't going to help anything."

"But she never—"

"No, let me talk. Believe me, I understand more than you think. I've been married to Corban for twenty-three years. And I didn't even know he was a secret agent for many of those years, but we have a sense as women when something is . . . off, don't we?"

"Yes, we do."

"COIL has so many enemies that our men have to keep

things secret, sometimes even from us, their wives. That's not out of spite, Eve. It's to protect us and to protect those in the field, men like your husband."

"Except Corban won't even tell me if Jesse's alive! Neither will Chloe."

"Did they tell you he's dead?"

"No."

"Well, it seems reasonable to assume they don't know, then. Do you want them to make something up to satisfy your demands?"

"Of course not, but he's responsible."

"You know better than that, young lady! Or are you just looking for someone to blame? Both of our husbands knowingly put their lives at risk every day to help others. It's been particularly crazy this past year. We've been attacked on a personal level, especially my family. Did you know I was abducted last year? My daughter and me? But I can't get into that right now.

"I don't have any confidential information about these circumstances, Eve, but I can tell you that a large operation is underway overseas right now. This situation has been a priority of Corban's for months. Coming here is usually the only way for me to see my own husband because he's been putting every hour into this. You wouldn't believe the resources he's drawn from other departments to address it, meaning: he's doing everything he can to bring your husband home in one piece. I don't mean to be short with you, but how can your stubbornness help anything? There's no conspiracy to keep you in the dark, Eve. Chloe's only doing her job. That's what Jesse would want, right?"

"But I . . ." Eve choked on a sob and leaned forward. Janice was there to hold the young woman as she cried. "I want to know if I should . . . hope or not. It just hurts so much!"

"Oh, sweetie. Knowing my husband pretty well, I'd say if he hasn't told you that Jesse is dead, there's every reason to hope."

"Do you really think he's getting him right now? There's nothing in the news about American hostages being paid for or traded or anything."

"No one will know anything for sure until they all come home together, okay? Now, you need to listen to Chloe. Her job is to protect our husbands. Their job is to protect those who are delivering the gospel of Jesus Christ. Sometimes, because of all the danger, we can't know much of anything. It's frustrating, I know, but we must be patient.

"Aren't you the woman who runs the prayer chain in Ohio? The Bible says that prayer gives us peace, even when we don't have an answer, because it shows our faith and trust in God when we do pray. You know this. I'm only reminding you. We have to stay focused even during the hard times."

Eve withdrew to dab at her tears.

"Everything you've said is right. I'm such a mess. I'm being so irrational."

"Nobody's blaming you. You're going through so much, you poor thing.

"Look, here's my personal cell number. Most of the people in this office don't even know I'm the boss's wife, okay? So, keep this to yourself, but call me any time you want. If I hear anything, or you hear anything, we can talk about it, okay?

"Believe me, I hear the same disclosures from Chloe, too. Sometimes, I don't even bother to ask where my husband is or what he's doing. Usually, Chloe's as much in the dark as we are, though. But God knows what they're up to and He knows we're anxious and impatient wives.

"It hurts, I know, Eve. Our men leave us and have no clue how much we miss and love them, but we must hang on. And when they do come home, we'll hold them so tight. Our guys just need our support so they can get back out there to risk their necks again to save many others. They're heroes, Eve, and God's shepherds through and through. So, we can't stand in their way. We can only stand behind them, and be thankful to be a part of their calling . . . because that's part of our calling, too."

"You have no idea how many there were?" Xacsin's green eyes were flashing. Arrogance poured from the abrasive, intimidating six-foot-tall bald giant, but Snake tried to appear casual and submissive.

They were inside Xacsin Castle, in an office above the two-car garage. A fire burned in a small hearth behind Xacsin as he sat at his desk. Hannah, Xacsin's bloodthirsty wife, stood to Snake's left. The short blond was emboldened when she was with Xacsin, glaring and daring anyone who crossed her. She was the only woman in the fortress, and she flaunted herself before all the men when Xacsin wasn't in their midst.

"Originally, we were tracking one man," Snake said,

"but it seems he led us into an ambush. There might've been up to ten men. They were all around us, like the others said."

"But, weren't you ahead of them?" Xacsin shook his head, his fierce eyes frowning at Snake. "What'd I hire you for?"

"I was hired to keep intruders out of the castle. That's what I did. It's a given that you also want me to keep your prisoners downstairs in their cells. We were attacked last night. But what do you expect? You've told me nothing about the strength of our adversaries. How can I take charge when you don't keep me informed? You've asked me to fight an enemy while I'm blindfolded."

"Watch your tongue, Snake." Xacsin tapped a finger on a pistol in his waistband. "You're not untouchable. I expect you to be ready for anyone and anything. Seeing as I have many enemies, I don't know who exactly might try to destroy us."

"It's not like we lost any men." Snake chuckled. "At first, I thought they were shooting paint balls at us. I don't think I've ever heard of any special ops using tranq pellets. Xacsin, I don't pry into your business, and I appreciate what you do here and what you've shown me, but you have a sophisticated enemy out there who'll beat us again unless I can fight back."

Xacsin studied Snake's face for a moment.

"Just tell him," Hannah said. "It's not like that group is more superior, anyway. He needs to know."

"Fine. We hate all Zionists, as you know—especially the active ones, always forcing their doctrine on us and the world—as if they were really chosen by God! I've communicated with real power, and those people definitely don't have it! The foolish blindly drink up their lies of Jesus, and the Jews have their agenda to pollute our race. All of this, we can fight; we *are* fighting. Downstairs, we have a revolutionary weapon to use against them. We can't be stopped! But we can be annoyed.

"There's a Zionist organization, COIL, out of New York City, that I targeted with my superior over a year ago. Hannah and her sister, Helena, were part of it all. Helena was arrested in Egypt, caught by the COIL organization. But I have two of their employees downstairs." Xacsin's eyes gleamed. "Another one died. He was weak; it wasn't my fault. You met one of them the other night."

"The big guy on the table?"

"Yes. I didn't believe his people would find us so easily, but one of my prisoners escaped two weeks ago. The authorities got their hands on him in a town a few kilometers west of here. COIL would eventually come, I knew, but I don't know how they found out so quickly. They're the reason I brought you in when I heard you were on the market. I know about your past, your disdain for the Jews and Christians in England. Together, we can exterminate this filth! The authorities, I can handle. Your problem is COIL."

"They're Zionists, you say, but not all Jews?"

"No, they're mostly Christians who take their religious scribble literally." Xacsin growled. "Many Europeans, some Americans, but they employ Jews, which makes them all Zionist trash. These self-righteous, cross-loving fools are trying to take over the world, Snake. Sometimes I feel like I'm the only one trying to stop them!"

"I hate them as much as the next Aryan, Xacsin, you know that," Snake snarled, "but they seem rather harmless with their little pellet guns."

"But they're not harmless!" Spittle foamed on Xacsin's lips. "Don't you dare say that! Their ideals are more dangerous than anything else. You don't know what these Christians can do! They even pray against everything I serve. Sometimes I wonder about you, Snake. I'm not even sure you're one of us because of some of the things you've said since you've been here, and questioning me . . ."

"How can you doubt my loyalties?" Snake stood boldly, seemingly unfazed by Xacsin's remarks. "My past speaks for itself. I'm worth any two of your men together. And if we were killing these captives of yours instead of merely infecting them, I'd be your number one exterminator. But you have this secret plan, so I can hold myself back for now. Though I'm not a visionary like you, I sorely hate the Semitic pollutants. That's why I'm here.

"So these COIL people were snooping about. Let them snoop. They won't get into the castle. Why? Because I won't let them! I'm still alive because I've never failed an employer. If I had failed, I would've taken myself out."

"Those are bold words, Snake, but don't underestimate COIL, even with their non-lethal toy guns. I've raised up others to fight them in the past, and my men were defeated. The founder of COIL is named Corban Dowler. He's surely working behind the scenes to destroy our plans—if he only knew what they were."

"We use live ammo, Xacsin. I'm not afraid of them."

"Very well. Get us through the next three weeks without incident, and we'll all be victorious. After that, you can burn this place to the ground for all I care. Until then, I'll be busy arranging everything for the next phase for our . . . patients. I even have a fresh bus load arriving soon, so we may need to double our cell capacity."

CHAPTER THIRTEEN

June was furious she'd been abandoned. Corban was responsible for her, the others had decided, so she was summarily left behind at the hotel with nothing to do. Scooter had met with Brauch to target practice. Memphis and Johnny were scouting for planes and choppers. Bruno and Rupert were setting up surveillance around the castle—which she'd be assigned to eventually, but not today. And Corban was nowhere to be found. Target practice, hunting for equipment, and whatever else they were doing—that's what she'd come for and she had experience in all that stuff! She knew she was missing out on some of the excitement and intrigue.

Checking the little radio she'd been given, she found no one was using the open frequency at that moment.

"Um, hello? Anyone there? Come in."

Sure, she thought, rolling her eyes. She wanted to be involved, but she didn't have a clue how to get involved.

"That you, June?" It was Corban.

"Yes!" Gripping the radio tightly, she shook with anticipation. "Where are you? I'm bored to death. The TV's in German, so I can't watch that. I can't go shopping since I have no Euros. What do you expect me to do?"

"Everyone's gone?"

"Of course. They all have assignments from you. Until the surveillance sites are set up, I don't have anything to do."

"And you want an assignment right now?"

"Well, yeah. I want to feel useful. Even when I was on assignment in Iraq, I didn't only carry a camera, you know."

"I'll be there in a few minutes."

Since she, like the others on Team Rahab, had brought nothing more than an overnight bag, June pulled on her only spare set of clothes—jeans, a t-shirt, and a black and white blazer. Shaking out her bun, she tied her hair back in a tight ponytail.

Now she understood they'd be in Germany for several weeks, though she didn't know why they could only carry overnight effects. They weren't in the bush! Why not stock up on laundry? But she knew better than to complain. Even if it was uncomfortable, she wanted to fit in.

This was the story she'd been waiting for—the inside scoop. For now, though, she was the outsider in more ways than one. June wasn't a real COIL operative, she was a single woman amongst mostly married men, and she wasn't even a Christian. The latter seemed to differentiate her more than any other reason. The men carried little Bibles, and on the plane, she'd spied them gathering in small groups to pray or discuss a passage of Scripture. She planned to include all this in her report, but as of yet, she hadn't scribbled any notes in her field tablet. Once she knew them better and they really trusted her, then she'd find the dirt on them.

Her room phone rang.

"Hello?"

"Come to my room," Corban said, then hung up.

June wasn't flustered by his briefness. She'd learned that Corban was a shaker and mover, nothing less. He wasn't unkind; he simply liked things to happen as efficiently as possible. After stowing her pack under her bed—ready to grab on the run—she walked down the hall to Corban's room. The door was open a crack and she slipped inside.

"Close and lock the door," Corban said from the bathroom where the door was ajar.

She obeyed then peeked into the bathroom. Bloody towels and a torn shirt lay strewn across the tile floor. His winter coat was also torn, soaked, and bloody. Corban sat halfway on the sink counter, twisting, trying to see a bullet wound across his ribs. There was dried, crusted crimson above his temple from another wound. He looked up.

"I made contact."

"I see that." She pushed through the door. "Face the wall. All your moving around isn't helping."

As she applied a washcloth soaked in alcohol, he didn't flinch. June noticed both recent and old scars covered his back, chest, and shoulders. Wounds were nothing new to this man.

"Why'd you go out alone?" She started working on his head. "Doesn't seem rational."

"That's how I operate . . . but you're right. I should've been more careful, but I had to check things out."

"You went to the castle?"

He didn't respond, so she didn't push. She finished cleaning his head and stepped back.

"You move much and that'll start bleeding again."

"Sew me up, then wrap it." He handed her a bag of pharmacy supplies. "I've got things to do."

"People will see your head bandage. Won't that draw a little attention?"

"I have a beret."

She sewed up his rib area first—twenty stitches. The fact that he was perspiring heavily told her he was hurting, but he didn't move a muscle. After wrapping his torso, she stitched and bandaged his head. Though it wasn't easy, she tried to keep the gauze high enough on his head to be out of sight when he wore his beret.

"Now, I don't mind patching you up, but I didn't come along to play nurse. And I didn't volunteer to come with you guys to sit in a hotel for a month, either."

"Actually, I'm thinking you should return to the States." He allowed her to help him into a clean shirt. "Maybe catch us on a calmer mission. It's going to get hairy."

"From all the scars on your body, I'd say you don't have missions that aren't hairy. All you deal with are the most serious of circumstances. Let me stay. I can handle myself. You have to trust me. Let me get involved."

Cleaning up the bathroom, she tossed the towels in the tub to soak. Corban sat on his bed and keyed into his laptop. Using a fax-scan-printer attachment, he printed out a form and handed it to her to read.

Like everything he seemed to do, it was brief. June signed the disclaimer without much reflection, agreeing to not hold COIL or its representatives accountable in any way for any number of injuries she might receive by her voluntary inclusion and investigation into COIL's Operation Rahab. Chloe had made her sign a general disclaimer before leaving the States, but this one was more serious.

Corban faxed the signed form back to Chloe, then printed out several pages of intel sent from a bulletin board system in England. He didn't object to June peering over his shoulder, but he moved too quickly through browser windows for her to catch much of anything. One thing she realized was that there was information pouring in from all over Europe and the States about Xacsin McLeery and his alleged service for someone named Abaddon. Of special interest was an updated infrared image of Xacsin Castle, which Corban studied intently before printing it out for the rest of his team.

Then, Corban wrote a report detailing his overnight adventure into the thick forest an hour north of Berlin. June read every word, even of Brauch's timely arrival to whisk him out of the forest. She was particularly awed by the fact that Corban had someone inside the castle already, someone named Snake, but he hadn't mentioned this to his team, probably for security reasons. He wouldn't divulge such information to anyone who didn't absolutely need it. It made her proud at the fact that he trusted her with such secret data no one else knew. He encrypted the report and sent it to Chloe, then shut down his laptop.

Picking up his radio, Corban pushed the button.

"Scheduled report time, boys. Bruno, this is Corban. Come in. Over."

"This is Bruno. What's up?"

"What's your status?"

"Setting up a hard link to the telephone relay box on the highway west of the castle. Should be done in an hour, then I'll be going into the woods north of the target. Over."

"Take backup. They're patrolling on ATVs for tracks in this snow. Over."

"Roger that. I'll see if Memphis or Johnny are free. Over."

"Good. Scooter, Brauch, come in."

"Scooter here. Talk to me, Boss. Brauch's right here, too."

"You guys find a range? Over."

"Yes, sir. Why didn't you tell me this guy's a better shot than me? Over."

"How're the NL-X1s? Over."

"Dead-on accurate, but how're we supposed to use them on this op? The castle's surrounded by forest with no ridges or hills nearby to shoot over the castle walls. Over."

"Get with Bruno. I want two sets of scaffolding set up nine hundred yards out. Over."

"That's gonna to be some tall scaffolding to see over the trees. Over."

"Anything else, Scooter?"

"Nope. We're out."

"Johnny, Memphis, come in," Corban called.

"Memphis here."

"Any progress on equipment? Even if we don't use everything, I want that list of machinery on standby. Over."

"We've got a double-prop chopper. Capacity of fourteen. Also, the couple buses you wanted. Oh, and we've got an electromagnetic pulse gun. Interested? Over."

"No, not right now, but flag it. Might need it another time. Over."

"Okay, I'll get with Bruno on recon later this afternoon. Maybe we can go over more of this. Over."

"Roger, Memphis. Take care. Corban out."

Corban told June they didn't need to check in with Rupert since the Berlin office supervisor had his own job to attend, including coordinating intel within his office. Rupert was involved primarily as support for this mission, arranging transport or hotels for the team. And the man had a radio if anything came up.

From a paper sack, Corban pulled a black beret and tugged it down over his bandaged head. Sticking his hand back into the bag, he hesitated, eyeing June with a mischievous look on his face.

"It'll take some sacrifice, but I have a job for you. You're sure you can handle yourself?"

June couldn't hold back a smile. She felt excitement course through her body. In past years, she'd hang-glided off cliffs in New Zealand, covered the war efforts in the Middle East, and scuba dived with sharks in the Indian Ocean.

"Just try me."

He produced a pair of hair clippers.

"I need to use you as a prop for one of my covers. From now on, your name is December."

"December. I see." June took a deep breath. "An undercover prop?"

"You've got the idea. I'd do it myself, but I really don't look good bald." He studied her reaction as he set a black body-art marker on the bed. "Or with fake tattoos."

Bernard Heisenberg liked to think of himself and his shop as an all-purpose stop, dabbling in just about everything and discriminating against no one. The men's department store southwest of Tiergarten Street in West Berlin thrived as a world class, black-market hub for anything from stolen manuscripts to human trafficking. He ran the local trade, claiming to be distant offspring of physicist, Werner Heisenberg. But Bernard knew many thought of him as nothing more than a thief and a fence, with little in common with the renowned scientist other than his name. Bernard rarely spent any time in his own shop, though. Usually, he was in his basement club where he served drinks and sent call girls to wait on wealthy clients who had yet to venture upstairs to partake of his other goods.

Upstairs in the store, he felt too vulnerable where the bright lights revealed his egg-shaped body and caterpillar eyebrows. Thus, Bernard preferred the darkness and strobe lights of the club below, which was open day and night. There, he could lurk and play lord over his empire, his ugliness masked by the dim lighting and the cigar smoke he puffed without pause.

This day began as any other, in the mid-afternoon when he descended a hidden staircase from his bedroom upstairs to the club office downstairs. He checked the books and took a few uppers—he always took uppers and always in pill form. Half the club regulars sported syringes in ankle holsters, but Bernard hated needles. After an hour in the office, he stepped into the wild throng of ecstasy and techno music where he danced with a few upper-class prostitutes and shook the hands of a dozen corporate men and thugs alike.

A lot of businessmen used his club to make deals. Sometimes the deals had nothing to do with him, but he still received a cut of everything. Those were the unwritten rules, and Bernard kept a book of names and scores. He used his leather-clad goons to handle the ugly work, if needed. The gangs that ran Berlin's streets could have the streets. Bernard's club was neutral ground—his ground. Everyone partook of his services, and no one would profit from his demise. A sly businessman above all, Bernard had a network that spanned the world.

He was behind the bar serving drinks and twisting to the million-Euro sound-system when one of his goons waved Bernard over to him.

"Some Englishman asking for you," the man yelled into Bernard's ear. Most of his goons were ex-convicts, so they were hip to the scene. Like their boss, they loved money and served him loyally for it. "I think the guy looks like a heavy."

The man pointed down the bar. A heavy was someone with both money and power, Bernard's favorite, but he couldn't see anyone who stood out. His goon put a hand to his neck and traced a jagged *S* below his ear. Bernard groaned, but it was nothing his man could hear over the vibrating music.

Moving down the bar, Bernard's eyes searched the throng and press of bodies for the Englishman who was sure to stand out in this atmosphere. But he was wrong. After a full minute, he realized he'd been looking beyond the Englishman because the bloke fit in too well. The Englishman wore black leather and a black beret. Though older than most of the day crowd, he was the right age to be a heavy from Britain. At only forty-three, Bernard considered anyone older than himself to be old school. This one with the beret was a little washed-up physically, but his eyes seemed keen and maybe a little cold. On his arm was a sexy woman in a stylish tank top, plaid shirt, and jeans. Her head was shaved, except for a strand of dark hair that hung from the front of her head to her left eye.

The woman could've been a meth freak or rocker by the way she was dressed, but there were a few things that told Bernard she was something special. For one, she looked healthy. White teeth shined through snarling lips, and her slender arms and neck showed signs of muscle. Her neck sported a couple tattoos: two lightning bolts on one side, not unlike Hitler's S.S. squad bolts. That's why Bernard had groaned when his man had shown the sign of the *S*. She and her Englishman were Nazis, part of the generation that believed such tattoos had to be earned. Maybe she'd killed a black or a Jew for her bolts. There was no doubt she was some type of soldier, a neo-Nazi, and maybe even the older man's bodyguard.

On the other side of her neck was an angled swastika so large it wrapped partially around her throat.

Bernard nodded his head toward the back hallway. Leaving the bar, he led the way for the leather-clad man and his vixen. Three of Bernard's goons fell in behind the

Englishman, one of which was a woman a little taller, though younger, than the shaved, tattooed stranger. Almost all of Bernard's people used meth and they looked it. What he would give for a pretty thing like this English broad to show off to clients—racist or not!

He opened a door next to his office. The two strangers and his three thugs filed inside with him and stood around a steel table surrounded by steel chairs. The door closed and sealed with a hiss, muting the club noise.

"I'm Bernard Heisenberg," Bernard said in good English, offering his hand to the man in the beret. "You look familiar. Have we met?"

The bald woman crossed her arms, her face expression set like stone as she stood a half-pace behind the man in the beret. Yes, Bernard decided, she was his bodyguard; she had the look. The beret man squeezed Bernard's hand as he shook it firmly.

"It was a long time ago, Bernard," the beret man admitted in an English accent. "I'm Cecil from Liverpool."

"Liverpool. Hmm. What brings you from the banks of the Thames?"

"Clever, but it's the Mersey River, actually." Cecil narrowed his eyes. "I wish I came for pleasure, but we have a bloody hazard on our hands. Doing some house cleaning. You understand?"

Nodding, Bernard knew the gang and mob lingo well enough. He looked past Cecil at the tattooed vixen. What was her name? Was she the cleaner who did the house cleaning? If she was an assassin, Bernard wondered how she killed her prey, and he wanted her even more.

"Whatever you need, Cecil from Liverpool."

Cecil reached inside his leather jacket and set an envelope on the table. Bernard stared at the envelope, but didn't reach for it.

"My policy is to . . . try to stay out of the Brotherhood's interests," Bernard stated. "Some of my boys are comrades, you understand, but while they're on the clock, they work for me and me only. I hope there's a purchase order in that envelope, Cecil from Liverpool, because it's about all I can give you."

"I have free information for you."

"Nothing is free, Cecil from Liverpool."

"Caution is free. For this information, you'll stand clear," Cecil ordered rather than requested. "A local has strayed from his racial purity. If he comes to you, deny him assistance. That's all we ask of you. He's a bloody traitor to his race."

Now Bernard was curious. Still staring at the envelope, he wished he could see its contents without actually touching it and becoming involved. A heavy from Liverpool was there to clean house? It could only mean that a local, also a heavy, had betrayed the white supremacist cause somehow. Bernard knew all the influential German neo-Nazis. Who was in trouble with the home office? If it were someone small—a nobody—he wouldn't be looking at Cecil from Liverpool. And, if it were a nobody who had betrayed his race, the vixen would've handled the nobody by taking him out. Whoever it was, it was someone big enough for this Cecil to isolate from Bernard, and surely others, before they killed him.

Though Bernard wasn't a racist, many of his clients stood on the left or right side of that line. He had Jewish clients, too—antiquities mostly—but he kept them quietly satisfied. They paid in gold or diamonds from New York, which was better than he could say for the Nazi clones who expected more than they paid for only because he was white like them.

His curiosity won out. He had to know who had betrayed the comrades.

After picking up the envelope, he unfolded five pages. Four were high-resolution photographs of a white man with red hair kissing and holding hands with a pretty black woman. The last page contained confirmation of the photographs and the subsequent investigative findings. Bernard felt himself go pale. He browsed the pages again, and then handed them to the goon on his right who also studied everything intently.

"I know this man," Bernard said. "He's a man of power in Europe, especially in this city. Though he has hair in this photograph, I know he keeps his head shaved now. But he's not the type to come looking for my help. He's in a different class of people, but with contacts everywhere. There are one or two spies of his in this club right now. It's a black-arts crowd, and witchcraft is one thing I don't dabble in, Cecil from Liverpool."

"Soon, he'll be desperate enough to go anywhere he can for help, especially once he goes on the run. Because of these photos, he's a marked man."

"Yes, I see." Bernard smoothed down his caterpillar eyebrows and looked through the pictures again. A Nazi in the arms of a black woman was quite condemning. "Xacsin McLeery with this woman—it hardly seems possible."

"We validated our information," Cecil said. "Even if it was a long time ago, it's him. His whole network is being dismantled since it's now polluted. Someone code-named Abaddon, perhaps his black-arts handler, is also on our list. When Xacsin decided to set up in Germany as a comrade, he had his past erased, but not very well. He killed this woman in the photo. A race traitor can't hide forever, though."

"Well, he's no client of mine. Seems like you guys could let him slip by," Bernard said. "I mean, after all he's been doing for your cause, as the rumors have it."

"There can be no compromise!" Cecil clenched his teeth. "We'll handle him, and whoever else is loyal to him. That's why I came to you first. No point in bystanders getting in my way, even if you're not a comrade."

Bernard beamed with pride. This was the closest thing to an actual compliment he'd ever heard from the likes of this man.

"The warning is appreciated. I'll be sure to pass the word. No one will help Xacsin McLeery." Bernard pointed at the bald vixen and his own female goon. "Now, what's it going to take to put these two in my ring?"

"My soldiers have better things to do than to entertain you, Bernard."

"Take the challenge, Cecil from Liverpool! I know you guys. You never hesitate to show your superiority. Coming all the way from your island, you have to give us a little demonstration! But we'll wait until the evening crowd shows up. That's where the real money is. We'll split the winnings down the middle, you and me, no matter what. Everyone'll place a bet. You'll see. They love these events. What's her name, anyway?"

"December," Cecil said without hesitating, "and you should know she doesn't usually leave her victims breathing."

"Oh, come now, Cecil from Liverpool, it's all in good fun, right? The first one unconscious. That's the rule—the only rule."

Cecil's face was expressionless, as he seemed to measure the younger, taller woman beside Bernard.

"What do you call her?" Cecil asked.

"Vulgar, as in the ancient Roman Latin." Bernard offered his hand to Cecil. "I'll have the ring set up. Say, midnight?"

"Xacsin can wait another day, I suppose." Cecil shook Bernard's hand. "We'll be back."

On the drive back to the hotel, June was quiet, making Corban uncomfortable. He opened his mouth several times, trying to find the right words to explain why he had to accept Bernard's challenge, but nothing he had to say justified the danger he just put her in.

"Look," he finally said, "I can stick you on surveillance up at the castle to get you out of the city. Bernard has people in this city, people who'll track us down if we don't show up tonight. Your safest bet is to let me get you out of the city, unless you agree to fly back to the States."

"Absolutely not!" She frowned. "If you hadn't accepted

the challenge, I would've, anyway. I can take that scrawny girl, Vulgar. Don't you think I can?"

"Whether I think you can or not, isn't the point. This isn't what COIL does. We don't fight for self-glory."

"Then let me fight to keep our cover. You know as well as I do, if I don't fight, Bernard may not even honor our deal about Xacsin."

"Oh, boy." Corban sighed loudly. "I think you're enjoying this too much."

CHAPTER FOURTEEN

"**C**orban, with all due respect, you cannot pit her against some club junkie of Bernard's! He doesn't have weaklings working for him—*I know!* June's a civilian. This is absurd! Listen, Corban, I don't tell you how to run business, but in this circumstance, you need to get her out of the country—after you wash that ink off her neck. And I can't believe you shaved her head!"

Rupert Mach was the only one amongst the COIL men who dared speak so boldly to Corban, though Corban was fifteen years his senior. Still in his leathers, Corban's bandaged head was now obvious, since his beret was on the bed. Behind Rupert, June was being drilled by Bruno and Scooter in the art of hand-to-hand combat.

June hadn't changed out of her December costume yet, either. She seemed to be enjoying the attention and appeared to be not the least bit concerned. In a few hours, she was to face a rabid and perhaps veteran fighter in the underground club as several hundred primal addicts watched.

"I know Bernard Heisenberg," Rupert said. "He wouldn't have set this up unless he could get something big out of it. This woman, Vulgar, she's probably a pro, Corban! Did you get a good look at her knuckles? See any scars? Disfigurement of her face? There's a guy I know who could drive June back to France by midnight. No sense in getting—"

"No," Corban stated firmly. "June made a good point earlier. If we pull out of the challenge now, we lose our cover. And the data I gave to Bernard would lose its validity. We need Bernard's gossip circle to isolate Xacsin."

"Xacsin was really with a black woman, huh?" Rupert asked. "That info was legit? Since it's all from six years ago, before he began the whole Abaddon bit, you think this will even affect him now?"

"It's all legit," Corban said. "His whole Wend gig now is new. Semi-new, anyway. But none of that matters if we don't show up at midnight tonight. We need Bernard's ability to pass on and vouch for the word that Xacsin is a marked man. It'll shut Xacsin down somewhat, not to mention shake up his nerves. His own people will begin to turn on him, or avoid him."

"He controls them. I don't think they'll turn on him."

"Well, he won't be able to hire anyone else, at least. His career is over—as a White Supremacist, anyway."

"So, you're going through with this?" Rupert shook his head in frustration. "I don't recommend it, but I guess it could work. Using June as a prop was a good move, but this? And you won't even tell us what happened to your head? Maybe that's what this is all about—you're simply not thinking straight from this head injury."

"It's an unorthodox move, Rupert, I admit that. Believe me, I wanted to avoid it, but now we don't have a choice. We have to proceed and follow through tonight."

"What if she loses? I mean, that's a probability."

"Hey, I'm right here!" June said from behind him.

"She's just a reporter!" Rupert said, ignoring her. "And you know she's going to get hurt."

"Maybe."

"Maybe? Okay, now we're getting somewhere. Then, you'll let me get her out of the city?"

"No."

"You're exhausting me." Rupert wrung his hands. "As it is, I have to work all night, running background checks on surveillance photos and evacuation routes. *All night!*"

"Actually, I want you and some of the operatives from your office at the club tonight."

"Are you serious?"

"Don't I seem serious?"

"All right. You pay the bills," Rupert said with resignation. "What do you need?"

"Bernard said he recognized me from somewhere. Most likely, it was from when I was undercover years ago. Whatever the case, look into his past to see if he and I may have crossed paths. It's a small detail, but not one worth getting killed for before we even get a chance at Xacsin Castle. Also, he's got twenty security personnel in the club and at least two outside. If he's up to anything questionable, I want to have him matched man for man."

"Well, are you taking Memphis and Johnny?"

"Yes, all my men."

"Okay, that's eight. I can double that, I think. It's a little late notice to find over a dozen men for an all-night op."

"Do what you can. I appreciate it, Rupert."

"Yeah, I know you do, Corban. We're all working toward the same goal. I've worked with Nathan Isaacson a few times over the years. I don't think I know Toad or Milk, but I understand why you're working us to the bone to get your guys back."

Rupert and Corban watched Scooter demonstrate on Bruno in slow motion how to knock out someone using a blow to the chin. June watched and listened to his instruction, but Corban felt confident she could handle herself.

"Maybe Brauch Schlenko should show her a few things," Rupert said. "He knows a thing or two that could save her from a drawn-out bout."

"June's not going to learn anything tonight she doesn't already know," Corban said. "And, she just might do all right. She doesn't look too worried."

"That's what worries me." Rupert frowned. "That girl should be scared to death. I know I would be."

"Well," Corban said, slapping Rupert on the back, "that's why we leave the brawling to the youngsters. Let's go over some of those castle photos while we wait."

Corban had kicked everyone out of his room to catch a few hours of sleep, but he was awake by eleven, suited up in his leather jacket and beret costume in minutes. He met June in the hallway.

"The rest of the team will be inside the club, so don't be distracted by familiar faces. They're only backup."

"What's your input on this fight?" she asked as they climbed into his car. "The others have all given me their two cents. I'd really like to hear yours."

Looking over at her, Corban didn't start the engine right away. She seemed a little nervous now. But in the ring, he knew that would turn into excitement from adrenaline.

"I'm worried that you may be enjoying this too much," he said.

"Actually, I'm a little flattered that you're letting this happen at all. I can't believe you trust me to do this."

"It's okay if you win. We'll all be happy with a win. Just try not to get too hurt. Either way, win or lose, the boys will whisk you out of there and into a car. Did Scooter teach you anything useful?"

"Not really." She smiled. "I know he meant well, though. When I was in the Army Reserves, I took all the *jujitsu* classes. They were only standard courses, and it's been a few years, but I think I know what to do."

"You'll do fine." Corban started the car. "If you get in a real pickle, just pretend to faint. That'll stop the fight. We don't lose or win anything from this fight; we only have to show up."

A few minutes later, they pulled into the alley behind the men's store. A valet took their car and they walked into the downstairs club together. Unlike many American or other European clubs, there was no weapons-check at the door. Almost everyone in the club was armed, but it was a known fact that if anyone drew a weapon, they would be blacklisted from the club, and no one wanted that. The club was the number one source in the city for all types of criminal paraphernalia.

Across the club floor, Corban spotted Johnny Wycke.

The bear of a man was nearly a head taller than everyone else. The floor was crowded with people jiving to techno music. The strobe light was disabled and several spotlights illuminated a circular fighting ring in the middle of the floor a few feet in front of the bar.

Noticing Bernard, Corban pushed through the crowd with June in tow. Seeming to be high on drugs, Bernard gave Corban a hearty embrace. They couldn't talk over the music, so they communicated through gestures. Bernard pointed down the bar at his prizefighter, Vulgar, as she climbed onto the bar. She raised her needle-marked arms as the crowd cheered.

Before June could protest, a heavy-set goon picked her up and hefted her onto the bar not far from Vulgar. June kicked aside a number of glasses as the throng whistled and cheered. Maintaining her scowl, she took off her plaid shirt and tossed it at a press of men trying to place their bets.

But Corban wasn't paying attention to her at that moment. Moving to the side of the bar, he put his back to the wall. He didn't do well in crowded rooms. It had something to do with his years undercover. There were too many unknowns here.

Brauch was twenty paces away, then Rupert. Bruno was near Johnny, and Memphis was there, as well. Scooter was ringside. They were all armed with NL-1s or NL-2s. Rupert's agents were scattered in the crowd, but Corban didn't know many of them by sight, especially in this atmosphere. No one looked like himself. Everyone was wearing his worst face and best disguise.

Corban even swept the crowd for Luigi Putelli. He liked

to think that Luigi had truly changed and was now an ally, but Luigi was still an unknown. It wouldn't have been out of character for Luigi to be there also, watching Corban. Luigi would be popping gum into his mouth and glaring at him from the darkened corners. Then Corban checked the corners for that very reason, but found no olive-skinned, bubblegum-chewing, potential assassin.

The betting continued, tallied intermittently on a whiteboard raised above the bar between the two fighters. Watching for a sign of anything out of place, Corban knew that meant he was looking for anything that appeared *normal*. Nathan would've loved this little exercise. The club was a circus of man's depravity, but the op itself was borderline out-of-control, and Nathan thrived in that unpredictable zone.

"Hang on, Nathan," Corban mumbled, "we're coming."

With the betting finished, Vulgar and June were lifted off the bar. Without touching the floor, they rode a sea of hands over the crowd to be deposited into the circular ring. Corban climbed onto a barstool to see better. Shaking out her limbs, June loosened up. The lights suddenly went out. The club was engulfed in complete darkness and silence as the music ceased. The spotlights were switched on, adjusted, and focused. June and her opponent glared at one another. Tension felt like electricity in the air. The crowd elbowed for the best view.

Vulgar wore her hair in a tight ponytail. Corban hoped June would think to use it as a handhold at some point. And he hoped the guys had reminded her that there were no rules in this ring—anything went.

Suddenly, high-pitched techno music started playing. The crowd cheered, screamed, and jumped up and down. The strobe lights flashed on. That was the cue. Vulgar's lanky figure rushed forward to make short work of June.

A look of steady determination replaced June's scowl, as if she were preparing to scoop a rival reporter. She could forget about pretending to be someone else now, Corban thought, and concentrate on fighting for her life and the team. As he prayed, he wished he'd reminded her that the team was supporting her.

Throwing a quick jab at June's head, Vulgar followed by a second. Dodging left and ducking right, June uppercut into Vulgar's ribcage. Retreating in a circle with a boxer's bounce, June kept her elbows tucked with her fists up to protect her jaw and nose.

In a sudden flurry of fists, Vulgar attacked. June covered up and backed away, the knuckles of her foe bruising her arms, but June didn't seem to notice; she was surely too energized to feel any pain yet. A blow landed hard on her right ear. She staggered sideways. The crowd screamed in anticipation. Gaining her balance, June dropped to the floor. As she dropped, she swept her leg around in an arc. Vulgar had expected a boxing match, but June delved into martial arts. Corban nodded his approval to no one in particular.

With her feet swept off the floor, Vulgar fell hard, landing on an elbow. Pain swept across her face. Smiling, June moved away lightly on the balls of her feet. Recovering, Vulgar circled more cautiously. Now she would know that all four of June's limbs were a threat.

They continued to circle, each waiting for the other to

attack. June took the initiative, but Corban realized it was a fake, a classic baiting. She rolled her shoulder and cocked her arm to throw a wide punch. Vulgar shot a jab at June's nose. Swinging her punch tight, June caught Vulgar's wrist then pulled the taller girl after the momentum of her punch, forcing a knee into her solar plexus as she bounded past.

June spun and bounced two light blows off Vulgar's head. Catching her wind quickly, barely fazed, Vulgar rushed at June in a meth-crazed frenzy. Batting Vulgar's grasping hands aside, June unexpectedly stepped close enough to slash sideways with her elbow into Vulgar's cheekbone, splitting it into a crimson gash.

Still, Vulgar didn't go down, though she was cut badly. She'd probably fought before, Corban guessed. Surely more than June had, but June was healthy, wiser, and in better condition physically. And June's arms had never seen the prick of a meth syringe.

Closing up protectively, Vulgar put her longer reach to use—jab, jab, hook. The hook caught June on the jaw. Corban prayed she had her teeth clenched for protection. Jab, jab. June took one on the brow. Vulgar jabbed again, but her second jab was met with stern resistance as June lowered her head to catch the jab square on her shaved hairline. Again, Corban nodded his approval. Evidently, June also knew the hairline was the hardest point on the human body. Recoiling in pain, Vulgar most likely broke a knuckle on that one.

Dancing sideways, June kicked hard at the side of Vulgar's knee. Their prizefighter was going down. She dropped her hands to catch herself as her knee buckled sideways. June darted close and whipped her elbow at Vulgar's other cheekbone. Instead, the blow split the younger woman's ear, as if an earring had been torn out. Rolling across the floor, Vulgar gripped her knee with tears of fury and pain in her eyes. Relaxing a bit, June backed up to the ropes. Several bystanders patted her on the back and urged her to finish Vulgar off. But June didn't advance. She watched amazed as Vulgar stood on her good leg, then painfully snapped her knee back into joint.

Limping now, Vulgar advanced. Warily, June circled away. Corban could see the crazed look on Vulgar's face. She charged and started to throw a punch. Instead, she wrapped her arms around June, encircling her shoulders and pinning her arms down. Then Vulgar head-butted June across the bridge of the nose. Blood spurted from both nostrils, making June cough and choke. Still, Vulgar hung on. The crowd screamed for more, and Vulgar gave her another blow to the nose before she released June with a rough shove.

Falling hard against the ropes, June bounced back into Vulgar. But Vulgar was ready. She used her uninjured hand to uppercut June on the chin, but she missed a solid contact. The blow slid up June's cheek as she twisted sideways. Landing on the floor, June rolled away from Vulgar as she tried to stomp June's head. Positioning her feet toward Vulgar, June kicked her away with both heels.

Vulgar grabbed one of June's ankles and dragged her away from the ropes. Then she twisted June's leg sharply, making June cry out. With what seemed like a final burst of energy, June pushed herself upright onto one leg, her other still in Vulgar's clutches. Leaping into the air, June spun around, throwing her good leg as high as she could. The toe of her boot connected solidly on the side of Vulgar's jaw. June crashed back down onto the floor while Vulgar was still airborne, flying backwards. Somersaulting in the air, Vulgar landed on her shoulder, then settled to lie motionless on her belly. She wasn't getting up.

June wiped her nose and mouth with the back of her hand as she rose to her knees. Spitting blood, she found her feet and stood panting. Jumping off his stool, Corban moved through the throng as they continued to cheer. Someone picked up Vulgar and carried her to the bar where markers were already being settled by the bartender.

Corban ducked into the ring before he realized Memphis was already there, smiling, with his arm around June's waist as others crowded around to congratulate her. If Bernard were going to try anything, it would be now, so Corban moved to June's other side to stand guard.

"I did it!" June fell against Memphis, getting blood on his jacket.

"You did good, December." Memphis held her up.

Hearing her cover name, June's scowl returned to her face.

"Her tattoo is smearing," Corban said in Memphis' ear over the techno music. "Get her out of here."

June saw Memphis' eyes, and panic crossed her face as she touched her neck.

"Hey, old man!" someone yelled at Memphis in German. "Don't tell me this pretty thing is yours!"

A young thug with blue hair loomed over Memphis.

Before Corban could respond, the giant of a man was plucked away and thrown to the floor. Johnny Wycke stood in his place.

"Get her outta here!" Corban shouted.

Latching onto June and Memphis, Johnny guided them toward the front exit. Corban moved back to the bar where he found Bernard.

"Never seen anything like her!" Bernard handed Corban a pile of Euros and a glass of cognac. "Where's the little wench?"

"Getting cleaned up." Corban smiled. "She'll be out on the dance floor as soon as someone sets her nose."

"Do you have any other vixens to show me, Cecil from Liverpool? I can set up the ring tomorrow night as well. The winter months are cold. We all need this kind of entertainment."

"Perhaps next time I'm in Berlin, Bernard Heisenberg. I'll make a note of it."

"Cecil from Liverpool—I won't forget you!"

Pocketing the money, Corban dumped the drink on the floor, then pretended to gulp it down. He squeezed through the crowd and out the front door. Scooter and Brauch were waiting for him outside to walk him to his car. Joining Memphis and June, they drove away.

When Corban arrived at the hotel, Memphis went to work on setting June's nose and cleaning up her other gashes and scrapes. With his physical education background, Memphis had seen enough high school injuries to do what he could, but he said her nose would never be the same.

"What was I thinking?" June moaned into the towel on her face. Fresh blood flowed down the front of her tank top. "How bad do I look?"

Memphis glanced at Corban.

"She did sign a waiver, right?"

CHAPTER FIFTEEN

Itching at the snake tattoo on his left arm, Alfred still wasn't comfortable with the serpent's presence on his skin. During the hours the slinger had gunned it into his flesh, he'd hoped the mission would be worth the life-long mark. As of yet, it hadn't failed him. Alfred no longer concerned himself with what he personally had to sacrifice—not after the tour Xacsin had given him of the levels under the castle's north wall.

In his head, he counted—four levels, fifty cells each. Most of the cells in the castle were full now. They'd brought in two more prisoners the day before, two Christian pastors from the coast. As much as Xacsin hated Jews, he also hated Christians. The recent arrivals were the lucky ones, Alfred figured. They'd spend a hellish time in the dungeon, then would be rescued relatively soon. Xacsin had shown him dozens of men that Dr. Stashinsky had infected with one virus or another. They were the unfortunate ones. Even if they were rescued, they wouldn't live long. But the recent arrivals would be saved. There were about fifty that would make it, he figured, including some who could be saved through intensive medical treatment. Yes, the nasty serpent on his arm was worth it.

Puffing on a cigarette, Alfred watched the guards on the

wall. They'd been shamed by the man in the forest a week earlier, and all had told Xacsin they'd been outnumbered by a whole force in the darkness that night. But the tracks in the snow didn't lie. Each of them knew they'd been bested by a single man—no doubt some sort of professional. And if that man would've used live ammo, they'd all be dead now. Secretly, however, Alfred was fascinated. That single man, he now understood, was part of the COIL unit due to storm the castle at any moment. If a single man could take down six of Xacsin's men in the forest, what could a whole unit do?

Xacsin's fear of COIL seemed justified, and Alfred couldn't wait to see the castle fall and the captives rescued. Even when the mission was over, he knew he wouldn't be able to tear himself from the work to which COIL so selflessly gave itself. Now he wanted to know more about the organization, to get involved, to know the man in the forest who had bested him physically and knew he was undercover.

Alfred dropped his cigarette and crushed it under his boot. Though he hated smoking, it was already part of his façade. He wasn't so delusional to believe he was stronger than such a vice, but he thought he might have an edge to quitting since he was doing it for a good cause in the first place. Hopefully, that would be enough. But he knew the Lord would help him regardless.

Walking casually across the castle keep, the courtyard was lit by a full moon this night, though a storm was in the forecast. His men on the ramparts stood out like gophers on a ridge, each of them an even finer target by the glow of their cigarettes. But it was of no concern to Alfred. He was doing the absolute minimum to make Xacsin happy—not disciplining the men much, only coordinating their repetitious watches on the wall, at the station house, or on patrol.

He opened the barracks door and walked quietly past the sleeping men to his end bunk. From a hidden Velcro pocket in one end of his duffel bag, he pulled his secure sat-phone. What he really wanted was a Bible, but that had been too risky to hide. The phone was risky enough since he'd been ordered not to bring one.

After tucking the phone into his coat pocket, Alfred went back outside to the north wall of the courtyard. Most of the guards avoided the north wall due to the two ventilation windows on the west end. The men were sure the diseases from below would infect them if they spent any time there, but Xacsin had installed a sealed door in the corridor to protect them from the bad air in the levels below. The vents were merely for intake. Alfred knew there was no danger of infection, but he played on the men's paranoia just the same.

With his back against the wall, he pressed the dial button on his phone. He'd already programmed the number and made sure service was available from that position. It rang twice.

"Zven's Laundry," a tired-sounding woman answered in German. "Who's calling at this hour?"

"James and John," Alfred whispered in code.

"Zebedee. Talk to me. I'm recording."

Taking the phone from his ear, Alfred held the

mouthpiece an inch from his mouth so he could speak directly and quietly into the mic in the darkness.

"Twenty armed men, more expected within a week from England. Begin at gate going clockwise. Tower north of gate: two men day and night. North wall: inside are four levels of fifty cells each. Each houses Christians and Jews. More arrive daily. Three-quarters with deadly infections. We are near capacity. Next, inside the wall east of the north wall is the exam room and operating room. Dr. Aleksandre Stashinsky is from Estonia, a biochemist in his sixties. His office and living quarters are next to his exam room. Then an equipment storage room is next. Door to courtyard here. Also, door to northeast tower overhead. Manned by pairs day and night. East wall: kitchen, then the mess hall. Door to courtyard, as well as to the southeast tower, also armed by a pair. The armory is next. Courtyard door. Barracks: door to courtyard and door to armory. Next, in southwest corner is the two-car garage. Xacsin's living quarters and office above. Then, the tower sits south of the gate, armed by a pair always.

"On the wall in thirds are three pairs on the roam day and night. Stashinsky thinks he'll be ready to release infected captives within thirty days. I stress—every captive will be infected by then. Two COIL men are below, both infected to some extent. All will then be transported and released in neighborhoods to infect the greatest number of civilians. You must strike within two weeks or consider a nuclear strike more merciful for this lot. The prisoners are not well. Every single day matters. Bring biohazard masks, suits optional. Expect heavy resistance. I'll disable RPG weapons, but small arms will be bountiful. God bless. Don't worry about me. Please hurry for their sakes. This is Snake signing out."

Alfred killed the power on his phone and shoved it into his pocket. As he had spoken on his phone, his eyes had played on the dark window above the garage: Xacsin and Hannah's quarters. The cold man with the green eyes had left earlier that day in something of a panic. He had a presence about him that gave Alfred a chill, so Alfred wasn't sorry when the man was absent, leaving Alfred in charge. His only order was to make sure the good doctor was safe as he continued his unthinkable acts in the northeast operating room where he was assigned an around-the-clock guard.

Oddly, Xacsin hadn't returned to the castle, which concerned Alfred. He wanted the mad leader inside the castle when COIL pounced.

"Hey, Snake! Send Mrs. McLeery up here to keep me warm, huh?"

Laughing with the others, Alfred groaned inside. Hannah had eyes that were as empty as Xacsin's. Her attitude toward COIL and the captives seemed personal, due to her sister's capture by COIL operatives in a past operation.

"I'm cold, too, Pudgel," Alfred yelled back. "Keep your eyes on the forest."

He crossed the courtyard and stood outside the barracks door as he smoked another cigarette, waiting for a split second to—

It was clear. No one was looking. Opening the garage door, he slipped inside and closed it softly. The men on the wall would think he'd gone into the adjacent barracks, but he had something else in mind. After passing the first of two SUVs, he climbed the stairs to the upstairs loft. He'd been up to Xacsin's office a number of times that week, but now Hannah McLeery was sleeping in the bedroom next door. Xacsin was gone, perhaps arranging any number of things for the release of the infected captives. His absence was one less thing Alfred had to worry about. He hoped the office might hold a clue to Xacsin's cloaked schedule.

Alfred flicked on a lamp. If he were caught now, it would be okay. The phone call had already been made to his employers, the COIL Agency. He'd done his job, giving whatever invading team they were sending an inside view. If he were discovered as a mole now, he could die with some resolve and peace. The lives in his care would soon be saved, his job complete. Anything else he could find out now was merely extra intel.

The desk computer was on standby. Sitting down in the chair, Alfred clicked the curser through a list of applications and documents most recently accessed. He couldn't risk the noise of the printer, so he would have to memorize whatever he found, if he found anything.

What he discovered seemed like very little at first: transportation schedules for infected captives. Alfred counted thirty different outlets that branched out to more than one hundred down the line, and Xacsin was organizing more. It would be impossible to stop the infectious diseases once the process began. COIL had to stop Xacsin before anyone left the castle! That was the only option.

But then Alfred found a four-page document full of

names and addresses, accessed as recently as that day, minutes before Xacsin had stormed out of the castle. Names and addresses, but for whom? Some were in Berlin, and some were in New York City. He clicked on links to adjacent photographs. The images were of surveillance quality, taken covertly. Alfred bit his lip. These could be kidnapping targets, perhaps future victims. But no, there were many women listed, and Xacsin wasn't housing women and children. And New York was too far away to be kidnapping people only to bring them to the castle for an infectious shot. Maybe there was another similar enterprise in the United States? He prayed not.

Opening an image titled "C.J. Dowler," Alfred saw a photo of a man, woman, and child. The child looked to be around six- or seven-years-old and seemed to gaze awkwardly off-focus. She was evidently blind. The couple with her were smiling and happy, maybe in their fifties.

C.J. Dowler. From where did Alfred know that name? He studied the man a little closer. Brown hair and eyes, average height, not very fit. Though it was an older picture, Alfred recognized him. It was the man from the woods. Corban Dowler—the founder of COIL!

Then the names and addresses all made sense. Alfred browsed the list. Yes. They had to be COIL people, the organization that Xacsin seemed to both blame and target more than anyone for their Christian activities. Xacsin wasn't satisfied that he was going to infect three continents with fatal diseases; he was going after his enemies specifically. And their families.

Alfred heard a noise. Someone was downstairs in the

garage. He closed out of an application and moved to the window to look down at the courtyard. No, no one was in the garage. There would've been light coming from the garage door windows. Maybe it was nothing. Maybe it was just—

"Find what you were looking for?" a woman's voice asked behind him.

It was Hannah. The hammer of a pistol clicked. Slowly, Alfred turned around. She flipped on the overhead light. Though she was in her nightshirt, Alfred's eyes were focused on the barrel leveled at his chest.

"Just nosing around, Mrs. McLeery," he said. "Didn't mean to wake you."

"What were you doing on the computer?" The gun didn't move.

"I'm an old addict. Chat rooms. Hoped you were wired to the net. No luck."

He met her icy blue-eyed gaze. She wasn't even five-five, but that gun made her seem much taller. The castle guards had said when she'd returned from visiting her sister in the South Pacific six months earlier, she'd come back mean and bitter, snarling at everyone, not only the prisoners. And she flaunted herself in front of the men in the mess hall, tempting them then threatening with death itself if anyone touched her.

She lowered the gun.

"I suppose this can be our little secret if . . ."

"If what?" Snake asked.

"Xacsin's gone," she purred, glancing over her shoulder at the bedroom. "But I've been lonely even when he's been here. Doesn't seem fair that he leaves us all alone, does it?" She took a step toward him. "You have to be lonely, too, Snake. That's what they call you, right? Snake? Call me Hannah."

"You're married, Mrs. McLeery. Let me just duck out of here. Have a good night."

"Wait! I'll have to tell Xacsin you were here then. We can't let this secret be one-sided. Don't you want to have something on me as well?"

Hannah hooked her hand around his neck and tried to pull his head down to her lips, but she was too short and he resisted. Without his help, she couldn't reach him. He stepped away, but she followed.

"Mrs. McLeery, this isn't happening. I have too much respect for your husband to mess around with you."

"*Respect?* Hah!" Turning away, she tossed the gun onto the desk, then rummaged through an envelope and handed him a photograph. "You respect Xacsin now? Him with a black girl, Snake!"

"This must be a fake."

"Yeah, right." She scoffed. "That's what he said, but I know graphics. And, I checked it out. It's for real. I trust the source I got it from, a contact of mine in Berlin. Everything we've worked so hard for is all on the line because he couldn't control himself ten years ago. Why do you think he left so quickly today? He flew to England to try to fix this mess, prove it's a fake picture. But it's no fake. There's even a team in Berlin from Liverpool, the rumor is, coming to take Xacsin out. They're saying he misrepresents the white race. After all the work we've done! It's more than a rumor, those people from Liverpool. Someone named Cecil. And you respect him, Snake? My own husband sleeps with blacks! I wouldn't be surprised if there were Christians and Jews in his background, too!"

"How could he keep something like this a secret?"

"I don't know. He had a life before I knew him, before my sister and I met him at a seance in Austria. So, he asked me to join him in his efforts to dispose of the racial filth that littered our world. My sister and her boyfriend, Branden Fairchild, made their own mistakes for this cause. Xacsin and I weren't going to make the same errors. Those COIL maggots were digging around in Xacsin's past, though. Must've found the picture, and turned it over to some purists in Liverpool." With both hands now, she wrapped her arms around his neck. "He'll probably never be back, Snake; he's out for revenge. Maybe Liverpool will kill him, but he would rather die than be taken alive by the COIL people, like they took my sister. Now, it's only you and me. We could continue the movement after the captives are released. You have the experience. I have the money. It could all start tonight, right now, you and me."

"What about the captives?"

"Nothing will change. Everything's been arranged. Dr. Stashinsky's in charge of that now. Oh, what's this?" Her hand was in and out of his coat pocket before he could stop her. She handled the thick antenna. "A satellite phone?"

Alfred grabbed for her hand, but she was already moving toward the desk. Knowing that she'd connected the dots in that split second, he dove for the gun as her fingers wrapped around the grip. Dropping his phone onto the floor, Hannah pulled the trigger before she'd completely aimed. The bullet ripped through Alfred's coat, into his abdomen, and out his left kidney. Rolling off the desk, Alfred collapsed heavily onto the floor. Panting, he ignored the disabling pain and pulled the phone close. He turned on the power and hit the redial button. If he was going to die, he had to warn the COIL operatives about the addresses he had discovered—that Xacsin was after their families!

The gun muzzle pressed against his temple.

"Give me the phone!"

Guards were now rushing noisily up the stairs to the loft.

The woman answered the phone, presumably on the other side of the world.

"James and John," he said in code, his breath coming in gasps. "Xacsin . . . is coming for your—"

Hannah pulled the trigger.

Though her eyes were burning, June Ellerman didn't take them away from the spotting scope mounted on the tripod in front of her. The scope was attached to a digital camera and lens, and it was focused on the forest road across the highway. Camouflaged, she remained hidden on the west side of the road as an SUV came into sight. She held up a button on the end of a fiber optic cable, which was attached to the camera. As soon as the SUV's occupants came into focus, she pressed the button. Their faces were captured at a range of two hundred yards. The lens was so powerful, whoever analyzed the surveillance photos later in Berlin would be able to count each facial pore, if they wanted to.

June remained motionless as the SUV pulled up to the highway. The driver looked both ways, then turned left toward Berlin. Little did they know, she was hunkered down in a camouflaged tent in the brush across the highway. Since she knew cameras, her current assignment was to surveil the road leading into the castle. Next to her, a propane heater kept the tent warm. The birds in the trees around her had accepted the intrusion of the tent and fought over seeds between patches of snow nearby.

It had been a week since June had fought in the underground club in Berlin. Her face was healing, though her eyes were still bruised and the bridge of her nose was probably scarred for life.

"December, this is Memphis. Come in."

Checking her watch, she saw it was two in the afternoon. Her shift was over. Now, as she'd done that whole week, she would take her photographs and notes back to Berlin. The intel would be sent via satellite to analysts capable of identifying the men in the vehicles coming and going from the castle. Other analysts in Berlin would do the same, then compare notes with New York, and try to make heads or tails of what Xacsin's next move was.

She picked up her radio.

"This is December. Go ahead, Memphis. Over."

"I'm coming up on you. Please confirm. Over."

"All clear. Come on in."

A moment later, the bushes rustled behind the tent. They kept their vehicles parked nearly a mile away on an old logging road and hiked to the covert post. June moved the tripod aside and opened the tent flap more than the crack required to shoot pictures. Memphis dropped to his knees and crawled into the tent, bringing pine needles and snow in with him. He lay on his belly next to her and studied her notes.

"Busy morning, huh? A dozen vehicles?"

"In and out, yeah. Wait."

June quickly repositioned the tripod as she heard an engine approach from the north. A commercial bus came into sight. She snapped two broadside shots before the bus turned off the highway onto the castle access road. After adjusting the focus, she took one last shot of the rear plates as the bus drove away into the shadows. Memphis watched as she jotted the time and description of the photos in her notebook.

"You ever think about making a career out of this?" he asked.

Looking up at him, she suddenly felt self-conscious, and tugged at her ski cap to make sure her baldness was covered. Thankfully, her hair was growing back quickly.

"Seems hard to imagine I could return to my old job after all this."

"What?" He chuckled. "No more investigative reporting?"

"Let me just say I'd have a tough time doing you guys justice no matter how long I worked on this story. The world can't understand what happens out here. This is real. You guys are real. The stories I write . . . I want them to be real, too."

"Is that why you've been so quiet this past week? Thinking about your priorities?"

"Is it that obvious?" She sighed. "The others are talking, aren't they?"

"They're only curious since you haven't asked for an interview for over a week. Don't get me wrong. We're glad you're not snooping about like we're newsworthy. Look at you. You've become part of the team."

"Well, not really." She frowned. "I don't really believe what you guys believe."

"Right." He positioned the tripod in front of his face. "So, what are your beliefs, Miss Ellerman?"

Though her shift was over, she made no indication she was ready to leave. Shrugging, she smiled sheepishly.

"To be honest, I never thought of it much before all this. I've never risked my life for anyone else before—just a good story here and there. I feel more alive than ever because of it, though."

"What about God?"

"God. Yeah. I don't know. I've made fun of Christians in the States my whole life. Much of what I've seen in America is pretty hypocritical. Most Christians might go to church and sit in a pew once a week, but they're otherwise no different from anyone else. They still lie, cheat on their taxes and spouses, break the law, and so on. That's only what I've seen in passing. In the last week and a half, what I've seen while living with you guys has me, well, refiguring my conclusions about genuine faith and Christianity. Maybe not everyone is a fake. Maybe there's more to it all."

"Keep in mind that your relationship with the Creator shouldn't depend on the good or bad actions of others."

"Oh, I know. But if I see something working for others, then I know it's real. For the first time in my life, I'm witnessing genuine people. It has me thinking there's something to the Bible after all—if it's taken literally."

Side by side, their faces were only inches apart. She suddenly realized he'd been watching her mouth as she spoke. He met her eyes, then looked away.

"I think I've been spending too much time in this tent. Sorry." Memphis needlessly adjusted the calibrations on the camera.

"What?" She nudged him playfully with her elbow. "Christians aren't human?"

"It's not that. I asked you a serious question and you were giving me a serious answer, which I barely heard. Sorry." Looking back at her, he swallowed nervously. "You were saying?"

She tilted her head slightly and kissed him softly on the lips. When she settled back, she saw him sigh with frustration.

"Now I'm the one who's sorry. Maybe we've both been in this tent too long." But she didn't bother to crawl out. "Let's change the subject. You're the only single guy on the old Flash and Bang Team."

"Well, Nathan's single."

"Okay, but I don't know Nathan. Besides, he's rather inaccessible at the moment, right?" She saw him flinch. "I didn't mean to sound heartless, but I don't want to talk about anyone else. I want to talk about you. When I asked Johnny about you, he said your wife passed away not long ago?"

"Yeah. A while back."

"What was her name?"

"Sammie. Samantha."

"You don't wear your wedding ring anymore?"

Memphis gazed at his finger where the mark from his band still showed.

"Not on missions."

"Do you still love her?"

"It wasn't even a year ago, June, but it seems like it was another lifetime. Since she was buried, COIL took me in and gave me a new place in life. It's helped me a lot. I was a P.E. teacher, you know? As a grieving widower, I was depressed to the point of inactivity. I lived like a hermit for days, not even showering. I needed to refocus. Don't get me wrong. I believe God can take us through any difficulty, but I was so torn up; I may have bordered on suicide. Sure, I loved Sammie, but after she was gone, all I could think about was myself. *Why me?* Why did God have to take her from me? How would I continue alone?"

"That's natural. You were hurt."

"No, I was selfish; I wasn't seeing the bigger picture. Even when Sammie was alive, I was selfish, staying in my comfort zone rather than listening to my calling. Sammie's accident shook me up, got me refocused after I cried my eyes and heart out to God."

"And this . . . team is your calling? Flying choppers and planes for COIL when you're not hiding in tents with cameras?"

"I was a good teacher, June, and I loved working with kids. But I've never felt so fulfilled before now. It's like

Special Forces Christianity, you know? Every day we fight spiritual battles. We can't handle these ops unless our hearts are in the right place. I've never been on the front lines of a war before, but I can tell you the spiritual front lines are more fulfilling than the physical. Here, we know we make a difference. My relationship with God adds a dimension to this lifestyle that makes it more complete. This is what matters."

"And that's what I'm missing," June stated. "Can I ask you a question?"

"Of course."

"Would it be selfish of me to, well, change my faith from basically nothing to what you guys have so I can feel more fulfilled as well? That's a stupid question, but I see you guys have something I've never seen before in anyone else. You guys, even your support people like Chloe, are active."

"It's not a stupid question, June."

"I've interviewed a few dozen special ops guys. They're all awesome and they do unbelievable missions. But at the end of the day, they're only soldiers who killed a pile of bad guys for people they don't know. And they have to get drunk to drown out their memories before they can go home to their cheating wives and rebellious kids."

"They have it that bad, huh?"

"Well, not totally, but don't get me started. So, my stupid question?"

"Right. A change of faith—selfish or not, just to feel fulfilled. It's not a stupid question. I wish more people would consider it. There are a lot of reasons why people decide to seek God, initially. The thing is, if the desire is genuine—the desire to be saved from yourself or your lifestyle—God kneads us like clay to become His vessels. In the beginning, most people are probably a bit selfish with their faith-seeking, I suppose, but when it's done in humility and brokenness, is that really selfishness? God is powerful and wise enough to straighten us out if we trust Him."

"Okay, then, I have another stupid question."

"Yeah?"

"I'm already thinking about the faith thing, so I can ask you this: would it have bothered you less when I kissed you if I was a Christian?"

"Boy, you don't skirt around the issues, do you?"

"It's the reporter in me. Well, I know we're getting friendly, I guess, and I've heard that it says in the Bible how a Christian should try to be with another Christian, not an unbeliever."

"And that's why you want to become a believer? Maybe we need to step back."

"Come on, Memphis. That's not the only reason. My life as a whole is quite a wreck. Look, I know you like me. Now I've told you I'm taking a good look at, well, the Cross. Let's say I'm giving you fair warning."

"How'm I supposed to concentrate on this op when you tell me something like that?" Laughing with him, she set her hand on his.

"You can love Samantha forever, Memphis. Just give me a piece of you, too, okay?" June gave him a peck on the cheek. "You're something special."

He didn't seem to know what to say, so she gathered her

things, the notebook, and the camera card, and crawled out of the tent. Glancing back inside, she caught him smiling like a schoolboy.

"Give me a few days with this decision, okay?"

"Um. What decision, exactly?" he stuttered.

"Jesus."

Memphis nodded, and she darted into the trees toward the car.

CHAPTER SIXTEEN

In the basement offices of Berlin's COIL headquarters, Corban walked through the desks of caseworkers. Though he wore a visitor's pass on his breast pocket, he was no visitor. He'd purchased the building, then hired Rupert Mach to run the office. Without an escort, Corban moved to one of the back rooms next to Rupert's office, then closed the door and sat in front of a computer terminal. There was a camera mounted on top of the plasma screen. The screen blinked at the touch of a key. Halfway around the world in New York City, Chloe turned to face her own camera in a secure conferencing booth at COIL's head office.

"Good evening, Chloe."

"Evening? I just took your daughter to school. It's barely after eight a.m. here."

"Oh, you've got Jenna for the weekend? I forgot. Any word from Janice?"

"She arrived in Cameroon last night and sent a digital. She's leaving Yaounde for a couple days to visit a clinic in the bush."

"What about hostiles in that area?"

"The Bight of Biafra is stable right now, Corban. You left me back here so you don't have to sweat the little things, right? Janice is fine. She'll be back on Monday.

194

You'll be back then, too, right? If all goes well this weekend?"

"Well, a slight change of plans. That intel we got from Snake moved us up, but there's a bad storm coming in that's forcing us to stand down until at least Tuesday."

"Not good." Chloe groaned. "Time means lives. Every hour counts, Corban."

"No one is more aware of that than me, Chloe, but we're expecting ten inches of snow over the next two days. Visibility is key. We'd have good cover in low visibility, but we can't approach the castle with our night vision in a storm, nor can we use our long-range weapons through a flurry of flakes."

"You're the man on the ground, Corban. What about Xacsin McLeery? Any sign of him in or out of the castle?"

"No, and this concerns me. It's as if he was warned; maybe he's been warned from day one. First, there was Paris. There've been other things as well, that might suggest . . ."

"Corban?" Chloe leaned closer to the camera. "Do you realize what you're saying? An inside leak? That gives me chills. You have to think back over the few you've trusted and figure out what the enemy may have discovered. To even mention this, you must have someone in mind. Whoever this someone is, we might be able to get a fix on Abaddon."

"Yeah, you're right. Maybe I'm getting soft in my old age. I do have a possible leak on this side of the pond, but I'm too terrified to admit it's him."

"Just tell me, Corban. So you're not implicated, I can

monitor him from this end. You need to focus on the op."

"I can't tell you yet. Not until I know for sure. And then I'll deal with it quietly."

"Don't do it alone, Corban. When you're sure, bring me into it. I don't want revenge, but I want to be there for justice. And if Abaddon is the inside leak, I definitely want to see him for myself, in cuffs, going to prison."

"We need to pray for the Lord's will on this, Chloe." Staring at his hands, Corban paused long enough to pray silently before continuing. "There's day and night coverage on the castle. After we tracked Xacsin to England, we lost him. I wish Snake could give us something more."

"He took a gamble calling us in the first place. And it sounded like the second call he made was interrupted. Hopefully, he'll call back. Who knows how many lives he's saved by risking his own."

"That's true, Chloe. But the gunshot you thought you heard might've been the end of Snake." Corban bowed his head. Snake had most likely been killed—so others could live. Gestures of sacrifice continued to play out around the world. But when would the bloodshed be avenged? "It's by Snake's intel already that I've been able to confirm what I suspect of our leak, and that could make a difference in the years to come. Snake knew what he was doing."

"After you hit the castle, and once you get all the captives to the hospital, if Snake makes it through this, I hope you can sit down with him and figure out where Xacsin is. That evil man's too dangerous to let get away, especially since we know he's connected to Abaddon. By the way, how's the hospital prep coming?"

"That's been Rupert's assignment, but according to him, the administration knows something's up. It's not every day a borough hospital is outfitted with quarantine specs."

"As long as no one panics."

"Thankfully, we've been able to avoid that, so far. Keep searching for Xacsin, Chloe. Get airport footage through MI-6 if you have to. We need to know what he's doing now and where he's going next."

"All right." Chloe studied her PDA. "Oh, CIA Deputy Director Buchanen called to make sure all was well since you missed your monthly meeting. I told him you were on assignment."

"Thanks. Did he have anything for us?"

"Just some background on Xacsin you probably already know. We now have confirmation from old email caches that Xacsin did indeed set us up in Malaysia. And Brandon Fairchild and Velt Plavanko—the two that Abaddon brainwashed to kidnap your family—still aren't talking. Neither is Helena. No surprises there. But the Agency did pass on that Fairchild, through Xacsin's counsel, hired an Italian assassin to hunt you last year. Might he be the one who shot you in Rome?"

"Hmm. Could be."

"They couldn't find any communication indicating Fairchild cancelled the hit on you, but the assassin is rumored to have died in Lebanon. Someone name Luigi Putelli. Anybody we know? Anyway, might keep an eye out for this guy, because his death isn't confirmed."

"Okay, I will." Corban acted as if he were taking notes, but he needed no notes about Luigi Putelli. He was hoping his old friend was still working in the shadows and hadn't returned to the darkness from which Corban had dragged him. Maybe, just maybe, the man who chewed bubble gum with gusto was somewhere near. "Anything else?"

"Well, I don't want to bother you with so much on your plate already . . ."

"Go ahead, Chloe. I'm snowed in here; I know the rest of the world's still turning."

"Maybe I can get one of the other teams to handle this. It's not even a COIL situation, not directly, anyway. Well, I guess it is, because there's a missionary family involved, but—"

"Chloe, you already texted me two days ago that all the teams are swamped right now with other assignments. If it's something I can handle while we're on standby, let me have it."

"All right. It's Sudan. One of the Darfur states isn't receiving their rations from the UN World Food Program again. South Darfur, actually, in the Red Sand Desert."

"So who called for us?"

"Roger and Judy Weston."

"Weston? Remind me."

"We transplanted them from Ethiopia eighteen months ago when they were run out of Addis Ababa. They were doing well in Khartoum, but recently got involved in the aid effort for the refugees in South Darfur. Ninety thousand people, mostly children, are in Kalma, the largest camp. World aid organizations are helping, or wanting to help, but even their food shipments have been intercepted by the Janjaweed, the Arab tribal militia. Several drivers have been killed. Even when the Janjaweed aren't raping and killing, they're stealing ration cards and burning them. These poor people are at the breaking point."

"So why doesn't the UN send in a couple thousand troops and take back the food?"

"A few problems with that. First, the food's hidden. We don't know where they're hiding it, so the aid programs are stocking a second shipment right now to replace the last, but they don't want to send it until they're certain it'll reach Kalma and the other smaller camps nearby. Number two, Sudan has again ousted a UN force in the name of peace talks organized by the African Union. Basically, no one cares about the two million displaced persons, not even their own governments, of which ninety thousand are starving to death as we speak. There was even a rally in Washington yesterday, but it wasn't on COIL's radar until Roger Weston called from a sat-phone we gave him for emergencies."

Corban's eyes were on his hands again as he mentally worked on the makings of a strategy. Chloe seemed to know to give him a few minutes while he came up with a plan. How could he make this hopeless situation better—at least for a while? Finally, he looked up.

"Where's this second aid shipment being staged?"

"The Upper Nile."

"Tell them to air drop it on Sunday at daybreak instead of driving it in. Drop it right on Kalma."

"Uh . . . the US Air Force would love to run an airdrop, but they're not exactly cleared for Sudanese airspace. Treaty talks have stalled everything. Besides, even if the camp did get the airdrop, the Janjaweed would ride in and steal it, killing people all the while. You can't solve Darfur's humanitarian problems in one day, Corban. No one expects you to. We can't cure the world."

"I hear you, Chloe." Corban nodded sadly. "But I think we can do better."

"There's nothing . . . I mean, we can't—"

"Let me call you back in a few minutes, okay?"

"All right. I'll be here."

Cutting the connection, he rose and paced the small room, then knelt on the floor.

"Lord, You know how torn up this Darfur region is. Right now, Roger Weston is probably telling the refugees to pray to You to save them, to somehow miraculously bring them food since no one else can. Father, You know my heart. Do I have the resources to handle this? Show me how, please. How can I help these people—Weston's people? Show me how to feed Kalma, and I pray that You use the rest of that disastrous atmosphere to somehow bring others to saving faith in You. Guide me, I pray, and guide Chloe. Watch over Janice in Cameroon—and us here as well. In Jesus' Name, amen."

Corban drummed his fingers on the desk as he reconnected with Chloe.

"Figure it all out?" she asked with a smile.

"Yeah, it came to me after I took it to the Lord. You ready to take some notes?"

"Seriously?" Chloe's smile faded. "You're gonna tackle this?"

"We have the time with the storm coming. If all goes

well, we'll be back by Tuesday to finish Operation Rahab."

"Okay. Tell me what you have in mind."

An hour after his talk with Chloe, Corban stood in his hotel room, the whole team gathered before him. They sat on the floor and on the beds, except for Memphis, who was on surveillance at the castle. The meeting was being recorded for his sake.

"Today's Friday. We can't do anything until after the storm passes, so Operation Rahab is being shelved until then." Several of them mumbled their dissatisfaction before Corban continued. "We're going to Africa—the Sudan, actually—for a short trip, assuming everything is ready to hit the castle as soon as we get back. Scooter?"

"Brauch and I are ready. Scaffolding is in place. The snow shouldn't faze it."

"Good. Rupert, you'll stay back here at the office to keep things moving forward. How are the preparations at the hospital coming?"

"Oh, a few staffing issues to address. We'll be ready by Tuesday for the infected patients from the castle."

"Okay. Johnny, you get choppers for backup?"

"Yep, and bio-hazard masks."

"Okay, is there anything that won't be ready for Rahab on Tuesday?" Corban paused and looked around the room. "Rupert, we're going to be covering a whole other mission now, so if you want to head back to the office, you can. We'll be out of the region for a few days, but we'll be in contact."

The German man rose to his feet.

"Just come back with enough men to make our efforts here worthwhile," Rupert Mach urged. "I can't stop Xacsin alone."

When the Berlin director had left the room, Corban laid out a map of northern Africa.

"Now, listen up. Operation Kalma requires our attention. Kalma, Sudan's largest refugee camp, is in South Darfur. Tribal militias have been intercepting food transports by track and truck, so we're going to make sure an air-dropped delivery is successful and not stolen." Corban sorted through a handful of papers. He handed one to Johnny Wycke. "Johnny, you're the lead with Memphis, piloting one of the oldest cargo planes in the world from the Upper Nile down to South Darfur to make the air drop. The aid organizations in the area will supply you with three or four volunteers to assist with the loading of the cargo, but they won't be flying with you. It'll be a dangerous flight."

"Exactly how old is this bird, Boss?" Johnny asked.

"This is a converted Boeing bomber, a YB-52, called a Stratofortress. Since you're looking for a date—it's a 1952 hunk of metal." Johnny shook his head and chuckled with the others, then Corban continued "But in defense, it was a prototype for the still-operational B-52 bomber. It was all we could borrow on such short notice. And, I think . . . it has wings."

Everyone erupted in laughter.

"Sorry, but that's actually the good news. Now, the bad news. Somehow, our militia boys in the area, called Janjaweed, got their hands on some SA-7, heat-seeking rocket launchers. As if the drop won't be tough enough flying an antique, you two get to dodge three-and-a-half-pound charges with a two-mile range."

The operatives were silent now with eyes wide, contemplating the seriousness of the situation.

"Moving on. Scooter and Brauch, pack up the NL-X1 sniper rifles. You'll be defending the refugee camp's eastern approach. The Janjaweed will be on horseback and it's likely they'll counter-attack after we make contact. Bruno and I will cover your efforts. Bruno, you're with Scooter."

"Oh, great!" Scooter playfully punched Bruno's shoulder.

"Brauch, it's you and me."

The ex-assassin nodded once.

"After ten minutes of convincing, Chloe and I managed to talk the colonel of a Turkish UN garrison into taking the Janjaweed off our hands, after—and only after—we've completely disabled them. The UN can't do anything else, under penalty of international tribunal, but their assistance is mandatory post-op when we're gone and the camp is otherwise defenseless. This is a short-term fix to a drawn-out conflict. Everyone knows that. The Janjaweed will regroup a month from now, but maybe, by God's grace, the peace talks will settle on some sort of treaty.

"Our objectives are to get to Kalma undetected, set up a drop-zone, defend the drop and the dispersement of food, knock out the militia with tranqs, and pull out after the Turks have taken up our post. The Janjaweed wouldn't dare attack a UN garrison, but that same garrison won't attack the Janjaweed unless provoked. As an impartial and non-lethal force, we're striking in absolute secrecy. Questions?"

"What about me?" June asked.

"We're risking our lives to buy these people only a few days, June. This is what we do. I'd tell you to stay here if I thought you'd listen, but you have that look in your eyes. In the cargo plane, you run the risk of being shot down. On the ground, you run the risk of getting shot by a Kalashnikov assault rifle. Pick your poison, or wait here for our return."

They waited for June's decision.

"Your new sniper rifles out-distance the AK-47, right?"

"By two or three times, yes."

"I'm not too hip on being shot out of the sky. I'll take my chances on the ground."

"Fine. The ground force will be armor-suited and booted. Everyone better make it back alive so we can finish up Rahab, or Rupert really will be trying to attack the castle on his own."

"Question, Boss," Scooter said. "Exactly how many Janjaweed are we talking about here?"

"Shouldn't be more than one hundred or so on horseback."

CHAPTER SEVENTEEN

Corban watched from the back of the van as it bounced along a barely discernible road that disappeared for yards at a time, its dusty, shallow ruts trampled by bony cattle and scrawny refugees. Bruno was assigned to drive the green jalopy across the wasteland of southern Sudan since he was the only black man on the team. And the green wreck had seen its share of warfare, so it fit the scene well.

Brauch, Scooter, and June sat in the back with Corban. At the far rear, Brauch sat on his forty-pound pack, his NL-X1 propped on his knees. If Bruno stopped and gave the word, Brauch would be the first to jump out to fire upon an enemy. He also carried an NL-3 rifle and NL-1 for close contact. When Corban had checked the packs, he saw that Brauch carried his night scope adapter for the day scope attached to the top of his sniper rifle, and he had two hundred rounds for the NL-X1. Everyone carried one thousand pellets preloaded in magazines for their NL-3 rifles.

Scooter sat across from Brauch with his own NL-X1 and similar gear. Beside Scooter, June was perched on her twenty-pound field pack. Corban prayed she could handle whatever was ahead. He had no idea how long they'd be defending Kalma; hopefully, it would only be a two-day op, but they had food, water, and gear for three days. Still, water would be carefully rationed in this desert.

Approaching Kalma from the west, then driving past a small refugee camp, it seemed that no one paid them any mind. It was possible the inhabitants were already starved to death, Corban considered, but they couldn't stop. They had nothing to offer these poor people yet.

June held her NL-3 rifle across her lap, trying to imitate what the others did as close as possible. It hadn't taken her long to recognize that Brauch seemed to be the most skilled operative among them. He rarely spoke as his chin was tucked and his eyes were constantly sweeping studying their surroundings. The next best was Scooter, June decided, but he wasn't as smooth as the German. Scooter had his own style, and though the others said he was a remarkable marksman and disciplined soldier, he had a careless air about him—most often evidenced by his mouth.

Across from June, Corban dozed as he leaned against the back of Bruno's seat. Corban carried two NL-3s, but June wasn't sure the aging man knew how to use them. His pack was as heavy as the others who were younger—and twice as heavy as hers—but judging by his physical appearance, she figured he wouldn't be able to carry it very far. She knew he was almost sixty. How did he expect to keep up with them?

Bruno also had two NL-3s on the floor next to his field pack. He was part of the old assault team with Scooter. June had heard them talk about it, so she knew Bruno could handle a rifle. Still, she wasn't sure who she wanted to stay closest to for safety. She hoped nothing dangerous happened at all and she wouldn't have to witness all-out warfare as she'd been so willing to do when she was safe in the States.

"Boss," Bruno called. He stopped the van.

Corban woke and leaned between the two front seats, keeping his head low in case an adversary was looking into the cab. He saw Bruno's concern. Before them was an ocean of single-roomed, plastic-roofed shelters. Dust-blown and foot-trodden, the road abruptly became a trail as it wound through the camp. Cattle and a few chickens moved between the dwellings, guarded protectively by starving refugees. The animals were obviously their last possessions. By the look on the few faces Corban could see, the animals wouldn't last the day. The people would need to butcher the animals to eat if they still had the strength to lift a butcher knife.

"This is Kalma," Corban said. "Drive to the center of the camp. Try to keep from stopping." He sat back down as the van chugged forward. "These people are starving. If you start giving them your rations, you won't be able to stop and we'll add your corpse to the rest of those who have no food. Keep your rations to yourself while we're in the camp. We can't save them if we have no food for ourselves. Do your job. That's all. When we're pulling out, give them the shirt off your back and the canteen off your shoulder, if you want. Just don't do it before we've finished our mission."

No one said anything. They didn't even nod in acknowledgement. Corban knew it was a harsh order, but he was right.

The Kalma camp was eerily quiet for housing nearly one hundred thousand people. It was the hottest hour of the day. Most everyone would be in the shade, but there still should've been renegade children darting about. Yet there were no children chasing chickens or laughing as they played tag.

Watching June from the corner of his eye, Corban wondered how she'd handle this exposure to the real world. She pressed her eye against a bullet hole in the side of the van, watching the camp as they passed through utter squalor. The few people they could see had bloated bellies, and flies swarmed their eyes, mouths, and nostrils. After a few minutes, June turned away.

"I can't bear this sight any longer."

"But you will," Corban assured. "You'll step up with us because no one else in the world can or will, ugly as it is."

"Here we go, Boss." Bruno stopped the van with a squeal of brakes.

Peering through the windshield, Corban saw the Red Cross emblem on a green army tent and a tattered aid banner on a makeshift, metal building.

"Everyone out," Corban said. "We're on foot from here."

Brauch and Scooter opened the back doors of the van and the team climbed out. A dozen curious refugees gathered to see who the strangers were.

June followed Brauch as he and the others secured a perimeter around the van. There could've been Janjaweed rebels around, though Bruno said he hadn't seen any armed horsemen on the drive in. Burdened with his pack and dressed in rusty-tan fatigues as the others, Corban approached the aid building. The door opened. Corban stopped and aimed his primary NL-3 rifle. A tanned white man raised his arms and froze. He had a brown beard, but the hair on his head was white and thinning.

"Roger Weston?" Corban asked.

"Yes, I'm Roger."

Lowering his rifle, Corban slung his weapon over his shoulder and offered his hand.

"My name is Corban Dowler." Roger lowered his hands slowly and hesitantly shook Corban's hand. "This is my team. Have you been in touch with the oasis? I don't see a drop-zone or a signal site set up yet."

"Drop-zone? Signal?" Roger shook his head wearily. "What are you talking about? I haven't heard from the Nile for two days."

"They were supposed to call you about an air drop. Did you get your wife out? Is there anyone else here with you?"

"Um . . ." Roger put his hand to his brow. He frowned. Starvation obviously plagued him as well. "Judy's out on her rounds. Two babies were born last week, but there's not much she can do. Who did you say you were?"

"Let's go inside." Corban took Roger by the arm and led him out of the sun into the building. Inside the small warehouse was a table, a few empty crates used for chairs, and two cots against the back wall. At one time, there were probably food pallets littering the dirt floor, but no longer. Taking off his pack, and, against his own orders, Corban pulled out a granola bar. "When was the last time you ate, Roger?"

"We . . . ate our last cornmeal two days ago."

Corban opened the wrapper and handed the bar to Roger.

"Split this with your wife. Eat it slowly."

Just then, the door opened and a thin young woman with white-blond hair strode into the building. She looked as weary as her husband did.

"Roger, what's happening? I'm not leaving these people!" Dropping a medical tote bag, she crossed the floor to her husband. He split the granola bar and handed her half. Tears flooded her eyes. "Who are you? We forbid guns inside this camp. Everyone's already dying. You don't need your weapons."

"A plane is dropping food by parachute at dawn tomorrow. My team and I will be fighting off the Janjaweed. I need you two to set up a drop-zone and food dispersement site. Gather your strongest dozen or so refugees to help you. Hopefully, we can avoid any riots or hoarding. You two have done this more than I have. We're only here to make sure . . ."

As their jaws slowly worked on their granola bars, they stared at him as if they were in a daze.

"On second thought, you two find me when you're ready. Just rest. We'll get started. You're gonna be okay now. So are your people."

Nodding, Corban patted Roger on the shoulder and exited the building. He climbed on top of the van and surveyed the view around him.

"Anyone in the Red Cross tent, Bruno?"

"A bunch of kids lying around. Empty, otherwise. Oh, and about twenty cases of expired malaria vaccines."

"All right. This camp is under the Westons' care, but they're in about the same shape as everyone else here. Scooter and Brauch, you two set up post on the east edge of the camp. It's about a quarter-mile that way. Take everything you have and dig in. The rest of us will set up the drop-zone here then join you."

Brauch and Scooter jogged away. June and Bruno stepped closer to Corban.

"Normally, when the supply trucks roll in here, they're three or four deep and piled high," Corban explained. "It makes for simple, mobile distribution. But we don't have that luxury. We're getting corn, rice, and potatoes in fifty-pound bags. Realistically, we can't expect much to hit the drop-zone perfectly, so we'll need to gather everything that drops and get it to the site we're clearing right now. As soon as Roger and Judy join us, we need them to organize the refugees to help gather and disperse the food once it rains from the sky. All these nearby shelters need to be moved back. I want one hundred square yards, with the aid building in the center. Okay, let's get going. This needs to be ready before midnight so we can join Scooter and Brauch. The Janjaweed could show up any time. And pray the provisions drop on target."

Bruno went northwest and Corban walked southwest to begin clearing back the huts from the intended zone, but June didn't move. She wasn't sure how to uproot the inhabitants when they didn't speak the same language. Watching Corban duck into the nearest hut, she decided he knew what to do, so she joined him at the shelter doorway.

"Food," Corban said repeatedly as he routed four children and three women. They could barely stand on their stick-like legs and the children began to cry. "June, help them gather their things. Use sign language. Once we move them, they can have their houses back."

June put a hand to her nose. It smelled like feces in the shelter, but she couldn't dwell on it. Corban disappeared into the next shelter. Holding her breath, June rolled up two rags that may have been blankets at one time, and set them in a woman's arms.

"Come." She motioned to the door as if they were going for a journey, then made eating gestures. "Food. Eat. Come on."

Already, she was sweating. It was over one hundred degrees and the air wasn't moving.

Corban and June worked in tandem down one line of shelters. Those in the next huts walked or crawled to their doorways to see what was happening. Some didn't move, even refused, having given up on life, their minds shutting down as the hungry beast of starvation completed its curse. The team carried the most desperate.

After they'd cleared the people from the first ten shelters, Corban put his shoulder against the first one and broke its earthen seal. Using handholds on either side, Corban and June picked up the dwelling and shuffled, skidded, and pulled it ten yards to the west to rest only a yard from its neighbor. Thus, the next shelter had to be moved twice that distance west.

By the time they started on the second row, several men who had a little strength seemed to understand their intentions and joined Corban and June in their endeavor. Others helped Bruno as well, and eventually, Roger and Judy came out to interpret and comfort the people being disturbed. Children who couldn't rise to their feet tugged on June's clothes from their knees as she passed them, weeping for food and attention.

As soon as Roger and Judy had control of the situation, Corban announced they were no longer needed in camp. He, June, and Bruno joined Roger and Judy in the center of the football-field-size drop-zone. Judy pointed at the sky, assuring a group of refugees that food would rain from the sky the following day. Roger had rounded up thirty of the strongest men and women he knew personally and gave them the responsibility of gathering the food sacks once they floated to the ground. Though they were the strongest of the refugees, they'd still need to carry the fifty-pound sacks in pairs, or by threes.

"Just before dawn," Corban said to Roger, "I want you to light fires on the four corners of this zone. Burn anything to help guide our pilots to this section of the camp."

"Who are you people?" Roger asked. "We were already preparing ourselves to meet our Maker."

"You contacted us a few days ago."

"I contacted everyone I ever knew for help a few days ago. Which ones are you?"

"We're COIL."

"Oh, you helped in Ethiopia two years ago. And you bought us a couple plane tickets out of the country before we met the machete. I thought you guys were Christians." He eyed the rifles with concern.

"These have non-lethal projectiles, like tranquilizers," Corban said. "Don't worry. No one's dying tomorrow. At least, not on the enemy's side."

"Tranquilizers." A smile cracked the man's lips. "That's ingenious."

"Roger, you know what you're doing better than we do here, so we'll go now. We have to go dig in and wait. Pray for us; we'll be praying for you."

"Thank you so much." Roger gave Corban, June, and Bruno each an embrace. "God bless you and keep you safe!"

June followed Corban as he led the way out of camp at a brisk walk. It was sundown and they hadn't taken a break since arriving, but Corban seemed as charged as if he'd just climbed out of the van. Each of them applied earpieces as they arrived at the edge of the desert.

"Scooter, report."

Three hundred yards to the north, a camouflaged figure stood and waved from his trench in the ground.

"All's clear, Boss. Nothing moving. Over."

"Brauch?"

"Nothing. Over," the German replied from nearly a quarter-mile to the south.

"Let's get in position before it's too dark. You two maintain our flank. We'll go out about two miles. I'm point. Bruno, you've got our six o'clock position."

Corban and Bruno tightened their pack straps. June followed suit, then Corban started east at a jog. She pushed herself to match his rapid pace a few yards behind him. Bruno padded softly in the rear. Far to the left and right,

Scooter and Brauch paralleled them step for step.

Fifteen minutes later, Corban called a halt. Winded, he took a knee. June and Bruno did likewise, though June nearly collapsed.

"Brauch, move two hundred yards south. Scooter, two hundred north. Let your superior rifle range cover the gap. Dig in and stay alert. Sleep in shifts. Thirty-minute reports. Go."

Bruno split away to join Scooter to the north. Corban walked south with June to join Brauch. It took ten minutes to find the German. He was already digging a foxhole with an entrenching shovel. Sitting on their packs, Corban and June ate their evening meal as Brauch finished his hole. Darkness consumed the desert as Corban began to use the same shovel to dig his own foxhole fifty yards ahead and north of Brauch. With the darkness came the chill of the night.

June welcomed her turn with the shovel and looked forward to relaxing in the safety of a foxhole. She dug in fifty yards behind and north of Corban. It took a half-hour to dig it as Corban had instructed her—large enough for two bodies in case someone had to retreat to her hole.

Finished with her refuge, she dropped her pack inside and collapsed in the three-foot deep by four-foot wide earthen bunker. She was hauling out her night vision scope equipment when Corban knelt next to her dirt mound.

"Brauch's taking the first watch until oh-one-hundred," he said in a low voice. "You take the one to four, then wake me up. Can you handle that?"

"Yeah. No problem."

"You doing okay?"

"Pretty tired already. And a little worried about Memphis and Johnny."

"They'll be okay. Johnny does this all the time, and Memphis, even though he's still a beginner, can fly a trashcan through a sandstorm. You might regret it, June, but I'm glad you decided to come along with us. You did a good job back in camp. With your help, we're saving thousands of lives."

"I keep saying this: it's hard to imagine continuing a life as a reporter in the city after seeing all this. In a way, I don't want my tour with you guys to end."

"Do you have your med-pak handy?"

She patted her breast pocket.

"Morphine, gauze, tourniquet."

"If Brauch and I get taken out, you're still within range of Scooter, so he can cover you if you want to retreat back to the camp. You were an Army Reservist and you've seen your share of blood, so I won't kid you, June. This operation is life and death. Any other ops commander would give you a cyanide pill right now because of what'll happen if the Janjaweed get their hands on you—I don't need to spell it out. But better and stronger than a cyanide pill is faith in Jesus Christ. We may meet our end here, so make sure you're straight with the Lord when you're at the end of the end. In situations like this, a man or woman is forced to contemplate eternity and standing before God Almighty."

"Getting straight with the Lord, you said. I don't really know how to do that. You're talking about prayer, right?"

Corban slid into the foxhole next to her.

"It's all about accepting the fact that Jesus died on the cross for you, June, and you make a conscious decision to believe you died to yourself with Him. After that, God's Spirit comes to live inside you, and you live for Christ instead of for yourself. What happens next is rather natural if your faith is genuine. He'll guide you through the obedience of following the Bible's plan of sanctification."

"That's it? No baptism? No ceremony?"

"No, it's that simple." He chuckled. "It's all about the heart, the inner man or woman. Jesus did the rest on the cross. All that other stuff other religions teach can't save a person. If it could, we wouldn't need God; we'd only need to do a little ceremony. There are other things God asks us to do as symbols and reminders of His Son's sacrifice, but that stuff can come later as you grow spiritually closer to Him."

"Did Chloe know this would happen? Did she let me come along with you guys because she knew I wouldn't be able to refuse a change of lifestyle?"

"Is it that obvious?" Corban chuckled again. "She probably had a pretty good idea what would happen. Between you and me, I took in someone last year who was trying to kill me. Once he saw the power of God using us, and how we risked our lives for others, I think his perspective on life changed, too."

"What happened to him?"

"He . . . helped us. Obviously, he didn't kill me. I like to think he's out there somewhere doing the right thing. But, why I'm saying this is, like him, you're seeing God working in us. Ten years ago, I wouldn't have risked my life for a bunch of starving refugees."

"That's what I want, that kind of passion, what you guys have. The connection with God to know with such conviction what to do. The selflessness. It's real. I know it is. I've been with you guys long enough to know you're not faking."

"And you're interested in Memphis, too, aren't you?"

"Yeah, but he's only part of it. On the flight into Alexandria, he showed me some sections in his Bible. I believe in Jesus. Now, I guess I just need to make it final or official or something."

"You're sure you're ready?"

June swallowed and took a deep breath. She looked across the desert plain. Even here, she knew there was a God. Even if she didn't know why bad things happened to innocent people, she felt that pursuing God would disclose some of those hidden truths.

"Yeah, I'm ready."

"Then let's pray. God sees and hears us, even in this desert foxhole." Corban looked up at the night sky, the stars blinking. The night was clear and cool. He took her hand in his. "I prayed this prayer almost seven years ago, and it changed my life. Pray what's on your heart, June; what you sense God has given you to say to Him."

"Okay." June also gazed up at the sky.

"Dear God, I don't have much of an excuse for not calling on You sooner, but here I am. I know I'm a sinner, but I believe You have a purpose in this world for me. Forgive me for my sins, please, for the sins that Jesus as

God died for on the cross. Fill me with Your Spirit and change my life. Thank You, Lord. In Jesus' Name, amen."

June finished the last few words through tears, then wrapped her arms around Corban's neck and cried on his shoulder. Such was her sorrow that she'd lived so long without her Creator. And such was her joy that she now accepted that enduring Life.

CHAPTER EIGHTEEN

For the first time in June's life, she knew she was going to heaven when she died. She didn't know much about the Bible, but she knew right from wrong and she knew—rather than felt—that God would teach her the rest, when she was ready. And for the first time in her life, she knew what she believed in. So many unknowns were now solved in her mind, and she ached to share that fulfillment with others. All she had needed to do was open her heart—to *believe*.

It was almost four o'clock in the morning. Every thirty minutes for the last three hours, June had taken turns running radio checks with Scooter, then Bruno, as they pulled watch shifts to the north. After Corban had left her foxhole around eleven, she'd nearly passed out from exhaustion and slept without moving, sitting upright and leaning against the wall of her hole. When Brauch woke her at one, June was instantly alert, ready to guard the team as well as the camp. For three hours, she'd browsed the rolling flatness to the east. The night scope made the view seem like daylight and she could see for miles—coyotes, a few wild sheep, but no humans.

Her watch beeped. She touched her earpiece.

"Radio check," she said. It was June's turn to query.

"Yeah, radio check," Bruno responded. "Nothing moving. Over."

"Nothing here, either. It's Corban's watch. I'll go wake him."

"Ten-four, December. Then catch a few winks until daylight. Might get a little busy today. Out."

June smiled. *December*. That wasn't a bad handle, though born from adversity. And the COIL team would never forget her bout against Vulgar in Berlin's underground.

One more time, she studied the desert, then crawled out of her hole. She walked swiftly, hunched over, to Corban's forward foxhole. No wonder she hadn't seen any movement from him. He wasn't even there!

His hole was large enough for only one body. She didn't like the idea of standing exposed, so she jumped inside. Through her scope, she checked for movement to the east and south again. There were no enemies on the prowl, but now she needed to find Corban. No need to panic. After sweeping the land to the west, she spotted him. Back about a mile, he was digging with the entrenching shovel. Behind and in front of him, spaced at fifty-yard intervals, were small piles of dirt from foxholes he'd dug. He'd been awake all night working! She kept her eye on him and cued her radio.

"Corban, do you copy?"

He stopped digging, checked his watch, then reached for his own comm.

"This is Corban. Go ahead, December. Over."

"Want me to keep watch? I see you're busy. Over."

"How tired are you? Over."

"I'm wide awake now. We've only got a couple hours until daylight. Keep doing what you're doing. I'll be fine. Over."

"Roger. Thanks. Out."

Picking up his shovel, Corban moved one hundred yards north, and started another foxhole. June watched the man dig for a moment, then returned to her own trench. She realized she'd greatly underestimated the COIL founder. He was more than just the brains behind the outfit; he was the brawn, too. But could he use the weapons he toted as well as the others could?

Between watching for riders and tracking Corban's activity, the last two hours of darkness passed quickly. Before six o'clock, she woke Brauch, and Bruno woke Scooter. Corban jogged past her and climbed into his foxhole, then they all waited and listened for the drone of a high-flying plane.

With daylight, Corban voiced a prayer on their comm-system. He even mentioned December joining the family of God, then they again waited in silence.

The sun rose. As he ran a radio check, Corban reminded everyone to have their packs ready to go in case they had to move suddenly—or if they had to ditch their packs altogether, to keep their ammo pouches and canteens no matter what.

"This isn't good, Boss," Scooter said. "The refugees are probably cooking the Westons for breakfast by now."

June glanced back at the camp. The plane was late, but the camp was burning something. Four columns of black smoke was rising from the drop-zone.

"Come . . . down there? Over," the radio crackled.

"You're breaking up, Memphis," Corban said. "Come again. Over."

Watching the blue sky to the north, June searched for an approaching dot. Memphis was up there somewhere. She mouthed a prayer for his safety.

"Corban, this is Memphis. Do you copy? Over."

On the far horizon to the east, a flash of light and a puff of smoke caught June's eye. A few seconds later, a dull thud of an explosion came to her ears. Two more blasts followed, then she saw the flying dot coming toward them.

"Memphis, we copy. What's your status? Over."

"We're on target. A little behind. Taking on fire from ground forces. Our heading is two-seven-zero at ten thousand feet. You guys asleep or do you have a welcome party for us? Over."

"The drop-zone is ready to welcome your gifts, Memphis. What's your ETA? Over."

The plane flew in from the east, which was wisest, June thought, since the Janjaweed would follow the plane right into their defenses. Obviously, Corban had done this sort of thing before.

"ETA: two minutes. You've got hostiles inbound. We've taken fire. Shrapnel has damaged the fuselage, but nothing bad. Over."

"Can you give us a head count of the enemy on the ground? Over."

"Yeah, Boss, this is Johnny. I'm looking at two waves of ground forces about fifty each—coming right at you on our tail. They're about five miles out. Over."

"Roger, Johnny. You should see our smoke. See you tonight. Over."

"I see your smoke. Thanks. Makes our job a little easier. Careful down there. We'll come back from the Nile as soon as we can. Out."

Two miles above the ground, the plane hummed overhead. A stream of two dozen parachutes caught air behind the plane, large bundles of provisions suspended beneath. They floated to the earth, over the camp. June sighed with relief that the Janjaweed hadn't downed the plane with their anti-aircraft missiles.

"Hey, Boss, what do our pellets do to horses? Over."

"Bruno, I don't have a clue, but you shouldn't be aiming at the horses. If they're five miles out, figure ten minutes from now until we see them. They'll be at a dead run, making for the camp. Hold your fire, team, until they're within range. Remember, these pellets only take them out for twenty minutes, so keep track of your downed targets. Snipers, your dart tranqs last an hour. Let's hope we don't need all that time. Radio silence unless there's something urgent. Have your flex-cuffs ready so we can hobble the targets as soon as we can. Over."

June stared motionlessly to the east. Behind them, the food crates fell upon Kalma. The people were surely rejoicing.

Ten minutes passed.

"This is Brauch. First wave is within my range. Over."

"Handle it, Brauch," Corban said.

❧

Since Scooter would systematically chisel away at the enemy's left flank, Brauch aimed carefully between two riders on the right. He squeezed off a shot, knowing that the five tranq darts in each round had a spread of five feet at one thousand yards. Different from the pellet guns powered by CO2, the NL-X1 rounds were explosive cartridges, so the darts covered the long distance swiftly. The round's velocity was subsonic, so the sound was distorted by the barrel's suppressor.

Unlike his violent past, Brauch didn't enjoy this work, but he knew he had the skills that others did not, so he applied what he knew to save lives. Brauch felt a bond with Corban Dowler more than he did with anyone else, even Rupert Mach. When he looked into the expressionless eyes of the old spy, Brauch sensed that Corban felt the same as he did—that it was a blessed burden to turn the skills of his past into skills that made a difference for God.

By the time Brauch worked the bolt action for another round, the water-soluble needles had traveled the two-thirds of a mile. He saw a horse stumble and knew his aim had been true. Two men slumped suddenly in their saddles, then fell off their horses. The Janjaweed seemed oblivious to the downed men as they continued their charge.

June watched through her spotting scope as Brauch took another pair down, then Scooter did the same from the left. The Janjaweed still charged, even with six men down. They whipped their horses mercilessly. The militia wasn't made up of blacks only. There were lighter-skinned soldiers as well, maybe Egyptians, June guessed, but all wore bandoliers over tattered, loose clothing—still stained with the blood and tears of their last victims.

Beginning to tremble, she scoped the background of this first wave, yet the second wave was still too far away to be seen through the dust of the first. June counted as Brauch and Scooter fired rounds. By the time they'd emptied their first twelve-round magazines, only six men remained in their saddles! Numerous horses staggered drunkenly, and some had lain down as the narcotic intoxicated them, yet it wasn't strong enough to knock the horses out completely.

Watching with the rest of the team, June saw the remaining six Janjaweed reign in their horses. The animals pranced about anxiously as their riders rallied and she assumed they were discussing their concerns over continuing the advance against an unseen force. The Janjaweed had halted at five hundred yards and surely couldn't fathom what foe was between them and the food they sought to steal in the camp. As the six riders talked about their options, the snipers had time to reload. The tranq spread would be much smaller now, so there would be no success in doubling up targets. Scooter and Brauch each took down one more man.

The four remaining horsemen spun their horses around and tore off to the east where the second wave of dust billowed closer.

"Cover me!" Corban commanded on the comm as he lunged from his foxhole. "I'm securing the downed targets!"

Alone, Corban sprinted across the desert to the east. On

his shoulders rattled one NL-3, a full canteen, and an ammo pouch. In his hands, he carried his primary NL-3 and dozens of plastic flex-cuffs.

"You'll never make it in time!" Scooter warned. "He should wait until after the second wave!"

"It might be too late by then," Brauch said. "When the first wave wakes up, we'll have more than we can handle on our hands, and not enough ammo. You'd better hurry, Mr. Dowler."

The second wave, however, was held up at twelve hundred yards as the four escaped riders from the first wave reported their crushed charge.

"He might reach them," Bruno said. "The Boss might even hobble a few, but he'll never make it back if those riders start charging again. Over."

Though Corban heard their concerns in his ear, he didn't respond. His lungs burned, but he didn't slow. He couldn't. If the attack lasted all day like he thought it would, the ones they'd already shot would wake up after an hour—as Brauch had suggested. They would surely rejoin the fight unless he hobbled them now.

Like a base runner sliding into home base, Corban slid to the side of the first unconscious Janjaweed soldier at five hundred yards. Like a rodeo roper, he worked quickly, pulling the man's hands behind his back, zip-tying them, then his ankles to his wrists. He dashed to the next one.

"You've got it, Boss!" coached Bruno. "We'll tell you when they're coming. Over."

Not looking up or acknowledging, he ran to the next and the next until he was at seven hundred yards where the first pair of riders lay, taken earlier by a single shot. Now he was closer to the enemy than anyone else. It wouldn't take the Janjaweed much strain to see through the rising heat waves that a solitary enemy was moving through their seemingly dead comrades.

"They're coming, Boss!" Scooter shouted. "Get back here!"

Mid-step, Corban froze. He'd tied only twenty of the forty-six strewn across the desert. He glanced at the few horses still about. Those that hadn't been hit had fled east with empty saddles, but those that were tranquilized were too drunk for him to ride back to his team.

Dropping to his knees, he tied one more soldier. Through the ground, he could feel the charge of pounding hooves coming behind him.

"Corban . . . *run!*" June screamed through his comm. "Just leave them!"

And Corban ran as if his life depended on it—because it did. He crunched the figures in his mind as he bounded over rippling sand and stone. The world's fastest thoroughbred could maintain an excess of thirty-seven miles-per-hour, and he was probably sprinting a little slower than half that speed. Still, AK-47 rounds danced all around him. The maximum effective range for the Janjaweed 7.62mm rounds was four hundred yards. They were closing on that distance fast.

"Bring them right to us, Mr. Dowler," Brauch said. "They're almost in my range."

When the Janjaweed crossed the thousand-yard threshold of the sniper rifles, Corban knew Scooter and

Brauch would open fire as one. Behind him, four leading riders fell from their saddles, but the charge didn't slow. Fifty riders bent low as they rode, partially hiding behind their horses' necks to offer hardly any target.

"I've got no shot!" Scooter said.

"Go for the horses!" Brauch instructed. "Or the riders' legs!"

The few riders who did sit up fired their assault rifles at Corban. Their aim on horseback wasn't accurate, but it took only one lucky round to send him sprawling.

Corban went down in a puff of dust. The riders—still eight-hundred-yards away—were closing in on the rest of the team.

June stared at the heap that was once Corban, now seeming to be lifeless. Her trigger finger ached for some firing time, but the range was still too great for the NL-3 guns. Wiping at a dusty tear, she tried not to hate the soldiers who'd raped and maimed so many and had now taken out their team leader. She wanted her involvement to be the ingredient that would finish the conflict and get Corban medical attention, if he was still alive.

"They're gonna trample him!" June cried out.

The riders headed straight for Corban's body. Many of the Janjaweed had been shot and had dropped from their saddles, but more than thirty still remained and kept charging.

Whatever the riders' intentions, the horses weren't blind. Instead of trampling Corban, they jumped over the fallen mass, their hooves barely passing over his motionless form.

June breathed a sigh of relief, even if short-lived.

At four hundred yards, the snipers picked off the horses and riders one at a time. Behind the riders, several Janjaweed were on foot jogging after their comrades since their horses were disabled. Every soldier had surely seen the provisions drop and wanted a part in sacking the camp.

Through her scope, June saw at two hundred yards the riders finally spotted the foxholes around and behind June and Brauch. They pointed them out to one another. But it didn't seem like they'd seen the holes several hundred yards to the north where Scooter and Bruno lay. Trembling with anticipation, June huddled in the bottom of her hole as bullets thudded into the sand around her.

Suddenly, there was a brief recess in the firing. She rose and pulled the trigger of her NL-3 at the eighteen remaining horsemen. At one hundred yards, the pellets peppered the horses' faces. The animals panicked and reared, then split off in every direction. Brauch started using his NL-3 since they were now in range. Scooter, from the far north, continued to shoot at the riders with his NL-X1, but the riders were in such disarray that he hit only one out of five shots. Fortunately, without radios, the Janjaweed had no coordination.

The pellets had an instant sleeping effect on the horses as they snorted the toxic vapors. As soon as the riders were exposed, June and Brauch pelted them in the head and chest.

Three riders managed to slip through the team's line of defense, and June twisted around to shoot at their backs. When the three Janjaweed soldiers noticed they were separated from their fellow riders, they circled north to regroup with others who had scattered, only to come face to face with Scooter and Bruno. A brief explosion of gunfire sounded as the soldiers attempted to pass the two COIL members. Two more riders fell.

Over a dozen men on foot jogged to the north to assault Scooter and Bruno. Near June and Brauch, downed horses littered the sand. Riders hid behind the horses, firing occasionally at the two defenders, but the sand piles on the edge of the team's foxholes were stopping the bullets adequately.

As if on some signal, the Janjaweed militants stopped firing and hid from sight behind whatever cover they could find. Four unscathed, riderless horses trotted southeast, but there were still one hundred men on foot on the plain, and nearly that many horses staggering or walking about.

June took advantage of the pause to gulp down some water. No telling when she'd get another chance to quench her thirst. As if to emphasize her thought, she heard Bruno speak through her earpiece.

"May as well get comfortable. They're gonna put up a fight. It's gonna be a long day. Over."

"Corban?" Scooter called. "Boss, you copy? Over."

There was no response. June picked up her scope. Though Corban hadn't moved, she saw movement farther east, beyond seven hundred yards. The first who had fallen in the initial wave were beginning to wake up as the NL-X1 tranquilizers wore off. *Had it already been an hour since the first shot?* It was now a little after seven in the morning. Those who woke were seeing corpses lying all over the plain. They gathered their gear and started to hike east. But those soldiers closest to the team of defenders were pinned down. The hog-tied Janjaweed screamed out their frustration at being bound, but no one could help them.

Two Janjaweed rose from behind a nearby horse and fired at June's foxhole in leapfrog strategy when four other soldiers rushed forward. Scooter was ready, as was Brauch, while June huddled inside her hole. One soldier scrambled back for cover as the other three fell in the first two seconds. June rose, staying at the ready in case they tried the same tactic against Brauch. This wasn't at all how she'd envisioned the battle—a virtual standoff. And Corban was down, isolated, and surely bleeding to death if he wasn't already dead. How would they make Operation Rahab in Germany a success without Corban?

At three hundred yards, four men rose from the sand and ran to join those in front of Brauch. As June watched, Brauch took out one of them before he had to hide from a barrage of rounds. But he received no help from Scooter's position this time as Scooter and Bruno had their hands full.

"December, this is Brauch."

"Go, Brauch."

"They're going to reach Corban's forward foxhole in front of me. His pack is still there. Over."

Licking her lips, June measured the distance to the hole. *Fifty yards*. It seemed like a mile, with death threatening every step. The hidden Janjaweed were so close!

"You want me to get it? Over."

"The pack can't fall into their hands. You're smaller and I'm a better shot to cover you. Over."

Yeah, that made sense, June figured. Corban's foxhole was smaller, too. It would make for a safer defense, if she could get there alive.

"If I get there, I'm not coming back," she said. "That's a lot closer to their shooters, east and south. Over."

"Take your pack. I'll cover you. Scooter, can you assist? Over."

"I can try. They're keeping their heads down. Over."

"December, count down for us when you're ready to go. Over."

"Roger." June fit her pack onto her back and checked her ammo and canteen. She wouldn't move too swiftly with all her gear, but she had to take it. "God, if You and I are tight now, I could use some help here. We're just trying to help the refugees. Amen." Touching her earpiece, she counted. "Five . . . four . . . three . . ."

"Wait!" Bruno interrupted.

The sound of a plane's engine reached their ears.

"One!" June said, and crawled out of her hole.

She wasn't going to wait. It was the perfect instant while the Janjaweed soldiers were peering skyward for the source of the engine, which they might mistake for an assault plane. June was halfway across the fifty-yard expanse before the first soldier saw her advancing. He raised his head and fired a volley. Sand popped in front of June's feet, but she couldn't stop now. She zagged to the left as Brauch slapped half-a-dozen pellets into the man's cheek and ear. Others joined in, rising from their cover much closer than June realized. Boldly, she ran straight at them, even amongst them, firing from the hip, not missing a step.

Fear showed on the Janjaweed faces closest to her. They were bullies, used to outnumbering and overpowering their victims. But here, surely to their dismay, was a woman with a gun, charging their concealed positions!

A round tugged at her fatigues and twisted her like a top. *She was hit!* Her heel caught on sand and she fell to the ground. Two rounds slammed into the pack on her back, tearing at her straps. Crying out in panic, she scrambled desperately the last four yards to the foxhole, and fell in headfirst, her feet kicking the air as she squirmed into her new defense. Gunfire peppered the rim of her hole, but she was safe for now.

June righted herself and shrugged off her pack. Shouldering her rifle, she mentally saw her target before she rose and fired. Corban's forward foxhole was at such a new angle that the Janjaweed flank was compromised. Many hiding behind horses from Brauch's angle were caught without cover from June's new position. There was a brief attempt by the soldiers to retreat from their fallible cover. Brauch joined June in peppering them with pellets until there was no one closer than eighty yards from June's foxhole, and over one hundred yards from Brauch's position.

"You all right, December?" Scooter asked. "Looked like you took one. Over."

She shrank into her hole and checked her pack first for damage. Her spare canteen was undamaged, but one ration pack of stew had been punctured, oozing thick gravy all over. Nothing serious.

"I'm okay. Over."

But she suddenly realized she wasn't okay. A bullet had grazed one shoulder blade. The burning pain began to surface as she acknowledged the warm wetness of blood mixed with sweat slowly running down her back. The team's fatigues were lightly armored, but the bullet had found its way between the plating and her skin, gashing her open before exiting the back of her heavy jacket.

There wasn't much she could do now without someone to help her. She could barely reach the wound with her fingers. Though she couldn't bandage it, she was able to use her belt to tighten it across her shoulder blade and chest, applying pressure to stop the bleeding.

Reloading her rifle, June poked her head out of the foxhole to keep watch. Brauch did his part with the NL-X1 to push the Janjaweed back from Scooter's position.

The Janjaweed settled into new defenses, and it was obvious they intended to wait out their enemies. As the minutes ticked by, more Janjaweed woke up. Some were too far away to see their comrades were making a stand, so they, like others before them, collected their things and turned to walk to the east. The team let these few go. But the enemy who were nearer found cover and joined the battle.

She glanced westward toward the camp. The plane they'd heard was now landing on the far side of Kalma. It was a small recreation plane—their ride out of this place. June wondered how long it would take for Memphis and Johnny to get suited up and come help them. No one was moving until then.

CHAPTER NINETEEN

Nathan Isaacson was running on the beach. The sandy, white beach reminded him of Daytona where he'd once taken leave during his Marine days. The water lapped against the beach and his ankles—green water, white sand, blue sky, and the wind in his hair. But if this was heaven, where were all the people?

He stopped running and looked around. Behind him, he saw a mob of people chasing him, though they were some distance off still. That's why he'd been running, but why were they chasing him? No matter. He'd better keep running lest they catch him. And they never would catch him because he'd always been a strong runner, even with a pack on his back.

Trying to move his legs forward again, Nathan found he'd sunk into the sand and was stuck up to his knees. Panicking, he clawed at the beach and glanced over his shoulder at the approaching mob. The waves of sand and water flooded him repeatedly. Grabbing at his thighs, he tried to free his body from the trap.

The mob was nearly upon him when he woke and his eyes flashed open. His heart beat wildly, adrenaline still rushing through him from the nightmare. *Perfect!* He had to use the adrenaline from his dream this time.

Lying flat on his back, Nathan was again on the table in the castle operating room. He'd been given his fourth "treatment" that morning, and like the other sessions, the doctor had left him alone afterward, strapped to the table. And just the day before, the idea had come to Nathan to use his adrenaline from his terrifying drug-induced dreams.

Dr. Stashinsky knew Nathan was exercising in his cell, but he didn't know how seriously. Even through his infectious night sweats, Nathan had forced himself to work out, oftentimes trembling uncontrollably with little fuel to feed his muscle fibers.

All this came together that instant. When he woke with the nightmare fresh on his mind, his senses and strength were heightened. He was stronger than the countless victims who'd preceded him, but their own thrashing and spasms had ensured his freedom.

The threads on the bolt had been stripped over the months of daily and nightly use. To his surprise, he was able to pull the Velcro strap loose before he applied all his strength to break the bolt free. Unstrapping his head and chest, he sat up and removed the strap from his other wrist. Next, he unstrapped his thighs and ankles. Though naked, Nathan jumped off the table, but fell flat on his face. He shook his head, fighting unconsciousness from the blow to his brow.

Rising shakily to his feet, Nathan eyed the doors—one left, one right. The one on his right led to the levels of cells. The mute escapee had ventured from that direction days ago, but he wasn't sure if there was a way out through there. *But naked?* Nathan had lost track of time, but he was sure he'd heard one of the guards say something about snow or winter outside.

He approached the left door. It was an unknown, but that's where the guards and Dr. Stashinsky always came from. The door was sealed with a protective flange. Nathan turned the handle to find it was unlocked, so he opened it a crack. Dr. Stashinsky was in a closet-sized chamber, suiting up in his biohazard gear. On the wall hung other white suits, masks, headgear, and oxygen canisters.

Nathan opened the door wide. Dr. Stashinsky looked up, his suit not yet zipped. His gaunt face froze in horror and his breath caught.

"What . . . have you done?" The old man's jaw trembled. "You . . .! My suit isn't on!"

"Welcome to the family."

The doctor didn't resist as Nathan grabbed him by the collar and pulled him into the exam room. The aged man's sunken black eyes bulged as Nathan stripped him of his suit and clothes, even his watch. When the initial shock had passed, the doctor tried to fight back, but Nathan easily slapped the man's hands aside.

"Please, don't hurt me! What're you going to do? You're my favorite patient. I can help you! Please!"

For the first time in months, Nathan pulled on clothes. They didn't fit, but they covered his nakedness. Though he couldn't button the pants at his waist, he got them zipped. Even after all his weight loss, he was still larger than the doctor. The shoes were too small as well, but Nathan forced his toes inside, letting his heels hang out.

"You've helped me enough, Doc. On the table. Now!"

Stashinsky whimpered as he climbed onto the table. Nathan pinned the naked man down and strapped him into place. Where the wrist strap was missing, he tucked the doctor's right arm against his side tightly under the chest strap. The old man thrashed about and gnashed his teeth at Nathan.

"You'll never get away with this! There are powers at work here that are beyond you! I will bleed you empty when they catch you!"

Not waiting to hear the rest, Nathan opened the right door and stepped into the lowest corridor of cells with the familiar stench. Closing the door, he silenced the doctor's threats and cursing.

Nathan was free. He could barely control his excitement. After checking the time on the doctor's watch, he shoved it into a pocket. It was ten o'clock—but morning or evening? How long had he been sleeping on the exam table?

The old bullet wound in his leg wasn't so sore anymore, but certainly stiff. Limping to the nearest cell door, he braced himself for what he might find and peered through a window into a cell. A man was curled into a ball in the far corner, a thin blanket carefully draped over one shoulder. But this man wasn't big enough to be Milk.

In the next cell was a small, white man, too white to be Toad; too small to be Milk. And Milk had shrapnel scars across his leg muscles. Nathan hustled to the next cell, then the next, continuing his search for the two Flash and Bang Team members who'd been captured with him in England.

Finding no one familiar on the bottom level, he cautiously climbed the stairs to the next. At the fourth cell, he almost moved on, then took a second look.

"Hey! Milk! Milk? That you?"

The malnourished prisoner rolled away from the rock wall. He was a skin and bones figure as white as . . . milk.

"Milk!"

Jesse "Milk" Patters squinted at Nathan peeking through the small window. Using the wall, he climbed to his feet. Bent over as if he were a one-hundred-year-old man, he approached the door.

"Who is it?"

"It's me! Nathan! It's Eagle Eyes! I just got loose. C'mon, Milk! We've got to get you out of there."

Gripping the door handle, Nathan tugged and wrestled with the lock, but it was secure. Frantically, he kneed the door, making more noise than necessary in his frustration, until his knee was bruised to the bone.

"Stop, Nathan. Stop it!"

Nathan reached his fingers through the tiny window and Milk met them with his own. He was so thin, so old looking, and he coughed every few breaths.

"We can find Toad and make a run for it!"

"No." Milk shook his head, tears streaking dirty cheeks. "I'm too far gone, Nathan. Leave me. Find Toad and go on without me. You have to. Tell the boss where I am. He'll come for me. You can make it without me. You were always the best man."

"I can't . . . leave you, Milk." Nathan choked on his words. It was unimaginable to leave a man behind. "No, I can't."

"Go! Listen. I'm not strong enough, and neither are you

to carry me. I've been sick a lot lately."

"We've all been sick. It's the experiments."

"They haven't started on me yet, Nathan. They've only taken my blood."

Nathan's face twisted with worry, fear, and then hope.

"Then, you might be okay if we can get you out right now! You probably just caught the flu, maybe tuberculosis. Nothing we can't treat!"

"No, Nathan. Go!" Milk's weak knees buckled, but he caught himself and leaned against the door. "If you go without me, you can save yourself and the rest. Use your head! And if you can't get Toad out of his cell . . . you'll have to go without him, too. You're our only chance."

"But the doctor could come for you at any time."

"I . . . can't . . ." Milk whispered an apology and slid down the door to the floor. "Go, I'm begging you. Before you're caught. Go."

Tears pooled as Nathan punched the door's lock. Maybe he could pick the lock with something, then carry him to . . . to where? They didn't even know where they were. Through the window, Nathan watched Milk roll away from the door, lacking the strength to walk or even crawl back to his corner. Looking up and down the corridor, it was so dimly lit he couldn't see the other end, but Nathan knew he had to go. The guard assigned to Dr. Stashinsky was sure to happen upon the operating room soon. At any moment, the alarm could sound.

"Forgive me, Milk," he whispered into the window. "We'll be back to get you. Give me two days, okay? Two meals, my brother. Count two meals—two potatoes—and

I'll be here for you. You know the boss won't let you die in here. Think of everything we've done for others in worse places. Just two days, Milk! You've got to hold on!"

Milk didn't respond, but Nathan was forced to move on. However, he couldn't leave without checking the other cells. Down all fifty cells on that level, then the next. He mistook a number of captives for Toad, but when they stirred, he saw they were strangers, though fellow sufferers.

At the end of the corridor, he climbed the stairs to the next level. Sorrowfully, he acknowledged so many more cells full of men, some even two and three to a cell, huddled together for warmth. But he found no one he knew. After doing the same on one more level, he came to a stone ramp that led toward a hallway where there was a sealed door. Nathan looked back. Had he missed any cells? Were he and Milk truly the only two COIL operatives held captive? Had Toad somehow escaped in England? His memory flashed back to London. He'd been wounded in Malaysia and unconscious so much of the time. Anything could've happened to Toad.

Nathan gripped an electrical lever and pulled it downward to open the sealed door. It slid sideways with a hiss, unlocking. The jailers surely wouldn't have imagined anyone getting out of their personal torture chambers, even though Nathan was certain the other escaped prisoner before him had to have come this way. He closed the sealed door, knowing its purpose was to keep the germs and diseases within . . . for now.

Moving down the hallway, he found a small window on either side. The mute man had been here, too, Nathan guessed. A castle courtyard lay to the left, a snowy forest stood out the right window.

Leaning against the rock wall, Nathan watched the courtyard for a few moments. It was almost eleven in the morning now. The sentries on the wall and others who lingered outside the two garage doors didn't seem concerned about any emergency; his escape hadn't been detected yet. Crossing to the other window, he measured the distance to the trees. A mere hundred-foot sprint would suffice, but even that distance seemed too far for Nathan right now.

He glanced from the ground to the sky. It had snowed recently and more bad weather was rolling in. Since he didn't know how far away civilization might be, he wasn't very keen on running blindly into the forest only to die in the snow. And he knew he was somewhere in Germany, but in which state?

All he needed was a phone. Once he contacted Chloe, Corban would send in a couple teams. Just how was he supposed to get to a phone, though? Nathan felt suddenly overcome and dizzy, and he slumped to the floor. He needed a plan, but while his brain wasn't firing properly, he couldn't proceed.

Since his team was often outnumbered, Nathan was used to overwhelming odds. But he'd often had superior technology, weapons, and intel. His wits were all he had to work with now, so he knew there was no room for error. Nathan did have the Lord, though; He was one Person he could go to for help. Whispering a prayer, he asked for some idea, maybe a way to mislead the enemy, to buy more time, or confuse them, to do the unexpected, to somehow get to a phone.

Then it came to him, even through the fog of disease that plagued his mind. Standing at the window, he studied the courtyard again. There were two four-wheelers parked against the wall opposite him. If he could get to one of those and get the castle doors to open, he would be free to speed away. But they had guns and it was daylight. He wouldn't be able to do it without the cover of darkness. So, he'd need somewhere to hide.

As he looked, two men exited a door in the opposite wall and climbed onto the four-wheelers. Both men wore fatigues and carried assault rifles. Nathan licked his lips. Where were they going? Maybe they'd do his job and come to him.

Sure enough, they started the four-wheelers and the castle doors creaked open. It was a routine patrol, Nathan figured. He watched as they exited the gate. One turned left, the other turned right, and the door closed behind them. The hum of their engines faded, then the sound came from behind him! With widened eyes, Nathan shuffled quickly to the window facing the forest. One of the four-wheelers patrolled along the outside of the wall below him!

Nathan had two seconds to think. It wasn't a conscious decision; more like a reaction. Planting a knee on the windowsill, he fell out, rather than dove. His hands reached out like claws. The driver of the four-wheeler flinched as Nathan fell on him from above, but it was too late for the gunman to aim his weapon or brace for impact. The bulk of Nathan's body landed on the guard's right shoulder. Rolling away in the snow, Nathan clutched at the driver's parka. Together, they stopped free of the four-wheeler, sank into two feet of snow and lay still, the ATV idling nearby.

A long moment passed before Nathan moved. Rising up on one elbow, he tried to remember why he wasn't in his familiar cell. The snow numbed his flesh. His mind registered the sound of the four-wheeler engine, and his escape became his priority once again. There was a man lying next to him. Nathan checked his pulse, found he was alive, then stole his bulky coat. After crawling through the snow to the four-wheeler, Nathan pulled himself onto the machine. Twisting the throttle, he turned the ATV around to head toward the front of the castle. There had to be a road leading away from the fortress near the doors.

Driving close to the castle wall, he knew there were guards above, possibly watching him even now. The parka was his only disguise. With his speed low, he rounded the northwest tower of the wall. A well-traveled road headed into the forest and away from the castle to the west.

Gunning the engine, his wheels spun through the powdery snow for an instant before catching. Snowflakes started to fall as he sped toward the road, then turned onto it. Someone on the castle wall behind him called out casually, then in alarm as he surely saw the shaggy face and long hair. Nathan sped faster as gunfire peppered the snow around him.

Suddenly, there was a gate and station house in front of him, and two armed men hurried to take their rifles off their shoulders. Cranking the handlebars to the right, Nathan bounced over the snow bank and nearly fell off. Then he crashed into a tree. The engine sputtered, but he gave it gas and it caught. Yelling and radio chatter came to his ears from behind him. He had only seconds. Bullets slapped the bank where he'd turned into the forest. It wouldn't be hard to follow him with such obvious tracks.

"Lord, I'm begging You . . ."

He threw the engine in reverse and pushed away from the tree. With fumbling hands, Nathan switched to drive and weaved through a dozen trees as bullets raked branches around him. The second four-wheeler was gaining on him. Turning left through a gully, he climbed over a snow-hidden windfall and bounced over a snowdrift. His left rear tire exploded from a bullet. The machine pulled to one side, but Nathan compensated and sped faster, barely squeezing his wheels between branches and tree trunks.

The ATV soared over another snow bank and back onto the road two hundred yards west of the gated checkpoint. With head tucked, he sped away on the ATV. Nathan prayed he wouldn't meet any vehicles coming from the other direction.

The road curved to the left and right, then straightened out. He saw level ground ahead and wondered if it was another road. Too late, he realized he was coming upon it too fast. But he couldn't slow down since the four-wheeler behind him was gaining.

A semi flew past on a paved highway in front of him, and then a car. *A highway!* Nathan hit the brakes before he ran into another speeding vehicle. Bullets zipped through the air all around him. Briefly, Nathan looked both ways. Left or right? He had to go now! It wasn't an option to outrun or out-drive his pursuer. The highway didn't help him any more than give him some sense of direction, and he certainly didn't want to put anyone else in jeopardy.

Pa-pa-pa-pa-pa!

Nathan didn't bother trying to find the source of the five muffled clicks. Even in his sluggish mental state, he recognized the familiar sound of an automatic NL-3 rifle. With the prospect of safety nearby, he hit the gas on his four-wheeler and crossed the highway in front of an SUV. He drove a few feet into the thick brush, then dove free of his machine.

Pa-pa-pa-pa-pa!

The pursuer returned fire, then the shots ceased altogether. Nathan lay on his back in a snow-covered shrub. Every bone in his body hurt, but if he died now, it was okay. He was free. *Thank You, Lord.*

"Hey, you okay?" a man called in German while cautiously creeping closer.

The voice wasn't familiar, but if this person had COIL weaponry, he had to be a friend. Struggling, Nathan forced himself to sit upright.

"Stay away! I'm infected! Keep back!"

The footsteps paused. A man peered around a pine tree, his COIL rifle leveled at Nathan. The man looked like he was barely twenty, but the fact that he wasn't an enemy, Nathan didn't care how old he was. He'd saved his life.

"Don't come near me," Nathan said. "A cell phone. Do you have a cell phone?"

"Of course." The young man lowered his rifle. "Who are you?"

His strength exhausted, Nathan lay on his back again, but all he could think about at that instant was Milk. They had to go back and get Milk!

"Throw me your phone. I'm a COIL operative. I need to call someone. And watch that road. There's a small army down there."

CHAPTER TWENTY

June's eyelids began to droop in the moments before her earpiece chattered.

"What's taking Johnny and Memphis so long?"

It was Scooter. Shaking herself to alertness, June once again trained her weapon on the desert. The sun was high and they were all growing weary of waiting, but they knew nothing would be decided that day in the desert until darkness had settled on them. Behind her, Brauch's NL-X1 fired a projectile at a Janjaweed soldier who'd woken from the second or third tranq shot he'd received that day. Every minute, another militant woke up. As soon as one stirred, Scooter or Brauch put him down for another hour. It was a round-eating task.

The Janjaweed no longer lay down cover fire before they moved. Though they had superior numbers, they apparently knew they were dealing with forces from the West with advanced technology. They surely waited for darkness, and as veterans of East African warfare, they were more patient than the COIL team.

"Anybody alive out there? This is Memphis. Over."

Though June wanted to talk to him, to hug him for coming to their rescue, it wasn't her place. Scooter was in charge since Corban was out of the picture.

"Corban's down," Scooter reported, "and we're running low on ammo. Over."

"Corban's down? How bad?"

"He was securing a few targets when that second wave swept over him. About four hundred fifty yards east from Brauch on the south flank. Hasn't moved in hours. We've got sixty or seventy Janjas scattered all over the plain. The boss tied a few of them, but those that didn't take off back to their camp are playing possum behind one another. A lot of their horses were taken out, but they've woken up since then and trotted off for water. Over."

"I figured as much. A few of the poor beasts wandered into Kalma," Memphis said. "The refugees are cooking horse stew as we speak. Where do you want Johnny and me? Over."

"Bring all the ammo you can," Scooter said. "Memphis, you go to Brauch and December on the southern front. Johnny, you come to Bruno and me in the north. We'll cover your approach with the last of our ammo, so you two better reach us. The real battle will begin at sundown. You copy all that? Over."

"We copy, Scooter. It's a long crawl out there, though. Over."

"Hey, it's December," June said. "Corban was up all night digging foxholes west of our position. I thought they were for our retreat, but they'll work for your approach. Must be twenty of them behind us. Over."

"Roger that, December. That'll help. You doing okay? Over."

"I'm all right. Over."

"Just get here before dark, Memphis," Scooter said. "Everyone in the camp get supplied? Over."

"Affirmative. Roger and his wife seem like pros at all this. We'll head toward you in ten minutes. Out."

June saw a Janjaweed soldier within her range climb to his knees and sight down his barrel at Brauch. She was ready and shifted her aim to the right to squeeze off a burst of pellets into the man's throat. He sprawled backwards, flinging his rifle two yards away. After mentally marking the man's position, she checked her watch. When he woke up in twenty minutes, she'd need to pop him again.

Using her scope, June checked on Corban. He hadn't moved an inch! Very near him, two hobbled militants struggled against their flex-cuffs. They'd been awake for several hours, but since they were bound, the team hadn't wasted their ammo to tranq them again. June wiped her brow. It was so hot. Some of the Janjaweed who were pinned down without canteens wouldn't get any water this day, either, but they'd live.

Another hour passed. Half of June's ammo was gone, and Brauch was down to his last couple magazines. Scooter was even more desperate. Without the NL-X1 long-range ammo, the enemy could crawl within one hundred yards all around them. Their thousand-yard arm had been the battle's difference, but they'd have no hope if they faced the enemy with only NL-3s. Their foxholes would be overrun within minutes after dark.

Scoping to the west, June saw two figures shimmering in the heat waves far away. Memphis and Johnny were working their way from hole to hole as they carried extra ammo pouches. Suddenly, bullets whistled over her head at Memphis.

"Pay attention, December!" Brauch growled.

Spinning around, she peppered a Janjaweed with pellets. He slumped back to the rocky sand.

"Sorry." June felt like a fool. They were all weary and stressed about the coming night, but the battle wasn't to the west! She had to stay focused.

The Janjaweed soldiers would know what Memphis and Johnny were up to, and they were surely figuring out they weren't fighting a foe who used live rounds. That made the murderers more blatant about their attempts to rise up and fire. A few of them began to rush forward as soon as they woke up. They'd get taken out, but within an hour, they'd wake up again and charge forward, getting closer every time. The COIL operatives weren't delusional about the inevitable, and that the inevitable would happen not long after dark. Many of the soldiers were now communicating in small groups, but since they were so exposed on the flat ground without even their downed horses for cover any longer, Brauch and Scooter were still able to take them out easily.

At four o'clock, Memphis and Johnny reported that they were nearly to their positions.

"Tell me where you want me. Over," Memphis said to Brauch.

"There's a two-man foxhole southwest of me." Brauch took a handful of sand and tossed it in the air. "See me?"

"Yeah, I see you."

"I have two rounds left. Over."

Johnny made similar arrangements with Scooter and Bruno as to placement. Scooter was out of NL-X1 rounds completely. While he was two hundred yards back, Memphis announced he was preparing a pouch for Brauch, then, with a final dash, he ran forward and hurled the pouch toward Brauch's foxhole. Several Janjaweed rose up to take him out, but Memphis dove into the designated hole as June and Brauch took down the targets.

"Cover me, December!" Brauch ordered.

He didn't wait for confirmation. June laid down cover fire as Brauch scrambled like a crab across the sand to retrieve the ammo pouch that had landed ten feet from his hole. Before June clicked on her empty magazine, Brauch was out and back. But she had only one two-hundred-fifty-pellet mag left.

Brauch quickly reloaded his NL-X1 and started attacking targets several hundred yards out who'd grown restless. To the north, Scooter was also resupplied.

"These guys are getting too close to me," June said. "What should I do? Over."

Since June was in such a forward position, the Janjaweed were charging her first—though only a few steps at a time. And every time they woke, they still managed to get off a few shots. The nearest had gotten within twenty yards of her post.

"Get back to me if you can," Brauch said. "You can cover me from here as things escalate tonight. Memphis can cover us both. Get ready, Memphis. She'll count down and move. Over."

"Roger. Go, December."

June wasn't very excited about moving again. The last time she ran for a different foxhole, she'd taken the wound across her shoulder blade. She wished there was an alternative, but there wasn't. Worse yet, she had to carry her pack as well as Corban's, and run fifty yards of wasteland back to Brauch behind her and to the south. Almost fifty pounds of dead weight would be in her arms, and her left arm hurt to move from the wound.

She strapped Corban's heavier pack onto her back and picked up her own. In her other hand, she carried what was left of her ammo pouch and her rifle.

"Three . . . two . . . one!" She rose to her feet.

The Janjaweed playing dead nearby didn't hear or see her for the first ten yards, but then they charged, shooting as they ran, trying to mow her down. June felt the jackhammer of two rounds hit the pack on her back. She tried to tell herself they were merely helping her forward momentum, but then a round zipped through the flesh on her neck. The impact spun her to the right as if she'd been punched in the carotid artery. For an instant, she blacked out, then came to on the hot sand as she was sliding forward on her back. Above her, the vultures circled. No, she wasn't sliding anywhere; she was being dragged. So, she wasn't dead yet. The vultures would have to wait another day to feast on her!

Brauch pulled her by her pack headfirst into his foxhole. Fortunately, June had kept hold of her rifle. The desert was quiet again; the Janjaweed had no target. Quickly, Brauch checked her for serious wounds, then gave her his gauze wrap to tie around her light neck wound. Thankfully, it wasn't bleeding much.

In the north, Scooter and Johnny joined up in the same hole as well, covered by Bruno in the rear. The team waited out the last few hours of daylight, sniping at any Janjaweed who twitched in front of them. They tried not to look at the buzzards overhead. Many of them swooped down to antagonize the flex-cuffed militants on the ground. A couple found Corban's body as a possible meal since he didn't even wiggle when they ventured close. At four-hundred-fifty-yards, Brauch took out two of the buzzards who pecked at their downed leader.

Everyone took a few minutes to eat in shifts and gulp down fluids. It would be their last for possibly hours.

An hour before dusk, Brauch used the handheld transmitter in Corban's pack to summon the Turkish United Nations garrison in the vicinity. He reminded them of their agreement if the team fully disabled the Janjaweed forces.

When dusk closed, several of the bound Janjaweed cried out in thirst to their comrades.

"Ignore them," Brauch whispered to June when he saw her shiver at their cries. "A man can live three days without water. It hasn't been even one day yet. They thirst, but they'll survive. One way or another, it'll all be over tomorrow."

Not responding, she watched the darkness close and the stars emerge. None of this seemed real. Not long ago, she was worried about her ratings, the next paycheck, the slide scanner she was going to buy, and the puppy at the shelter she wanted to bring home. That was the old June, she reflected. Now, she was December.

"Get your night scopes out if you haven't already,"

Scooter said. "These guys will be slowly moving closer, thinking darkness will cover them. They don't seem to have night vision of their own."

June and Brauch clipped on their night scopes. Brauch's was an adaptor on his existing riflescope.

"No one's moving," she whispered to the ex-assassin.

"Be ready," Brauch warned. "They'll come all at once. I've seen this many times. African fighters are experts at both night stealth and silent coordination. This is as you Americans say—'the calm before the storm.'"

For thirty minutes, no one moved, even those who had awakened. For good measure, Brauch and Scooter tranquilized those nearest.

Still, the Janjaweed waited. June stared through her scope in shades of green and gray at a man she knew was only playing dead. He was eighty yards out. His face was turned toward a number of other Janjaweed behind him. She aimed carefully and shot him once on top of the head. A harmless round to get his attention. When he looked up, she shot him in the mouth. Again, he drifted to sleep.

Another soldier over one hundred yards out used hand signals to convey orders to the others. In the darkness, his fellow soldiers could barely see his signals, but the team with night vision could see as clear as day. Something was about to happen.

"Brauch . . ." June breathed.

"I see them. They don't know we can see in the dark yet, but they will. Let them get to their feet first. Hold your fire."

They rose as one, sixty militants with rifles rose silently

from their bellies to their knees, then to their feet. These ghosts were experts at killing silently, snuffing breath and life. Staying in a crouch as they moved, making smaller targets, they crept forward with stealth that would shame a panther.

"Come in, Brauch. This is Memphis. Over."

"Go, Memphis," he whispered back.

"You say when. Over."

"Watch for the first one to fall. Get your packs on. We can move back in the darkness as they come. Don't assume we can defeat them all in the first wave. Over."

Carefully, Brauch aimed at the rear-most Janjaweed within his range. He pulled the trigger. That man went down unnoticed by the others. Memphis and June understood without being told, and opened fire on other militants toward the rear of the company. But their clicking chambers raised an alarm. The Janjaweed realized their forces were being dwindled behind them by their foes.

With a scream, the first man charged, then the others with him. Brauch started firing more rapidly at the army rushing at them. He picked at their farthest soldiers as June and Memphis concentrated on the nearest. Everyone who charged screamed so loudly, the disorienting noise terrified June. Their muzzles flashed fire and thunder. Though she fired, her aim was off as she stared at the wall of bloodthirsty men.

"Go to Memphis!" Brauch ordered June since she wasn't helping. Her ammo was low already, too.

Dragging her pack and carrying Corban's on her back, she slithered on her stomach from the foxhole and started toward Memphis. She couldn't see him, but she could hear the vague clicking of his rifle between the thunderous bursts from the Janjaweed rifles.

Suddenly, everything was quiet. The attack had lasted less than sixty seconds. June froze halfway to Memphis. What was happening now? Was it over?

"Careful," Brauch warned on his comm. "We got about half of them. They're playing with us."

June turned her head to the right, opening her neck wound again. She felt a trickle of blood and sweat stinging her flesh. There didn't seem to be any enemies near her, but it was too dark to know for certain. Her eyes couldn't focus on the shapes nearest her. A pile of dirt was only ten yards away, but that couldn't be right. Letting go of her pack, she put her riflescope to her eye. The focus was all wrong. Had she bumped her scope? All she could see through the night scope was a man's face. His blinking eyes and brow filled the scope. Apparently, he was waiting for another order to attack, because he didn't seem to be disabled.

But it was no illusion; he was the mound of dirt only ten yards away! June swallowed hard. He would've killed her if she hadn't realized him as the enemy first. She aimed at his chin and shot him. The sting of the pellet caused him to rise to his knees, then he fell sideways. Behind her, Brauch continued to fire the NL-X1 intermittently.

Crawling forward on her elbows, June whispered her arrival to Memphis before she tumbled into the foxhole with him.

The Janjaweed came with a vengeance then, some from the back who'd since awakened. It was all June and

Memphis could do to cover Brauch as his foxhole was overrun. Finally, Brauch couldn't remain in his forward position any longer. Firing his NL-3 from the hip, he retreated toward Memphis and June. The Janjaweed were blind, but like bats, they could hear the NL weapons clicking and they fired in response.

"Get back and cover us!" Memphis ordered June.

Scurrying out of the hole, June made room for Brauch, and he slid in next to Memphis. The enemy was too close now to use the NL-X1. The team fired frantically at chests and faces through their green scopes. Once June reached one of the retreat holes, she turned and gaped at the number of Janjaweed rushing their positions. She fired in short bursts, paused to slap in another mag, then continued. In her scope, she saw Memphis fall into the foxhole, then get back up. Brauch shoved him out of the hole and covered him as he fell again, then crawled toward June.

For the first time, June considered the suicide pill other ops teams would've had. If the team fell into Janjaweed hands now, no one would be able to save them. But June remembered Corban's words. *Faith was better than cyanide.* God was with them, no matter what happened.

Suddenly, when the enemy began falling into the team's forward foxholes and there seemed no hope left, they heard a shout in the Janjaweed Arabic language. To June's amazement, the Janjaweed in her scope turned to fire to the east. June stared in fear at the plain, afraid she might find a secondary attacking force, which made little sense. But beyond the militants, a lone figure was walking at an angle toward them with a rifle in each hand. He was firing each of them, but no flashes came from his muzzles.

It was Corban.

Rising from her foxhole, June charged the Janjaweed who were now caught in the crossfire. She didn't know how Corban was still alive, but she wasn't leaving him out there unprotected and alone to finish off the last of their foes.

Brauch saw the same ghost, and from three sides now, they counter-attacked the remaining eight still-standing Janjaweed and put them all to sleep within twenty seconds. If Corban had been one minute later, the team would've been killed. The Janjaweed never saw from where Corban had come.

When the last man had fallen, silence once again fell upon the desert. Corban moved forward with both NL-3s cradled in his arms, aiming at each fallen shadow in turn, until he reached Memphis in a foxhole that Corban had dug nearly twenty-four hours earlier. Brauch jogged over to join Corban and June.

"You guys call the UN Turkish force?" Corban asked first.

Stepping close to Corban, June saw the right side of Corban's head smeared and matted with sand and blood, his earpiece cord cut by a bullet that had nearly killed him.

"About an hour ago," Brauch said.

"Good. Let me use your radio." Brauch handed Corban his earpiece. "This is Corban. Scooter, you copy? Report. Over."

"Scooter here. Took a little siesta on us, huh, Boss? Over."

"Listen up. The Turks'll be here within the hour

expecting a force of subdued Janjaweed. Take your flex-cuffs and move out together to lace them all hand and foot. Watch out for sleepers. Don't be afraid to fire on them as a precautionary measure. Get moving. Over."

"Roger. We're moving."

June was the team's southern-most chosen lacer. Corban and Memphis moved warily through the Janjaweed ranks as June went from man to man and bound each soldier. Brauch stood at a distance with his NL-X1, covering the whole operation. Whenever there was a soldier in question, Corban or Memphis fired pellets at June's next target. They ventured far out into the desert where Corban had hobbled the others early the previous morning, until everyone was bound and their rifles were collected.

By the time the Turkish armored personnel carriers rumbled up to them from across the plain, June was stumbling from exhaustion. The Turkish commander, in his blue helmet, spoke halting English with Corban, then deployed a dozen men to collect the arms and the Janjaweed prisoners.

Together, the seven-person COIL team headed to the Kalma refugee camp. They could barely walk and were too tired to talk. Each of them was wounded, but they were thankful to be alive.

CHAPTER TWENTY-ONE

Nathan Isaacson opened his eyes. Whimpering, he tried to focus, fearful that he was back on the doctor's experimentation table.

"Water . . ." he whispered in a dry, raspy voice.

Someone held a cup with a straw to his mouth. Nothing was familiar around him. He was in a white room with a lace-curtained window on his left. Sunlight warmed his cheek. This wasn't the castle. His eyes drifted upward to his attendant's face, then he used his tongue to push the straw from his mouth.

"Corban." Nathan tried to sit up.

"Don't get up, son," Corban said. "It's okay. I wanted to be here when you woke up."

"You . . . shouldn't be here." It took great effort for Nathan to speak. "I'm infected with . . ." He shook his head to clear it. The four-wheeler had crashed in the brush. Someone had helped him. When he couldn't connect with Corban on the borrowed cell phone, he'd left a message. "What's happening?"

Corban, with his head bandaged, pulled a cushioned chair close to the bed.

"You're in a rented suite in West Berlin, Nathan. No one else knows about it. I need to talk to you about Xacsin

Castle. Do you think you can talk?"

"Xacsin Castle?"

"The place where you were held is owned by a man named Xacsin McLeery. He's working for the man we know as Abaddon—the same one who trapped us in Malaysia. Listen, Nathan. I need to know how you got away."

"They . . . left me. The doctor was careless. I . . . escaped. I . . ." His memory flashed back. "*Oh, no!*"

"What? What is it?"

"Milk! How could I?" Nathan choked on a sob. "I left him. I had to. I couldn't break the lock . . ."

"Milk is alive?"

"Yeah. But I couldn't open his cell."

"He's in one of the cells? Which level?"

"Second, um, level. From the bottom. I think the fourth cell from the stairs. How could I leave him?"

"It's okay, Nathan. You had to. We're gonna get him out tonight."

"We? Who else is with you?"

"Bruno, Scooter, Memphis, Johnny, and a couple others."

"Toad. Where's Toad? Did he get away in England?"

"Seems that Toad died in England, Nathan. He probably put up a fight, knowing him, to keep you and Milk alive."

Nathan looked toward the window as he processed the hard news.

"It was all a trap, Boss. First Malaysia, then England." He groaned. "Wait. A woman . . . she's in the castle. She said something about Helena from Malaysia. They're sisters. All this has something to do with that."

"Helena's still in prison in the States. From our intel, Helena does have a sister named Hannah." Corban stood, opened a file, and showed Nathan two photographs. "This is Xacsin. What about him? Is he there?"

"I've seen him." Nathan nodded. "I know those green eyes. It was a while ago, maybe á couple weeks, when I saw him last. But I've lost track of time."

"That's okay. How about this one? His name is Snake."

"Yeah. Yeah, he was new."

"Did he talk to you?"

"No, but I could tell he wanted to once. What day is it?"

"Wednesday."

"Wednesday . . . then, I think it was last Friday. I'm not sure, though. A guard was taunting me. Snake. Yeah. The woman, Hannah, killed him. They said Snake was a spy. He was one of ours?"

"Rest up, son." Without answering his question, Corban rested a hand on Nathan's shoulder. "I've got a nurse taking care of you. I'll try to stop by tomorrow night, all right?"

"Wait, Boss." Nathan clenched his teeth and took a deep breath. "How bad is it?"

"How bad is what?"

"My . . . condition. Give it to me straight."

"Nathan, there's nothing we can do about your leg. You'll probably limp a little for the rest of your life, maybe have to wear a brace, but knowing you, it won't slow you down."

"But, what about, you know, my body?" Nathan held up his arms to show the scars and scabs from needles, even the identification tattoo. "They pumped everything but refined ricin into my veins."

"You'd be in a hospital if you had anything chronic, Nathan. We had x-rays taken, tissue samples, blood . . . Your lungs show signs of scarring. So does your liver. But there's no trace of anything that caused the damage. We even had you checked for TB. Since the guy you gave the blood-message to had TB, we figured you'd at least test positive for exposure. But you're clean, Nathan, through and through."

"No, the tests are wrong. It's got to be a trick. The doctor, um, Stashinsky, they called him—he's experimenting to create a virus delivery system through living tissues, through people. And I was one of them. Milk will be next."

"We had you tested thoroughly, Nathan."

"That . . . doesn't make any sense. I was near death from it!"

Corban picked up a Bible off the bedside table and set it on Nathan's chest.

"You know I don't believe in staged or sideshow miracles, but God can do anything. Some things we'll never understand. You're living proof that God's not snoozing. He's not done with you yet, Nathan Isaacson."

Nathan picked up the Bible and stared at its cover. Then he looked into Corban's face.

"Boss, you have to get the others out. There's so many in that place. They hadn't started on Milk yet, but they will soon. You don't have much time."

"I know. We're going in tonight. Operation Rahab.

Snake got us all the intel we needed to do this, and you've confirmed what he said. Anything else you can remember? Something that will help us?"

"The castle's closed up pretty tight. I counted eight men on the walls that I could see—and more in the towers. I'm sure there's more."

"There are."

"Besides getting Milk out, do one more thing for me, would you?"

"What's that?"

"Get that doctor."

"I will."

"You're going on this one yourself?"

"Well, you've left some tough shoes to fill as team leader, but I'm giving it a shot. Listen, there's one other thing before I go." Corban glanced over his shoulder. "No one knows you're alive."

It took Nathan a couple blinks to process the news.

"Okay . . . What about the guy who found me?"

"One of the Berlin COIL agents. But I coached him. He won't say a word. He's the one who set us up here. I was in Africa for a couple days, and while I was gone, we killed you off."

"Hmm, I see. I guess that explains why no one else from the team is barging into the room right now." Nathan sighed, already guessing what was next. "Knowing you, Boss, I won't be seeing friendly faces for a while, either."

"It's up to you, Nathan. We can still bring you back. I acted while I could; it was an opportunity. Now it's up to you, but you need to decide right now. Otherwise, Scooter's going to be trying to find you in the castle tonight."

Turning his head, Nathan looked out the window.

"I'm a soldier, Corban, not a spy, if that's what you have in mind for me."

"Yeah, you're right."

"But you could teach me what I don't already know."

"You need to be sure about this."

"Hey, I know it's not easy to kill off a man's identity, but you've already done it. I don't have anybody, Boss. You've already thought this through. I'm perfect for it. I could become anybody, go anywhere, infiltrate anything, with no history."

"Nathan, it's a lonely life. I've lived it, I know. But the Lord will stick closer to you than a brother."

"By the sound of things, you have something in mind for me already, don't you? An operation that no one else can handle?"

"Yeah." Corban smiled. "Something like that."

"Then count me in."

"All right." Corban moved to the door. "We'll be in touch."

"Hey, Boss? Tell the guys I said I loved 'em before I passed on, would you?"

"Of course. I'd be glad to."

"And give me a nice burial, huh?"

"You got it, Eagle Eyes."

The team was waiting in Corban's hotel room in Berlin when he entered. He took one look at their steely gazes and knew they were ready for this special op. They all had small wounds from their excursion in Sudan—June's neck was still bandaged and Bruno's forearm was wrapped—but nothing that would keep them from the Rahab op.

"Boss, the weather's clear," Scooter said. "It was clear last night, too. Please don't tell us we're waiting on the weather again."

Corban sat on the edge of the desk next to a lamp.

"No, we're going in tonight."

"Yes!" Scooter cheered.

The others shared his enthusiasm—all but Brauch, who sat quietly in the corner behind a thoughtful Rupert.

"While that may be good news, I have some bad news. It's the only reason we waited until today." He frowned. "Another prisoner from Xacsin Castle escaped while we were gone to help Kalma."

"*What?*" Memphis gasped. "I didn't read any reports about that!"

"Why didn't we hear about this sooner?" Scooter asked. "Sorry, Boss. I'm just so anxious to—"

"We're all anxious. Let me finish." Corban searched for words. His concern was obvious, so no one interrupted. "Nathan was the escapee. They . . . couldn't save him." Everyone stared in shock. "He was too overcome with disease. We had to . . . burn the body. I have his ashes. We'll have a funeral when we get back to the States."

Bruno, elbows on his knees, bowed his head. The tears flowed. Scooter gripped the edge of the bed. Even June dabbed her eyes though she'd never known Nathan.

"Did you talk to him?" Johnny asked. "Or was he too far gone?"

"Yes, I talked to him. But he didn't say much; he didn't know much more than we already knew. He did ask that I tell you each how much he loved you." The room was quiet for a couple minutes except for a sniffle now and then. "And he said Milk is alive."

"Milk! Oh . . . that means they got Toad in England," Memphis said. "His fiancée isn't going to take that well."

"Fon's a strong woman," Corban said. "But our concern is for Eve Patters now. Tonight, we have an opportunity to bring her husband home. Milk is on the second level, four cells from the stairs, according to Nathan. We get him out and make these two lives—Nathan and Toad—worth their passing. Rupert, are the authorities ready?"

"I have a detective on standby, but he doesn't know any details. All I have to do is make a phone call and the police will move in. One look at the inhabitants of the castle and arrest warrants will be issued, no matter how popular or powerful Xacsin was around here. And the hospital is ready to receive up to two hundred for quarantine. That should be enough witnesses to put Xacsin and his men away for a long time."

"Except we're still not sure where Xacsin is," Corban said. "Somehow he knew we were closing in. He abandoned his fortress, even his wife, Hannah, who Nathan confirmed is Helena's sister."

"Helena." Scooter growled. "Her sister's as sick as she is?"

"She is. Besides attacking the Christians and Jews, this has been Hannah's own little private revenge session against us for taking her sister captive after Malaysia, so add her to your list of targets tonight. The doctor should be at the castle as well. We've gone over everything else. Let's do this and go home. There are a lot of people out there who need us. Abaddon has done a good job of interrupting our primary objective. I didn't put COIL together to be consumed with its own affairs all the time. Every day we're busy here is a day that Christians in other countries are dying."

Corban eyed each of them in turn. Rupert wasn't going with them, as Corban had arranged. He would handle support and monitor communications from Berlin. But the rest of them would be staring death in the face in a few hours.

"Bruno, lead us in prayer, then we'll gear up."

"Sorry, Corban." Rupert Mach held up his phone and started for the door. "There are a few things I need to take care of before tonight. I apologize, everyone. This can't wait."

The others moved aside to allow Rupert to pass. Corban stared after the leader of the Berlin office for a few seconds, then snapped back to the moment.

"Okay, Bruno, pray for us to remain focused on God's will through this. There's no sense in hating these people who've attacked us. They're simply lost souls. Pray that something we do tonight, in some way, might turn someone's heart around for the Lord."

"Hi, sweetie. How was your trip?"

"Good," Janice answered her husband on the phone. "Got a lot done. I half-expected to find you back home by now, though. Chloe's not telling me anything, so I know what it means when you call like this, Corban."

"I know you know, and I know you worry, but I had to call, anyway."

"I'm glad you did." She sniffed. "Is it late there?"

"About seven. Jenna is okay?"

"Yeah, but she misses you. Chloe spoiled her while I was gone. I wasn't sure she'd want to come home with me!"

"Tell her I miss her, too." It was no mystery why he was calling. When he was able, he called when he was about to face possible death. And Corban knew Janice understood there were times he couldn't call her, for safety reasons. But he was thankful for the times he could speak to her remotely, even if it was only to say goodbye. "I love you, Janice."

"I love you, too, Corban. You, um, won't be long now?"

"Not long. Tell Jenna that I love her."

"I will. Please . . . be careful."

"Yeah, I will. Goodbye, Janice."

"Bye-bye, Corban."

Corban clicked off his phone. Alone in his hotel room, he took a deep breath. In a perfect world, he would be home right now. That's what he wanted—peace, security, and a week of solitude with his two favorite girls. But while there was nothing wrong with rest and relaxation, he knew God had given him the responsibility of shepherding others. It was his burden, his blessed burden.

He stood and zipped up his fatigues—shades of white and gray to blend in with the snow and forest terrain around the castle—then checked his pockets, gear, and weapons.

Lastly, he took off his wedding ring and set it on the Bible on the dresser. He hoped to be back soon to pick them both up. Kneeling beside the bed, he whispered a prayer to his God.

CHAPTER TWENTY-TWO

June had never seen Xacsin Castle except in pictures, but she knew the fortress and surrounding terrain as if she'd grown up in the area. Between Snake's intel, and intel from satellites Corban supplied them with, there wasn't much of the castle the team couldn't sketch by hand. And because they were so prepared, the darkness of the night wouldn't impede their attack.

Kneeling in the snow beneath a birch tree, June trembled—not from the cold, but from excitement and anticipation. She certainly preferred this setting to the openness of the desert. Here, June and the team could move through the two feet of snow in relative silence within the security of the forest. With the castle's hourly patrols in mind, she and Corban approached the castle from the north.

It took a few seconds to locate Corban to the east in her night scope, but he was there, waiting for radio confirmation that the others were in place before the two of them proceeded. She and Corban were to attack the station house first. Then, they would move up the road, Corban on one side and June on the other, to the front of the castle. The others would initiate their own offensives from their respective positions.

Listening intently, June could barely hear the slight hum

of a plane engine somewhere around eighteen thousand feet, she guessed. The castle guards wouldn't suspect a thing. To them, it was probably just a passing plane, but it was actually quite another thing. Using a plane that Memphis and Johnny had procured in the last two weeks, Brauch had arranged a pilot to fly Bruno over the castle. In fact, June figured Bruno probably wasn't even in the plane anymore. Wearing armor-plated fatigues, the big black man was to parachute directly into the castle courtyard.

Meanwhile, Scooter was eight hundred yards to the northwest and Brauch was the same distance to the southwest. The two had secured platforms and scaffolding sixty feet off the ground amongst the tops of the pines. Both platforms were anchored at four points and were large enough for each sniper to lie on his belly and aim at the castle. They were high enough to see the four towers, most of the walls, and some of the courtyard.

"Memphis in place. Over."

"Johnny in place. Over."

The two pilots were to be on the north and south ramparts. They had telescoping ladders to scale the fifteen-foot heights as soon as the walls were clear of men. Corban and June wouldn't be able to enter the castle until the front gate was opened.

"This is Bruno. ETA, sixty seconds. Over."

That was the cue for Corban and June, and they started forward again. There was no need for overnight packs, only ammo pouches, so they weren't burdened by other gear. They moved swiftly, like phantoms through the trees, their NL-3s shouldered and leveled.

Spotting the station house, June circled right to approach from the front as Corban arced left to attack the two guards from the rear. Pausing, she scanned the post thirty yards away.

"Wait one," she said to halt Corban. "I see only one. Over."

"Move in. I've got the second. Over."

June didn't hesitate, confidently stepping over the snow bank into the road. She knew to trust the man now; she'd seen him in action, defying all odds. The guard still hadn't seen her, even though he faced her direction, his gloved hands working a lighter at a cigarette in his lips. Once close enough so she wouldn't miss, June aimed three inches under the glowing butt and fired a burst of five pellets. The man staggered backwards, clutching his throat, then fell over. Running up to him, she covered the station house as she advanced.

Corban appeared from behind the gate. He gave her the thumbs-up signal. She returned the sign, then picked up her target's rifle and hurled it off the road into the snow. Slipping one glove off, she flex-cuffed her downed target's hands and feet, then moved around the gate to join Corban. Motioning for her to take the right side of the road, he took the left. Together, they jogged along the road toward the castle.

"Bruno here. I'm—ugh!—in the lions' den. Over."

Looking up, June saw the shimmer of a black parachute canvas disappear behind the southwest thirty-foot tower. Almost simultaneously, one of the two sentries in that tower fell where he was standing. She assumed he'd been taken out by Brauch from over a half-mile away.

As machine gunfire split the quiet night, June dove behind a tree then jumped back to her feet when she realized she hadn't been spotted yet. The gunfire was directed at Bruno inside the castle. Glancing at Corban, he was pointing something out to her. Looking up, she saw a satellite to the right of the great castle gate, probably to service the castle office. Then she noticed a weathervane on a pole to the left of the gate. Nodding, she didn't wait for Corban's signal to fire. When she was within range, she fired at the satellite, causing noisy pinging sounds. They hoped to take the guards' attention from Bruno. Corban did the same at the weathervane, drawing fire almost instantly. The plan was for Bruno to catch the sentries on the wall with their backs to him. It seemed to be working. A man on the wall went down, then another in the northwest tower. The team voiced their progress on their comms as they advanced.

The castle gunners quickly overcame their surprise and focused on their visible targets—Corban and June, Memphis and Johnny, and Bruno on the inside. Scooter and Brauch were too far away to be noticed or even suspected. They would be able to patiently scope for stationary targets. Since they were without pressure, it seemed they were taking out a target with every round. This was different from the team's experience in the desert. Here, men ran to and fro on the walls, hid behind the battlements, ducked, and popped up unexpectedly to shoot. Thus, Scooter announced on his comm that he would shoot over the north wall at crouching enemies on the south wall, and Brauch could do the same, hoping to take their foes out with a tranquilizer in the back.

The towers were danger zones for the team, though, as Xacsin's men fled to the security of the elevated structures when they realized their enemies had the upper hand. Since the front doors were still closed, Corban and June withdrew into the forest as gunfire from the towers made their stand impossible in front of the castle.

The gunfire waned as the snipers continued their seemingly invisible assault. Memphis and Johnny joined June and Corban in their retreat into the trees.

"Four down by Scooter. Over," he reported.

"Brauch has five confirmed. Over."

"Johnny taking the north wall . . . now. Over."

Still in the woods, June moved southeast around the castle toward Memphis' southern position. He battled with two guards on the wall who remained hidden in a blind spot from their two snipers. Stepping from the trees on Memphis' left, June peppered the top edge of the wall with pellets. When one raised his head to see who else had joined the assault, Memphis shot him. The second guard turned and ran to the southeast tower.

Memphis ran forward with his collapsible ladder. June covered him as he leaned the ladder against the wall.

"We're coming, Milk!" she hollered in her excitement. The men had given her a photo of the white-complexioned field agent in case she came upon him. Like in Africa, her heart was thrilled at the idea of selflessly helping those she didn't even know.

Dashing up behind Memphis, she climbed the ladder

first as he steadied it. The plan had been for her and Corban to enter through the front doors, but Memphis and Johnny hadn't scaled the walls fast enough, and Bruno would be in desperate need of help by now. There was constant gunfire from inside the courtyard.

June's head crested the south wall. Already on the north wall, Johnny ran to the west side where the northwest tower seemed to be secured. Both eastern towers were spitting fire from the better-concealed tower windows. Memphis climbed up behind June and they knelt on the walkway. A ricochet bullet whined off the rock at her foot. She poured pellets into the southeast tower window.

"Get back! Get back!" Memphis yelled over the deadly rounds.

She understood and ran toward the southwest tower over the castle gate. There was no other cover on the walls. After reaching the tower door and stairs, she covered Memphis as he retreated to her. He ducked inside the tower's safety to reload.

"You see Bruno?" he asked.

As June poked her head out then pulled back, the courtyard image registered the split-second visual.

"Yeah, I saw him. He's pinned down below us behind the four-wheelers outside the barracks door."

The hum of gears made them jump, then they realized Johnny was opening the double doors from the other tower for Corban to enter the castle.

"This is Memphis. June's with me in the southwest tower. We can't take either eastern tower. Too much firepower and no cover. Over."

"Scooter here. I have no shot. The enemy is hidden inside the towers now. Over."

"Brauch is blind as well. They're not exposing themselves. Over."

"Roger that," Corban said. "I'm immediately outside the front gates. Cover me as I make a run for the equipment room. Bruno, you there? Over."

There was no answer for a few seconds.

"Yeah, I'm against the barracks wall. Took one in the left shoulder, but I'm able and willing to help. I'll cover you against the northeast tower. Over."

"Good. Johnny, close the doors once I'm inside. I don't want anyone sneaking out. Here I go. Three . . . two . . ."

Memphis and June fired on the southeast tower window that faced the courtyard as Bruno and Johnny fired on the northeast.

Below Memphis and June, Corban sprinted through the doors and along the inside of the north wall to the door that led to the equipment room. Thanks to Snake's intel, it was a layout he knew as well as anyone. He collided with the door at full speed, his shoulder taking the impact. Gripping the knob, he whipped the door open but jumped aside as a muzzle flashed from within the darkened room.

Behind him, a bullet fired from a tower, slammed into the wall, and speckled him with rock fragments.

"Cover me, Memphis!" he shouted.

Corban tugged a flash and bang stun grenade from his belt. After pulling the pin, he tossed it into the room, hoping he didn't ignite any ammunition stores or other explosives.

He closed his eyes and covered his exposed ear. *Boom!* From the back of his belt, he took a small gas mask and slipped it over his face.

Charging headlong into the room, Corban fired from the shoulder as he went, raking the walls, stores, and shelves with pellets. Turning to his right, he put his back against the wall and stood in silence. He used his night scope to scan the darkness and spotted a guard huddling behind a half-dozen bags of flour. The guard blinked rapidly, still disoriented from the grenade, but he held an SKS assault rifle. That was enough for Corban to fire a burst into the man's chin. Then, he searched the rest of the room for a second foe. Finding none, he flex-cuffed the downed man.

"Equipment room secured. I'm entering the doctor's quarters. Over"

"This is Scooter. Brauch, you can cover both towers better than me. I'm on my way to the castle on foot. Over."

Easing the door open a crack, Corban peered into a lit room. There was a cluttered desk with a lamp and a twin-sized bed in the corner. He entered with a quick sweep from right to left, but the room was empty. Crossing the room cautiously to the other door, Corban turned the handle slowly. Anticipating gunfire, he threw the door open and stepped clear of the entrance to the exam and operating room, but no gunfire came from within. Taking a quick look inside, he stepped through the doorway, then aimed his NL-3 at a black-eyed old man wearing thick glasses.

"Dr. Aleksandre Stashinsky, Nathan Isaacson sends his regards."

"Don't come any closer!" the man warned in German.

He wore a white biohazard suit with the helmet off so he could hold a pistol against his temple. "Stay away! Just let me leave!"

"That's not happening, friend," Corban said softly. "Put the gun down. Come on, Doctor. It's all over."

Corban tensed to shoot Stashinsky with a tranquilizer when the biochemist pulled the trigger. Blood spattered the room. The body crumpled in a mass of red and white. Sorrowfully, Corban shook his head as he lowered his gun.

"May God have mercy on your soul." He touched his earpiece. "Exam room clear. Stashinsky is down. I'm assaulting the northeast tower now. Over."

As he passed back through the doctor's quarters to the equipment room, Corban heard the gunfire outside. He found a ring of keys on the unconscious guard, then crossed the dark room to a steel door set into the back wall. The second key he tried opened the lock. Pocketing the keys, he tugged the door open. A draft of cold air hit his face. Gunfire echoed from a spiral rock staircase leading to the tower's platform above. Moving forward under a single light bulb, he paused only to unscrew the bulb in case someone happened down the stairs.

Above, the gunfire ceased. That meant Scooter had found cover in the tower with Johnny. It seemed like a standoff, the two short towers against the two taller towers. But the enemy failed to realize Corban had breached their defenses. He aimed up the steep stairs as he ascended slowly. When halfway up, he whispered into his comm.

"Johnny, distract the northeast tower for twenty seconds. Over."

"Roger. Go in two . . . one . . . go!"

The gunfight broke out again above him, so Corban bounded up the remaining steps two at a time. He reached the overhead wooden hatch and drew a foot-long crowbar from the back of his belt. Fitting it into the flange that encased one of the two trapdoor hinges, Corban heaved on the crowbar, causing the wooden flange to splinter. Dropping the crowbar, he used his head to open the hatch enough to slip a stun grenade through the crack. Allowing the hatch to close, Corban descended four steps. Above, men cursed and yelled as their gunfire ceased.

Boom!

Corban lunged up the stairs, then thrust one hand through the broken hatch to force it open against its last hinge. Instead of two men, he found three, their senses disabled as they fired blindly out the tower's two windows. Since they could neither see nor hear, Corban immediately fired into their chests and necks.

"Northeast tower clear. What's the status of the last tower? Over."

"They're holding tight," Memphis reported. "Four making a stand. I think they're low on ammo, though. Over."

Securing his three disabled foes with flex-cuffs, Corban tallied the targets: nine taken at the beginning by the snipers, two at the gatehouse, two in each west tower, two more on the south wall, and one in the equipment room. That was only eighteen.

"If there are four in the tower, we're still missing a couple," Corban said. "I'm expecting closer to twenty-five.

I had three in this tower. Over."

"Probably in the barracks," Bruno said. "A few stragglers I've been trading shots with. Over."

"Bruno, can you meet me at the mess hall door? I'm out of flash-bangs to take the tower. Over."

"Boss, the prisoners must hear us coming," Scooter said. "They're making an awful lot of noise."

"Scooter, Johnny, drop over that wall to the hallway below. Make sure nobody is making a last ditch effort to take out the captives. Memphis and December, pound the last tower when I tell you. Bruno and I are taking it. Watch the barracks door for those stragglers. Don't forget, they have access to the armory. Over."

Corban picked up his crowbar as he descended the stairs.

The captives above were making so much noise—yelling out their door windows, hitting and kicking their doors—Milk knew something was happening. He crawled from the warmth of his rock to his cell door. This wasn't the first time he'd witnessed the others acting so rowdy in the last six months, but this was the loudest they'd ever been.

Sobbing breathlessly, he joined the ruckus, pounding weakly on the bottom of the door. Milk sobbed because it was time—time for Corban to arrive. Nathan had said two meals, and two meals had come and gone. This had to be a rescue attempt!

He pulled himself up the door and put his ear to the little window, his frail legs trembled as he stood for the first time in two days. Between bouts of yelling from his neighbors, he heard bursts of automatic gunfire echoing down the corridor. There was a raging battle somewhere above them, but Milk couldn't stand and listen for long. Sliding down the door, he sat on the floor to rest his legs. His sleeping rock in the corner was losing its heat. When he was about to crawl back to his bed, the corridor became eerily quiet.

Pushing upward, Milk clung to the door to hold himself up. He strained his vision to see up and down the corridor. Gunfire rattled once again above, then ceased.

What was happening?

A shadow came down the corridor. It was a short man in a gas mask and fatigues. Milk recognized the practiced movements of a wary commando, one he'd worked with on countless missions all over the world. The man stopped in front of Milk's door then visibly counted the cells from the stairs. Eagerly, Milk waited for the soldier to recognize him.

The masked man put his gloved hand to his ear as his eyes locked with Milk's eyes.

"This is Scooter, Corban. I've located Milk. I'm looking him in the face . . . Roger that. Out."

Corban and Bruno took the last tower. While the castle now seemed to be secure, there were several sections yet unseen. June stayed in the southwest tower to cover the castle as Corban, with Bruno and Memphis, moved on the armory, barracks, and garage. Bruno had a gunshot wound in his left shoulder that made it useless, but he was running on adrenaline still, his rifle cradled in his right arm.

When they stormed into the armory, they didn't risk throwing a flash-bang inside, but the storeroom was empty of men. There was a closed door that led into the barracks from the armory, and a door from the barracks leading into the courtyard. Bruno backed Memphis as they stood outside the courtyard entrance to the barracks, and Corban readied himself at the armory door.

"Three . . . two . . . one . . . Go!"

Kicking the door open, Corban stood clear as rounds zipped past him into a rack of rifle magazines. Suddenly, he wanted out of the armory, but he'd committed himself. At the other end of the barracks, Bruno and Memphis barged through the door. The room inhabitants were torn between two fronts and caught in the crossfire. Corban fired as he ran from the armory into the barracks, dove onto a bunk, bounced onto the floor, and landed on his back. A bullet gashed across his chest like a branding iron, but he forced it from his mind.

He crawled under a bunk, then stood abruptly, throwing the bunk at the guards holding their ground in the middle of the room. Three guards ducked as the bunk frame nearly knocked them over. Corban rushed forward after the bunk. When the nearest guard raised his head again to fire, Corban was two paces away. The man's eyes bulged as Corban attacked. Farther into the room, Bruno and Memphis rained pellets at the three guards.

Jumping through the air to shove the nearest guard's muzzle away, Corban then tackled him inside the ringed barricade that was their cover. He wrestled with the guard and kicked another. The third went unconscious from the barrage of pellets. The second rose up to shoot Corban, but he collapsed from the pellets as well. Memphis stood over him and fired on the man who Corban had in a headlock. A misplaced pellet smacked Corban's shoulder. There was no avoiding the inhalation of vapor. Corban's grip relaxed on the man under him and he felt himself slipping. As he drifted to sleep, he slid off his foe in time for Memphis to finish the job.

$$\maltese$$

"Boss, you okay?" Bruno called from the door.

Memphis flex-cuffed the three.

"He's okay. Um, friendly fire," Memphis said. "Twenty minutes till he's awake, right?"

"Yeah, but he won't be happy. Pick him up and bring him outside."

Pulling Corban over his shoulder, Memphis took him out in a fireman's carry.

"This is December! I hear a vehicle engine! Is that you guys?"

As Memphis was too burdened to move quickly, Bruno spun on his heels and ran from the barracks. Next to him, the garage door broke apart as an SUV crashed through it. The vehicle surged into the courtyard and turned toward the castle's closed gate. The SUV rammed into the double doors, but it didn't have enough speed for much of an effect. The doors cracked, but held sure.

The driver's door opened. A pistol emerged first. Three deadly rounds fired into the ground as the driver found her feet. Bruno fired his NL-3 with his good arm. The shocking impact of pellets on her wrist caused the pistol to fall from Hannah McLeery's hand. She stood unarmed as Bruno skidded to a stop in front of her. It wasn't so dark that Hannah couldn't see his face from the courtyard lamps.

Swinging at him, she tried to claw at his eyes. He backed away and aimed at her chin.

"I'm not afraid of you!" Hannah hissed and cursed at him in English. "Go ahead!" She raised her arms. "Shoot me. I know you won't kill me. You'll never win. First, you caught my sister, and now me. So what? You think you're making a difference? Where do you think Xacsin is right now? Abaddon will never stop fighting against you filth!"

"Where's Xacsin, Hannah? Tell me. And who is Abaddon? We'll get them soon enough, anyway."

"No, you won't! It's too late! Is Corban Dowler here?"

Bruno narrowed his eyes.

"Why?"

"Take me to him. I have a message from Abaddon."

"Corban's busy, but if he wasn't, he'd tell you to shut your mouth unless you have helpful information."

"I'd like to see his face when he finds out his little blind brat is being butchered right now. Abaddon has protected us before, but your God can't protect your families from Abaddon!"

With a grunt, Bruno shot her in the throat. She choked for breath, then slumped on the cobblestone. Memphis was quick to bind her.

"Hey, Bruno," June called from the tower above him. "What'd she mean about getting butchered?"

He didn't know, so he didn't respond. Bruno walked back toward the barracks door where the four-wheelers were parked. Corban was positioned against the wall. Their team leader had taken a bullet in his chest plating, but his body seemed uninjured. Surveying the castle, Bruno tried to guess what Corban would do at this point.

"Scooter, I think the castle's secure. The boss took some friendly fire. He'll be back around in fifteen. Over."

"Roger. We've got a mess of prisoners down here. Rupert, you listening? Over."

"I'm waiting near the highway. You ready for us? Over."

"Bring in the cavalry!"

Bruno sat down next to Corban and doctored his own oozing shoulder as Memphis cleared the SUV from the gate and parked it back in the garage. Then Memphis went out to the checkpoint gate to raise the arm for the first of a convoy of vehicles. Government agents mingled with COIL men and women from Berlin as they poured onto the castle grounds. They all wore germ warfare suits. Corban's team recovered as Rupert took charge and led the way to the prisoner levels.

Next to Bruno, Corban stirred. He awoke calmly and sat upright against the wall to watch the commotion. Xacsin's guards were rounded up, identified by the flex-cuffs. Hannah was one of the first to be loaded into a police van with multiple cages. She was still unconscious, but many of Xacsin's skinheads had regained consciousness to claim their innocence or proclaim their hatred.

"You need to make a call, Boss," Bruno said beside Corban. "Hannah said something about Xacsin going after your daughter. Sorry, but the word 'butcher' was used."

Corban's face was grim as he drew his sat-phone from a rib pocket. His chest was bruised and throbbing, but his pain didn't matter when it came to the safety of his family. He hit redial. It rang and rang. The answering machine picked up, but he clicked his phone off without leaving a message. After dialing another number, Corban listened to it ring twice.

"Good afternoon. This is Chloe."

"Chloe, it's me. It's an emergency. Xacsin is after my family again. That's why he's not at the castle."

"Okay. I'm on it."

Click.

Narrowing his eyes thoughtfully at Rupert Mach, Corban watched as the man organized a number of medical aid workers to enter the compound's dungeon levels. The Berlin COIL agent and ex-spy had been in the shadows of many COIL operations, but was always there when Corban couldn't be. Like now, Rupert was quick to assume leadership.

Groaning inside, Corban closed his eyes. *Not my family, Lord. Please, not my girls.*

CHAPTER TWENTY-THREE

Xacsin McLeery sighed with satisfaction as he finally heard a key in the front door. It had taken him several days to find Corban Dowler's family, but he'd done it. Abaddon had helped him. He was here to bring Corban to his knees. Corban was as cautious as a cat, but Janice, his wife, had led him straight to their new residence when she'd returned from Cameroon the day before. Breaking the Dowler's bathroom window and climbing into the house had been easy.

From the living room, Xacsin moved to one of the three back bedrooms that belonged to the blind girl. He was humiliated that his men had caught these two only months ago, but had failed to use them effectively against Corban. Now, he'd get even and finish what he'd started with Abaddon years ago—to destroy those who served their Christ.

Standing against the wall, he sniffed at the air. Since Xacsin hadn't bathed in two days, Jenna, the blind girl, wouldn't be able to see him, but she might smell him. Let her smell him, he thought, as he drew his automatic pistol. Only a split second was needed—first, the blind girl, and then the wife. That's what Corban had done to him—taken everything he'd worked so hard for under Abaddon. Not that he cared so much about losing the castle, or even the endeavors he'd left behind in Germany. It was the fact that Xacsin had been forced to shame Abaddon, whom he'd served from his youth.

The girl and woman were moving about the house. Xacsin had already turned the phone ringer off so there'd be no interruptions. And if it went well with the daughter, he'd take his time with the mother. Abaddon had taught him that—how to hurt his enemies through the ones they loved.

Holding his breath, Xacsin heard someone walk down the hallway toward the room in which he was hiding. Which was it, the wife or the girl? Whoever it was strode past to another room. That was okay, Xacsin assured himself. Sooner or later, Jenna would come into her room. He had all night; he'd simply be patient. Abaddon would give him patience.

Xacsin was born for moments like this: the purging of weakness from his race and the world. And now nothing stood in his way. Corban had drawn all his resources to attack the castle. COIL had probably taken the castle by now. Even if they hadn't, he knew Corban was still in Europe. Everything had worked so perfectly.

The person walked back up the hallway. The footfalls were heavier than a child's steps, he thought. So, it had to be Janice. But where was the daughter? Why hadn't she come to her room?

Panic coursed through Xacsin's mind. Something was amiss. It was too quiet in the house. There was no sound of a radio or television. He knew he had the right house. A Braille Bible was on a child's desk near his knee. Maybe only the mother had returned home? Maybe Jenna had been dropped off somewhere? *Fine*. Taking a deep breath, he settled his nerves. Okay, no blind girl to squeeze into oblivion. It was just him and Janice.

Leaning away from the wall, Xacsin peered down the hallway through the cracked doorway. *What was this?* Frowning, he saw gum wrappers littering the floor of the hallway in a line down the middle of the carpet. *Gum wrappers?* They hadn't been there earlier, had they? He clenched his teeth. What was happening? Perhaps he hadn't noticed them earlier when he'd moved from the living room.

No matter. They were only gum wrappers. Slipping quietly into the hallway, he stepped on a couple wrappers. What was it about the wrappers that gave him chills? Feeling uncertain, he wanted to contact Abaddon for advice. Abaddon always had answers. But Xacsin didn't have time.

With his pistol held at waist level, he crept down the hallway. Xacsin followed the gum wrappers sprinkled every few feet. Passing the linen closet, he craned his neck toward the living room and saw Jenna and Janice sitting together in the same easy chair. He could see their profiles as they faced something barely out of his sight, maybe the television. At last, he had them. Their end had finally arrived. It would also be the destruction of Corban's will to assist those who preached about their Jesus. This would break him!

Looking down at the floor, Xacsin saw the gum wrappers led directly to the chair in which the girls were sitting. It made no sense!

"You like gum?" a man's deep voice asked from behind him. "Drop the weapon. Now!"

Xacsin flexed his jaw muscles. *Cursed gum wrappers!* He'd been so distracted by them, he hadn't thought to look to his right to check the kitchen! After hanging his pistol on his trigger finger, he let it drop to the carpet. It was okay. There was a backup revolver in his ankle holster. Looking up, he saw Janice glaring at him as she led her daughter out of sight. *No!* This was all wrong! How had he been trapped when he'd come to trap them?

Slowly, Xacsin turned to see a lean, bald man with olive skin standing against the kitchen counter, chomping a large wad of gum. Who was this man? How had Corban known to guard his family?

Quickly sizing up the stranger, Xacsin figured he outweighed the gum-chewer by a good forty pounds, and was taller by an inch or two. The man had no obvious gun or weapon. He stood with his thumbs hooked inside his waistband. Relaxing, Xacsin wished he wouldn't have given up his gun without checking the stranger first. But he'd win yet! This man was of no consequence—he couldn't be; Abaddon hadn't warned him about any such danger. Xacsin would dispose of this character and take care of Corban's girls yet!

"Who are you?" Xacsin asked.

"No one special, but I've dealt with your kind before. I thought I'd never get another chance to honor Mr. Dowler by safeguarding his family. For months, I've been watching this house. Then, you came."

"You don't even know who I am, do you?"

The lean man shrugged and blew a bubble. The bubble popped loudly.

"Doesn't really matter. Soon, you'll be gone, and nobody will care."

"Just like that?" Xacsin smiled. "If you're the one who stopped my men last time they were sent for Corban's family, then I know you were shot. Are you that man?"

"My scars won't let me forget, but I'm not overly grieved to have experienced it. It has helped me see the important things in this life. I was an assassin, a killer like you. But God changed even me."

Xacsin studied the ex-killer's eyes. The man seemed sure of himself. But Xacsin licked his lips, tasting triumph. There were only three yards separating the two men. He could reach down and grab his pistol before the stranger could do anything.

"You may as well go for it," the bald man said, somehow reading Xacsin's thoughts. "I'll have to take you out, anyway."

"I'm going to kill them!" Xacsin snarled. "They've been given to me for a greater purpose. But first, I'm going to kill you."

"Show me."

Swiftly, Xacsin kneeled to reach for his pistol grip. But, like a rattler, the lean man's belt buckle snapped forward. Jumping backwards, Xacsin dodged it, but the belt swept again, this time slashing across his cheek. Seconds later, Xacsin fell onto his side, his arms no longer responding to his commands. Stunned, he stared up at the man now standing over him. *How had he been outsmarted? Xacsin was an ambassador of Abaddon! This was impossible!*

"Abaddon is my god!" he exclaimed, struggling to stand. "I thought—"

"That . . . was your problem," the bald, ex-assassin interrupted as he refit his belt. Then he moved into the living room where Jenna rushed out to embrace him.

Xacsin crumpled to the floor as he drifted off to sleep.

Brauch Schlenko cleaned his glasses with a handkerchief as he stood against the wall of COIL's Berlin headquarters. Nearly all the employees had left for the day, and the night shift, a skeleton crew, was filing in the front door. The field agents and caseworkers were already applying themselves to their normal tasks as if Operation Rahab had never happened.

But Operation Rahab wasn't quite finished, Brauch thought to himself. At least, not for him. Corban had spoken to him privately after the taking of the castle, and told him in secret the identity of Abaddon. It still caught Brauch's breath, but he had listened carefully to Corban's evidence, and there was only one thing to be done now: expose Abaddon.

Brauch looked up as Berlin's director, Rupert Mach, shrugged into his overcoat and headed for the door.

"What're you doing here, Brauch? I thought you were off on some mission for Corban. That's what he said, anyway. Figured you'd be halfway to Mongolia or somewhere."

"No, this is my mission." Brauch opened the door for Rupert. "I'll walk you to your car."

"I was thinking of putting a down payment on the old castle. What do you think?" Rupert reached in his pocket for his car keys. "We could turn it into our own little COIL fortress."

"I'll mention that to Corban since I'll be the new Berlin director."

Rupert stopped in his tracks, still three paces from his car. He turned to face Brauch. The wind blew flakes of snow across the lot.

"What's that supposed to mean?"

"Someone was leaking information to Brandon Fairchild a year ago, and Xacsin McLeery's computer at the castle had classified COIL information, information that we narrowed down to you."

"That's ridiculous! What is this nonsense? Why isn't Corban here to accuse me to my face?"

"Because he said he didn't trust himself to have you only arrested. This is my first order of business—dirty business."

"This is a mistake, Brauch. You know me. You've worked for me since before either of us were Christians!"

"Only Chloe, Corban, and you knew we were changing planes in Paris three weeks ago. There've been a lot of little signs that gave you away, Corban said."

"Corban said? Come on, Brauch! Listen to yourself! You're going to listen to him when we've been friends for—"

"It's ugly, I know. Do you know what decided your fate? That last night we were gathered in the hotel before Rahab went down. You didn't want to stick around for prayer. As careful as you've been, Abaddon, something that simple exposed you for who you are. Simple but powerful prayer."

Brauch watched Rupert's face turn from calm to a twisted snarl.

"You'll never prove anything." Rupert backed to his car. "For decades I've been here, and I have too much work left to do to be destroyed by some scumbag like you! I know the dirt of your past, how many you've killed and maimed. You're the one I've always been able to call a friend. Come with me now, Brauch! I promise you, I'll show you the resources at my disposal that will leave Corban's network looking like an anthill! Brauch, we can change the world, and crush the weakness that thrives under their God once and for all! We don't have to live in bondage any longer. Listen to me! I'm your friend. I wouldn't lie to you."

"You've lied to us all. However you've done this, whomever you've allowed to take root in your soul, I won't stop praying for you, Rupert. Yes, I was a terrible human being. You know that better than anyone does. But you also know that Christ changed me. And if He can change me, He can change you."

"Change?" Rupert mocked with laughter. "I'll never change!"

Rupert lunged at Brauch, the older man's keys between his fingers like spikes. He thrust the keys towards Brauch's eyes. Brauch took a step back, then grabbed Rupert's wrist and twisted him around. Now behind Rupert, Brauch held the traitor close to whisper into his ear.

"You were like a father to me. I should've seen the darkness in you before now. But, I don't hate you, Abaddon. I pity you."

Two police cars drove slowly into the parking lot.

"A jail cell won't hold me, Brauch. I have powers that transcend this world! How do you think I brought everyone together against COIL the last couple years?"

"Then transcend this," Brauch said, and he thrust a tranquilizer dart from an NL-X1 rifle into Abaddon's backside.

Rupert gasped and struggled, then was still. The police officers rushed forward and took the man from Brauch's arms. Brauch shook a sergeant's hand, then turned away toward his new office as he palmed his phone.

CHAPTER TWENTY-FOUR

"And because we know Nathan 'Eagle Eyes' Isaacson and Quin 'Toad' LuDao had accepted the gift of salvation from Jesus Christ our Lord, we know we'll see both of these men again. Brother?"

The speaker, a missionary on furlough from the Philippines, moved aside for Corban to stand between the two caskets of Nathan and Toad. The caskets were both symbolic and empty. Only Corban knew the details behind each. Normally, he would never speak without disguise in front of such a group of civilians; he preferred anonymity. But Chloe had insisted, and the family of Toad wanted it that way. Corban was the commander-in-chief of COIL, which made him, in a sense, responsible for their deaths. And while Toad's fiancée, Fon, was there with Toad's family, Nathan had no mate or direct blood relatives, but he had plenty of brothers and sisters, nonetheless. What was left of the Flash and Bang Team was gathered around the caskets. Milk, still recuperating from malnutrition and tuberculosis, sat in a wheelchair next to his wife, Eve. Bruno and Scooter stood with their families as well.

June and Memphis, alone except for one another, stood on Corban's right. Chloe and her husband, Zvi, stood on his left. Janice and Jenna were behind Corban, as well as a few others who had known Nathan and Toad through their church or COIL.

"We loved Nathan and Quin," Corban said. "Some of us cried and bled with them in distant lands. Their whole lives, they seemed to be at war, at conflict with the world. But when we look closer, we see they loved their enemies. Refusing to compromise, they saved the lives of both friend and foe. They were strong, stubborn men for their God. When we stood beside them, they stood a little taller than we stood, not because they were proud, but because they were humble, and gave in service to their Lord and others. Quin and Nathan knew what it meant to serve Christ, and they followed in His footsteps when they laid down their lives. Proof of this is before us. *There is no greater love than when a man lays down his life for his friends.*

"We'll miss you, Quin. We'll miss you, Nathan. But we praise God for the goodness you both left in your wakes— your joy, your confidence, your faith. Until we meet again, my brothers."

Corban stepped back and gripped his wife's hand.

The gathering slowly dispersed after the side-by-side caskets were lowered into the ground. Near this same burial plot, a dozen other COIL operatives had been laid to rest who'd died while assisting others. And there were even more, like Alfred, or "Snake," who went unclaimed in death, but Corban would always remember their sacrifice. He wept for them when he was alone.

Soon, the families left the graves until only the closest friends—Milk, Bruno, Scooter, Memphis, June, Chloe, and Corban—remained over the gaping holes. Johnny had wanted to be there, but a shipment of Bibles for Libya had demanded his attention. Memphis would be joining him soon to continue their work together, doing recon and staging for COIL operatives worldwide.

June was going through the steps of joining COIL officially as an employee under Chloe—a position worthy of her talents. Milk was on indefinite leave, requiring time to recoup, as his wife, Eve, endured chemo. Bruno and Scooter, the last two of the team, had already joined another COIL team formed from other ex-military Christians from America and elsewhere.

The Dowler family had moved again, taking up residence in another Queens neighborhood.

Turning, Corban peered across the huge Calvary Cemetery in Queens, burial site to nearly three million people. On a knoll a quarter-mile away, he saw two tall men standing among the many headstones. The two had been there through the whole funeral, but were careful not to approach too closely. Though they were too far away to identify, Corban knew who they were. He knew one was bald and would be chewing gum, and the other had slanted eyebrows and leaned on a cane.

Alone, Corban strolled toward the two figures on the knoll, leaving the others behind at the gravesites. His phone rang and he saw it was a dreaded call he was expecting. He answered it.

"Hello, Corban, this is Brauch. I hope the funeral went well."

"For funerals, it was fine. We'll miss those two."

"Well, Rupert is in custody. Operation Abaddon is

finished. When will you be back in Europe?"

"That depends on the next bout of strife against Christians. You'll be hearing from me, Brauch."

Corban approached the two men on the knoll.

"Good to see you up and around, Nathan," Corban said, stopping a couple paces from the two.

Nathan flexed his knee, now in a knee brace.

"I'm feeling better."

"You two got my message, I take it." He nodded at Luigi Putelli. "I can think of no one better to teach you what you need to know, Nathan."

"I'll miss the old days, Boss."

"We all will."

"Did that Xacsin fellow ever lead us to Abaddon, by any chance?"

"It seems he did." Corban nodded. "Someone from COIL recently picked him up and turned him over to the Germans, along with the rest of Xacsin's people. We can't let our work—your work, the Lord's work—be interrupted by the Abaddons of this world, Nathan. I'll see you in Australia in a few months, and put you where you need to be."

"Okay, Boss, I'll be ready."

Corban gave one last look and nod at Luigi, then walked back down the hill, rejoining his people at the gravesite. When he glanced back a moment later, Luigi and Nathan were gone.

Endnotes

D.I. Telbat brings your attention to Samaritan's Purse, a ministry serving the persecuted, victims of war, poverty, natural di-sasters, disease, and famine. You will find the following information on their website at samaritanspurse.org.

"Samaritan's Purse has done our utmost to follow Christ's command by going to the aid of the world's poor, sick, and suf-fering. This earns us a hearing for the Gospel, the Good News of eternal life through Jesus Christ."

Mission Statement

"Samaritan's Purse is a nondenominational evangelical Christian organization providing spiritual and physical aid to hurting people around the world since 1970 . . . serving the Church to promote the Gospel of the Lord Jesus Christ."

~

"For we do not preach ourselves, but Jesus Christ as Lord, and ourselves as your servants for Jesus' sake." (2 Cor. 4:5, NIV)

~

Programs Bless Children & Families Displaced by ISIS in Iraq

ISIS remains in control of large areas of Iraq and many thousands forced from their homes remain in desperate need. Samaritan's Purse has airlifted food and housing supplies as part of efforts to help thousands of families displaced by jihadists, and is now moving beyond immediate relief to programs that focus on long-term needs.

Our recent work builds upon longstanding efforts to help those in need in northern Iraq, a region where we have been actively offering relief since 2007. This work continues to grow, and beneficiaries include those from Christian, Muslim, Yazidi, and other backgrounds. Please continue to pray for the people displaced by the terrorists, and for an end to the violence wrought by the militant jihadists.

Massive Relief Effort Continues in South Sudan

As the fictional COIL team provided protection and help to the refugees in Sudan in *Dark Hearted*, Samaritan's Purse provides real help for real needs. How they minister in Sudan:

Samaritan's Purse (SP) continues to help meet the needs of hundreds of thousands of people in desperate need. The continuing turmoil has displaced about 1.9 million people, cutting off many from normal food supplies and basic services. All this comes as nearly a quarter-million refugees, mostly from Sudan, are struggling to survive in South Sudan.

Persevering to help relieve suffering, the work of SP is done in Jesus' Name, saving lives now and for eternity, and people are open to the Gospel. SP is working in a number of locations, providing relief in a variety of ways. Programs in one camp:

Unity State

The Yida refugee community numbers around 73,000 individuals, primarily who've fled the Nuba Mtns in Sudan.

SP is the only UN Refugee Agency's Water, Sanitation, and Hygiene (WASH) partner for Yida, located about 15 miles from the Sudan border. We maintain 14 boreholes in Yida, providing 1 million+ liters of clean water per day. We offer hygiene training, distribute hygiene items, and provide sanitation.

In coordination with the UN World Food Programme, Samaritan's Purse also manages and distributes monthly food rations— lentils, sorghum, oil, salt—for the entire camp as well as a nearby settlement of over 14,000 more refugees.

We also run a nutrition center and 5 mobile clinics that offer malnutrition screening and treatment for young children.

The active SP ministry team teaches Christians and Muslims to read the Bible through literacy courses. We also partner with local churches to show the Jesus film as an evangelism tool, offer prayer and support for suffering refugee families, distribute Bibles in the local language, train church leaders.

Further south, SP conducts monthly food distributions for over 21,000 South Sudanese affected by the political conflict. We have also provided seeds for planting and installed two surface water treatment systems, providing access to clean water for an estimated 4,000.

Our aviation team, based in Eldoret, Kenya, provides significant logistical support.

Please continue in prayer for the people of South Sudan and our staff who serve them. Pray for peace for this troubled nation, and that many would come to faith in Christ.

Other Samaritan's Purse Ministries

Samaritan's Purse provides water, food, and temporary shelter, meeting critical needs through their emergency relief programs. Visit the SP website samaritanspurse.org to learn more about the following and their many other ministries:

Operation Christmas Child – The world's largest Christmas project of its kind, OCC uses gift-filled shoeboxes to share God's love with needy children around the world. Since 1993, SP has collected and delivered more than 113 million gift-filled shoeboxes in over 150 countries. Shoeboxes are collected in the US, Australia, Austria, Canada, Finland, Germany, Ireland, Japan, New Zealand, Spain, Switzerland, and the UK.

World Medical Mission – The medical arm of SP provides "first-class treatment in the Name of the Great Physician through our medical projects," supplies mission hospitals with much needed equipment and supplies, places volunteer Christian physicians, dentists, and other medical personnel in mission hospitals and clinics around the world, staffs a biomedical department and warehouse, sends hundreds of doctors abroad on short-term assignments to help meet the phys-ical and spiritual needs of people in impoverished nations. Many of our mission hospitals are desperately in need of additional medical staff. Visit online for ways you can help!

Crises and Disaster Response, home and abroad – When victims of war, poverty, disasters, disease, epidemics, and famine cry out for help, SP stands ready to respond at a moment's no-tice wherever disaster strikes. We specialize in meeting critical needs throughout the world, often working through ministry partners already on the scene. We provide food, water, shelter, medicine, and other aid in the Name of Jesus Christ.

Construction Projects – Our projects provide shelter for families who lost everything in disasters, education opportunities to help break the cycle of poverty, facilities for physical and spiritual healing, and places to build up the body of Christ.

SP is on the Front Lines Against Modern-day Slavery

Human trafficking—the exploitation of men, women, and children in order to gain a profit—is a crime against both humanity and our Creator. This modern-day slavery has become a global crisis with an estimated 27 million victims. Some are taken by force, others are deceived by promises of a better life. In the midst of this dark plague of evil, SP is making a difference in the Name of the Lord Jesus Christ. Thousands of people in scores of villages have gone through our safe migration programs that teach the dangers of believing in these false promises. Please join us in praying that God will use our ministry to help bring justice & shine the light of the Gospel.

"Let my heart be broken with the things that break the heart of God." —Bob Pierse, Samaritan's Purse Founder

"Perfect justice for the poor and oppressed won't come until our Lord returns and puts all things under His feet, but in the meantime, we're going to do all we can in the Name of the Lord Jesus Christ to help the suffering and the weak."—Franklin Graham, President and CEO of Samaritan's Purse

Please visit samaritanspurse.org for more information on the many ministries Samaritan's Purse provides in the name of Jesus, and see how you can help make a difference.

~

Note from the Author: I'm so thankful for Samaritan's Purse and many other like-minded organizations and countless individuals who reach out to our suffering brothers and sisters. If we can't participate in activities firsthand, we can take part through prayer and giving when and where we can.

Pray for the many believers who face persecution around the world—for God's protection, provision, and strength. And pray that God will use these afflicted believers to reach even their tormentors with the Gospel of Christ. —D.I. Telbat

ABOUT THE AUTHOR

D.I. Telbat desires to honor the Lord with his life and writing. Many of his books focus on persecuted Christians worldwide—their sacrifice, their suffering, and their rescues. He is best known for *The COIL Series,* and his post-apocalyptic series, *STEADFAST: America's Last Days.*

David studied writing in school and worked for a time in the newspaper field, but he is now doing what he loves most—writing and Christian ministry. At this time, D.I. Telbat lives in California but keeps his home base in the NW US. You can find his complete bio at ditelbat.com/about/.

On his Telbat's Tablet website, David Telbat offers FREE weekly Christian short stories, or related posts, which include sneak-peeks of his books, his novel news, author reflections, and occasional challenges for today's Christian. Subscribe to his blog at ditelbat.com to receive his stories and novel news right in your inbox. Also, receive exclusive subscriber gifts.

Please leave your comments wherever you bought this book. Reviews tremendously help authors, and David Telbat would love to hear your thoughts on his work. He takes reader feedback into consideration as he makes his future publishing plans. Thanks for reading!

Made in United States
Orlando, FL
31 August 2022

21799469R10189